'But Miss Sutton claims her waters were never associated with miraculous cures,' Westfield said, turning towards Glory as if for confirmation.

'And I spoke the truth, as far as I can tell,' Glory said, hesitant to contradict the Duchess.

'All mineral waters are known for their healing,' the Duchess said with a wave of dismissal. 'But those from Queen's Well are unique in their benefits.'

'And what might they be?' Westfield asked.

The Duchess smiled slyly. 'The waters here have a certain propensity for bringing about unions.'

Glory blinked in surprise, while Westfield looked dubious.

'Unions?' he asked.

'Romance, dear, romance.'

AUTHOR NOTE

I hope you like my latest Regency, set at a faded spa resort with a rich history—and a mystery. As my readers know by now, I'm fascinated by old legends, hidden treasures, and secrets of the past, and I love creating my own.

Although Queen's Well is my invention, spas were once the prime destination for members of fashionable society eager to 'cure' various ailments. They enjoyed the polite company and entertainments provided, along with drinking and bathing in the mineral springs. And, since such waters were thought to have healing powers, other rumours might have swirled around them, long forgotten, just waiting to be revived...

GLORY AND THE RAKE

Deborah Simmons

First published in Great Britain 2011
by Mills & Boon, an imprint of Harlequin (UK) Limited,
Eton House, 18-24 Paradise Road, Richmond, Surrey TW9 1SR

© Deborah Sieganthal 2011

ISBN: 978 0 263 88787 7

Harlequin (UK) policy is to use papers that are natural, renewable and recyclable products and made from wood grown in sustainable forests. The logging and manufacturing process conform to the legal environmental regulations of the country of origin.

Printed and bound in Spain
by Blackprint CPI, Barcelona

A former journalist, **Deborah Simmons** turned to fiction after a love of historical romances spurred her to write her own, HEART'S MASQUERADE, which was published in 1989. She has since written more than twenty-five novels and novellas, among them a *USA TODAY* bestselling anthology and two finalists in the Romance Writers of America's annual RITA® Award competition. Her books have been published in 26 countries, including illustrated editions in Japan, and she's grateful for the support of her readers throughout the world.

A previous novel from this author:

THE DARK VISCOUNT

Praise for
Deborah Simmons

'Simmons guarantees the reader a page-turner...'
—*RT Book Reviews*

'Deborah Simmons is a wonderful storyteller and brings historical romance to life.'
—*A Romance Review*

'Deborah Simmons is an author I read automatically. Why? Because she gets it right. I can always count on her for a good tale, a wonderful hero, a feisty heroine, and a love story where it truly is love that makes the difference.'
—*All About Romance*

For Ruth and all of the book club members: Darlene, Ellie, Frances, Grace, Kim, Melissa and Pat. Thanks for your support and for many memorable afternoons.

Chapter One

Glory Sutton slipped into the Pump Room, blinking in the dimness. She should have brought a lantern, for the curtains that were drawn to foil gawpers also kept out the light of the fading day. But she hadn't realised how late it was when she'd remembered that she had left her reticule here.

The workmen had gone, but the smell of fresh paint lingered, making it easy to envision the final touches that would enable the spa to re-open. Queen's Well had been in her family for centuries, and Glory took pride in her efforts to preserve that heritage.

But a low noise made her glance warily about. It was just the creaking of the old wood, Glory told herself, yet she renewed her hunt for her reticule. Although she had never been the type to start at sounds, since arriving in the village a month ago, she'd been aware of the mixed feelings of the residents.

That alone wouldn't unnerve her; what did was the sensation she often had that someone was watching her. She didn't mention it, for her brother Thad would say her feelings were proof of the enmity of the locals. And Aunt Phillida would only worry—or faint dead away. Neither of them shared Glory's hopes for the spa and would seize upon any excuse to abandon the once-thriving well she was trying to revive.

Although Glory kept her concerns to herself, she had slipped a small pistol into her reticule. The precaution would have horrified her aunt and her brother, but Glory's father had instilled in her the good sense to watch out for herself—even in such a seemingly benign locale as the village of Philtwell.

However, a pistol would do no good, if she did not have it at hand, Glory realised as she turned to scan the deserted room. The shrouded furniture made the place look ghostly, as well as shielding her view, and she had to swallow a cry of surprise as a stray draught caught at a sheet. Finally, she spied a dark object lying on one of the benches that lined the walls. Had she put it down when inspecting the refurbished pieces? She couldn't recall. Perhaps one of the workmen had moved it there.

Hurrying into the shadows, Glory reached for the item, relieved to feel the soft material of her bag and the heft of the weapon inside it. But then she heard a noise again and spun round in alarm, for it sounded like the creak of a door.

Had someone followed her inside? Glory was tempted to call out the question, but held her tongue.

Who would be entering a darkened building that had been closed for decades? It might just be a curious villager or one of the workers returning, but something made Glory shrink into the shadows.

A glance towards the main entrance showed that it remained firmly shut. However, she had come through the rear of the building, using her key. Had she left the door open? She had so much on her mind, so many details to tend to before the re-opening, that she might have been careless. The wind was sometimes fierce in Philtwill and could be to blame, Glory told herself. Still, she slipped the pistol from her reticule and inched behind the sheeted tables, keeping to the edge of the space.

But the rooms at the rear of the Pump Room were even darker, and Glory cursed her own foolishness as she shied away from the shadows. Finally, she saw the door standing open ahead and moved towards it, eager to leave the eerie atmosphere of the building. Hurrying over the threshold, Glory released a sigh of relief, only to catch her breath again as a shape loomed up in front of her.

Jerking backwards in alarm, Glory lifted her weapon with a shaking hand and called out in an even shakier voice, 'Stop, or I'll shoot.'

'Excuse me?'

The low drawl wasn't what Glory had expected, but she was not about to lower her guard. 'Stand right there. Don't move,' she said, inching away from the presence. Although it was lighter outside, tall sycamores shrouded the Pump Room's exterior, and she could see little except a dark form, tall and menacing.

'Do you know who I am?' it asked.

Although definitely male, the figure was too large to be Dr Tibold, who had made himself a nuisance with his insistence that the well waters be given freely to all—so that he could more easily line his own pockets.

'No,' Glory said, even as she wondered whether the physician had hired some thug to ensure her submission. Her heart thundered and her grip on the pistol faltered. This fellow seemed too smooth, his speech too refined, to be a ruffian, and yet all her instincts told Glory that, whoever he was, the man was dangerous.

'Should I?' she asked, with more bravado than she felt.

'I assume that's why you're robbing me.'

Glory blinked in surprise. 'I'm not robbing you,' she protested. But in that unguarded instant he made his move, knocking the pistol aside and pulling her to him.

The weapon fell to the ground and Glory found her back up against the man's body, while his arm closed tight across her chest, holding her fast. Gasping at the startling intimacy, Glory felt her wits desert her. Although rarely at a loss, she was bombarded by unfamiliar sensations: the man's obvious strength, the hard form pressed to hers and the heat that enveloped her.

Even as she drew in a sharp breath, Glory was

assailed anew by the scent of warm male tinged with a subtle cologne. Her heart thundered, her pulse pounded and then there was a brush of warm breath on her hair as though of a whisper…

'What the devil?' Thad's shout rang out, cutting off whatever words Glory imagined she might hear. And she blinked as her brother appeared on the path, silhouetted against the setting sun. 'Unhand my sister!'

'Work in tandem, do you?' The deep drawl close to her ear sent shivers up Glory's spine. She told herself it was because the villain didn't seem the least bit wary of Thad charging to her rescue. The voice itself, rife with confidence, had nothing to do with the peculiar quickening of her body, a loss of control that alarmed her more than anything else.

But perhaps that's what fear did to a person, Glory thought, although the man had not hurt her, simply disarmed her. In fact, she appeared to be in more jeopardy from Thad, who suddenly launched himself towards the stranger, despite the fact that Glory was standing in front of the man, unable to move. Her assailant, a bit more aware, quickly set her behind him.

'Don't make me regret this,' he said, as he released her, and Glory wondered at the kind of thug who would set her free. *Perhaps one who thought far too highly of himself*, she mused as he faced Thad.

But the man's confidence was not misplaced. Even in the dim light, Glory could see that Thad's efforts were clumsy and erratic, while his opponent's were perfectly controlled, as practised as a boxer's. Although that was not unusual, for even Thad wanted to take up the gentleman's sport, this fellow had the skills of a professional. He could easily have been one of the bruisers who were paid to bloody each other in a milling-match, and Glory feared for her brother's life.

Indeed, Thad was soon knocked to the ground, and Glory cried out in protest. Automatically stepping towards him, she nearly tripped on the forgotten pistol. Relief swamped her as she leaned down to retrieve it.

'Stop right there!' Glory shouted, and this time her hand was steadier as she pointed the weapon at Thad's assailant.

But neither male paid any attention to her threat. Thad sat up, rubbed his jaw and eyed his silent foe with what might have been admiration. 'Where did you learn to fight like that?'

'Gentleman Jackson's.'

'No! Really?' Thad said, his voice rising with excitement. 'I'd love to learn from the master, but my sister doesn't approve. Instead, she dragged me here to the ends of the earth, where there's nothing for a game fellow to do.'

As Glory watched dumbfounded, Thad's opponent stretched out a hand to help him to his feet. 'So you've taken up thievery?'

'What? No! I'm no thief, but what…what are you?' Thad asked, apparently coming to his senses. His tone changed to a challenge as he straightened. 'What were you doing with my sister?'

'I was wondering why the door to the supposedly closed Pump Room was standing open when your *sister* threatened to put a bullet in me,' the man said.

They both turned towards Glory, who got her first good look at her assailant as the setting sun struck him. Tall, dark and good looking, he was dressed immaculately and reeked of power, wealth and arrogance. Or was it simply confidence? Shaken, Glory drew in a sharp breath.

'Who are you?' she asked.

'Since circumstances have conspired against a formal introduction, you may call me Westfield,' he said, with a slight nod.

'You're the *Duke of Westfield*?' Thad's voice held both awe and horror, and Glory might have swayed upon her feet, had not the nobleman reached out a steadying hand—to turn away the pistol she was pointing at him.

Oberon Makepeace, fourth Duke of Westfield, shot his cuffs, straightened his neckcloth and headed up the slope to Sutton House, none the worse for the attempted assault. He tucked the small pistol he had collected into the pocket of his coat, the better to avoid any further unpleasantness. Neither the young man nor woman had put up much argument at that point, and Oberon had made good his escape without the fear of a bullet in his back.

He had not been expecting such an encounter, here on the outskirts of nowhere, and he wasn't sure what to make of it. Although the effort had been clumsy and easily foiled, Oberon could not discount the possibility that there was more to what had transpired than met the eye. And it was that prospect, among other reasons, that kept him from tossing his young perpetrators in gaol.

Oberon had learned long ago that people were not always what they seemed, and while the young woman looked like any other empty-headed daughter of the local gentry, genteel ladies did not point pistols at strangers. She might be passing as one of her betters, so that she and her so-called brother could run some kind of swindle, and, if so, they might have stumbled upon Oberon by chance. After all, he had arrived only an hour ago.

However, chance was something Oberon viewed with scepticism, and he tried to remember who knew he was travelling to the village of Philtwell. He hadn't told many of his plans, just put it about that he had a family engagement. But his mother might have spread the word. She was responsible for the outing, having insisted that he accompany her to visit an ailing relation. Although Oberon had suggested others in his stead, including the family physician, the dowager was adamant. Nor had she accepted what she termed his 'social commitments' as a viable excuse.

Acceding to her wishes, Oberon had endured a lengthy journey on barely passable roads to reach Philtwell, a rustic backwater far from civilisation.

The village boasted little more than a rutted main street lined with dilapidated buildings, including the remnants of Queen's Well, a spa once favoured by Queen Elizabeth. Never a particularly fashionable watering hole, it had not enjoyed the success of Bath or Tunbridge Wells, and its heyday had long passed, its waters closed.

And yet, someone had been skulking about the Pump Room, and not just anyone… At his first glimpse of the shadowy form, Oberon had reacted more strongly than was his wont. Perhaps it was the threat she had presented, but the ennui he had felt since leaving London disappeared, replaced by a surge of excitement, sharp and unfamiliar. He told himself it was only the sudden appearance of a new challenge, a puzzle, here, of all places.

And if the enigma came in a slender body that fit perfectly against his? Oberon frowned. Obviously, it had been too long since he parted with his last mistress or he would never have been so affected by a slip of a female. Far more important than her appeal was the fact that she carried a pistol and had threatened him with it. That made her both foolhardy and dangerous—and worth further inspection, along with the village itself.

Philtwell's remoteness would be an advantage to those who would meet away from prying eyes, and in the past, many had gathered at spas to hatch their plots. But today? Oberon shook his head dubiously. He was probably clutching at straws in order to occupy himself. Yet, as he left the outskirts of Philtwell to turn into drive of Sutton House, he watched the shadows for any signs of movement.

Nothing loomed ahead except Randolph Pettit's residence, a sturdy brick building that was small by ducal standards, but would serve well enough for a short stay. Although a couple of centuries old, it had a clean look, thanks to some additions and improvements over the years. More were needed, especially inside, and Oberon wondered just how well his mother's cousin was situated.

He slipped in a side entrance to avoid any scrutiny and to determine whether he showed any signs of his recent adventure. A quick assessment in his bedroom revealed nothing except a dusty coat, which could be easily remedied by his valet. Reaching into his pocket, Oberon removed the small pistol and deposited it in a bureau drawer.

Looking down at the weapon for a long moment, Oberon wondered whether he should have questioned the young woman more closely. But too much interest on his part would be remarked, and he could not afford to show his hand even in such a distant locale as Philtwell. However, he had no intention of dismissing the incident, and he was already thinking ahead as he called for his valet.

Country hours were kept at Sutton House, which meant an early supper and a long evening of boredom to follow. But now Oberon's senses were alert, and the upcoming meal became like so many others, an opportunity to listen and learn and ferret out the information he sought.

However, when he made his way to the dining hall, Oberon found it deserted. Obviously a part of the original structure, the room remained much as it must have looked when built. Although most of the house had been refurbished, here the dim lighting cast only a faint glow that did not reach the corners. The furniture, too, was heavy and dark, Oberon noted, as he walked slowly around the perimeter. He was approaching one wall where the paint appeared to be mottled with age when he heard footsteps.

Turning, he saw only his mother on the threshold. 'Your cousin is unable to join us?' he asked, masking his disappointment. It appeared he would learn little about the locals tonight.

'Not yet,' she said. 'But he does seem to be improving.'

Oberon wouldn't know, having been shooed away from the sickroom of a man he could not recall. And he wondered, again, why his mother insisted that he accompany her when she would have been better served by a physician, companion or man of business who could put her cousin's affairs in order, if necessary.

But he was here, whether he liked it or not, and he took a seat across from his mother, hoping that the food would be palatable.

'Did you enjoy your walk?'

Accustomed to hiding his reactions, Oberon gave only a non-committal nod in answer, for he was not prepared to share the details of his unexpected outing with his mother, at least not now. Perhaps not ever.

'Did you see the Pump Room?' she asked. 'That's where your father and I met, you know.'

Oberon nodded. Despite her sharp wit, his mother seemed to have succumbed to nostalgia. Since receiving her cousin's summons, her usual pragmatic comments had been replaced by such reminiscences, and Oberon was not quite sure what to make of them.

'I understood that it is no longer in use,' he said.

'Yes, not long after your father and I were here, the spa was struck by a fire that consumed some of the buildings and resulted in its closure. That's when the owners sold Sutton House, but it seems they held on to other properties.'

'And yet I thought I saw some activity there,' Oberon said, carefully.

'Perhaps it was the Suttons. Randolph says they have returned to rebuild and re-open Queen's Well.' She seemed absurdly pleased by the prospect, while Oberon wondered what kind of fool would attempt such a venture.

Although watering holes like Bath still had their adherents among the elderly and barely genteel, the Prince Regent had made the seaside, most notably Brighton, the fashionable destination. And from what little he had seen, a lot of money would be required to make Queen's Well presentable, with little prospect of return.

'And did you meet anyone when you were out?' Something about his mother's innocent tone made Oberon suspicious.

'I hardly think I would be approached without

an introduction, even in such a place as Philtwell,' he said.

His mother loosed a sigh of exasperation, whether directed at her son or the strictures of polite society, Oberon did not know. And he had no intention of finding out. Instead, he turned the conversation towards the village in the hopes of finding out what he could. But his mother had not visited Philtwell in decades, making her less than knowledgeable of current residents, including a pair of possible thatch-gallows whose names Oberon had not obtained. At the time, he had not bothered to ask, suspecting they might answer falsely.

Now he wondered whether they played some part in the revival scheme. And if he was more intrigued by the female half of the duo, Oberon told himself it was because no woman had ever held him at gun-point. Whatever else he had felt when subduing his opponent was not something he was ready to admit, even to himself.

Glory would probably have remained where she was, gaping in shock, had Thad not hustled her away. So scattered were her wits that she had walked some distance from the Pump Room when she remembered the open door.

'Thad, wait,' Glory said, halting in her tracks. 'I've got to go back and lock up.'

'Well, I'm coming with you,' he said. 'It appears that you can't take two steps on your own without getting into trouble.'

The statement was ludicrous coming from Thad, but Glory didn't argue. She was too grateful for his presence as they turned back towards the Pump Room. She had never been wary of the place before, but now the deep shadows gathering under the trees seemed ominous and menacing, as though anything, not just a handsome stranger, might be hiding there. Waiting. *Watching.*

Glory tried to ignore the sensation, but a creak revealed the door was still swinging, and the back of her neck tingled. She wished she had her pistol back. Fie on the Duke of Westfield for taking it! But surely he hadn't been the one creeping about the deserted Pump Room.

Or had he? Now that she had recovered from the shock of his identity, Glory realised that a title was no guarantee against bad behaviour, and she shivered. Somehow the thought of the tall, dark and attractive duke intending harm was more disconcerting than some nameless, faceless pursuer. Was he mad or simply…bad?

Pushing aside such speculation, Glory stepped towards the opening, only to flinch at a sudden flash of brightness. She whirled around, smacking into Thad, in time to see a lad passing by with a lantern. Seizing upon the opportunity, Glory sent Thad to borrow the lamp, so she could see what she was about.

Thad grumbled, but did as she bid and was soon holding the light near the open door. Fingering the key, Glory was wondering whether they ought to look inside, just to make sure the place was empty, when something caught her eye.

Leaning forwards, she stretched out her arm to keep Thad where he was and knelt down to get a better look. The mark was just outside the building on the first of the flagstones that led towards a gravel path. Crouching close, Glory saw it was in the shape a curve as though the painted outline of part of a boot heel. Tugging off one of her gloves, she reached out to touch the mark and lifted her finger. *Fresh* paint.

'Lud, Glory, I think you've gone a bit too particular about the damned well, if you're bothered by something back here that no one can see without crawling on the ground,' Thad said. 'Just lock the place and let's go home. Isn't it enough for one evening that you assaulted a duke?'

Ignoring the question, Glory snatched the lantern from her brother and carefully walked over the threshold. Inside, she found another stain and then the source: a drip that had landed on the floor.

'Here's where they stepped in it, but when? And who?' Glory asked aloud.

'Are you playing at detective now?' Thad asked, with a snort. 'What can it matter? Are you going to sack the workmen for a stray drop or two?'

Glory did not answer, but found her own lamp in one of the rear rooms, so that she could return the lantern, along with a coin, to the boy waiting patiently at the exit. Once he had hurried away, Glory closed the door and turned her attention back to the marks.

Although they could have been made by one of

the painters who had left the building before she had returned, Glory felt certain that was not the case. And she took a good look through the entire place, Thad at her heels. With her brother beside her and even the far corners and heavy curtains illuminated by her lamp, the Pump Room no longer seemed threatening. Nor did she find anything amiss.

'Lud, Glory, what's this about?' Thad asked when they stood back in the main room.

Glory drew a deep breath. 'Why do you think I pointed a pistol at Westfield?'

'I don't know,' Thad said. 'You've gone barmy over Queen's Well? And what were you doing with a gun anyway?'

'Don't say anything to Aunt Phillida,' Glory warned.

Thad snorted. 'I'm hardly likely to tell tales, especially since I don't care to lug her lifeless form about should she hear that you were threatening a duke,' he said, with a frown. 'Why did you do it?'

'When I came back to fetch my reticule, there was someone in here, hiding in the shadows.' The tone of her voice made Thad look over his shoulder in alarm.

'*What?*'

'It's not the first time I've felt like someone was watching me,' Glory said, explaining the odd sensations she had experienced since they had arrived in Philtwell. 'And that's not all. The men who were hired to tear down the remains of the burned buildings aren't doing the work. It's as though someone is hindering our efforts to re-open the spa.'

Having finally given voice to her suspicions, Glory felt a sense of relief, but Thad appeared both uneasy and sceptical. Finally, he shook his head. 'Well, I wouldn't put it past some of the locals to turn a blind eye to work, especially considering the attitudes we've seen from them.' He paused, and Glory waited for him to try to talk her out of her plans. Again.

However, when he spoke, it was not about 'Glory's Folly', as he had dubbed her efforts to revive the family heritage. 'The villagers might be up to mischief, but Westfield? I can't see him sneaking about here in the dark, intent upon attacking you.'

Although Thad's dismissive tone made her suspicions seem ridiculous, Glory was fairly certain someone had been inside the building with her, someone who hadn't made his presence known. And it chilled her.

Perhaps Westfield was not the thug she had originally thought him, but that didn't mean he wasn't involved. Glory shivered at the memory of being held tightly against him, disarmed and helpless. And if she was suddenly flushed with heat, as well, it had nothing to do with solid feel of his muscular form or the scent of him, so very close…

Drawing in a deep breath, Glory pushed such thoughts aside. 'I don't know,' she admitted. 'But I'd like to take a look at his boot.'

Chapter Two

The Dowager Duchess of Westfield paused before the bedroom door and knocked gently. Although she thought she heard movement, there was no answer. In other circumstances, she might have left quietly, in order not to disturb the occupant, should he be sleeping. But Letitia only knocked louder.

'Come in.' Randolph's voice was frail and breathless when he finally answered, and Letitia slipped inside, closing the door behind her. The curtains were drawn, and she peered into the dimness of the room, finally spying the man lying prone among the covers of the elaborately carved four-poster.

As she approached, he turned his head slightly and groaned, as if in pain. Then he opened his eyes and focused upon her.

'Oh, it's only you,' he said before abruptly sitting up. 'I hope you've brought me something to eat. The broth they're giving me isn't enough to keep a sparrow alive.'

'I'll tell the cook we need to build up your strength,' Letitia said.

Randolph sighed. 'Well, please do. And I am ready to be rid of this room, as well.'

'Not yet,' Letitia warned. 'Oberon is not slow-witted. He's already giving me the eye. If he finds you've recovered, he might leave, which would bring us to nothing.'

Randolph protested, 'I would think my health would be worth something.'

'Of course it is, but the only reason I brought Oberon is because of the girl, and I won't have him slip away without throwing them together.'

While Letitia was pleased to see Randolph's illness had passed quickly, she was not about to relinquish this opportunity. When he'd written to her that the waters of Queen's Well might be available once more and that the new owners included an interesting young woman, she had seized upon the prospect like a drowning man, investing all of her hopes and dreams in someone she had yet to meet.

'I'm sorry I ever wrote to you about her,' Randolph said, reaching under his pillow for a deck of cards.

'No, you aren't,' Letitia said, pulling over a small table, which he used to deal out hands. 'Because you know as well as I do that it's high time Oberon settled down.'

Randolph nodded. 'I agree, but I would have preferred simply to throw a lavish entertainment and invite both your son and the promising prospect.'

Letitia shook her head. 'He wouldn't have come. I could barely get him here by claiming you were at death's door. You don't know how stubborn he is. He's just like his father.'

When Randolph lifted both brows in a sceptical glance, Letitia sighed. 'All right, he might have inherited a bit of obstinacy from me,' she admitted. 'But if he thinks anyone's trying to put forth an eligible female, he turns his back upon her. Literally.'

'Well, did he run into her last evening?' Randolph asked, taking up his cards.

Letitia frowned, as she took her cards. 'I don't think so. He didn't say, but then he's not the most forthcoming even at the best of times.'

'Cool. Quiet. Strong,' Randolph said. 'Far too handsome, and with a bit of stand-offishness that is like catnip to the females. I would think he'd have no trouble finding a duchess.'

Letitia made a sound of derision. 'Oh, he's had mistresses. Don't think I'm not aware of them! But he won't have anything to do with marriage-minded misses or their mamas. Too arrogant, by half, I'm sure.'

'Just like his father,' they both said at once, and Letitia smiled fondly.

'That's why I wrote to you and asked you to keep an eye out for someone here, where I met my husband,' she said, though at the time she'd had little hope that Queen's Well would ever resume operation.

'I cannot assure you that they will get on,' Randolph warned.

But Letitia refused to be discouraged. 'Well, I can assure you that a typical débutante would be no match for him. Why, he'd chew them up and spit them out before they knew what he was about. He needs someone attractive enough to hold his attention, but strong enough to stand up to him, an independent young lady with a mind of her own.'

'Like the one his father married,' Randolph said.

Letitia smiled. 'Perhaps,' she acknowledged before growing sombre. She hated to interfere, for she was not a meddling mother, but she had given her eldest son plenty of time, and he was no closer to marriage now than when first weaned. She shook her head. 'The Makepeaces are not easy matches…'

She had not even finished before Randolph nodded and spoke what was on his mind. 'Which is why we need the waters.'

Stepping outside, Oberon viewed the cloudless sky and surrounding peaks with a jaundiced eye. Although not one to admire the picturesque, he was reminded of just how long it had been since he'd stayed at Westfield, the family seat. He knew a sudden yearning for those rolling hills, followed by other yearnings for all that went with a home, and paused in surprise.

He had put such desires behind him long ago, so why they should strike him here and now, he didn't know. Perhaps it was all his mother's talk of meeting his father at Queen's Well. They'd had a devoted marriage, but at what cost? Oberon had seen his mother's devastation at her loss, and he remembered his own pain at the death of his father. It had left him vulnerable to those who did not have his best interests at heart, and he'd vowed never again to be that…weak.

And he had never been tempted to break that vow. Most of the women who pursued him were cold and calculating, seeking the title of duchess as a business transaction. The younger ones and those less determined were usually vapid, pretty vessels that held nothing of worth. That was the sum of feminine society, at least in the circles in which he moved, an endless round of balls and routs and salons peopled by many of the same faces, the same deceits, the same falsehoods, year after year.

Oberon shook his head at his bleak thoughts. What the devil was ailing him? He had slept like a stone and eaten an enormous breakfast, unusual behaviour that his mother claimed was brought on by 'the air'. And now he was sunk in introspection of the kind for which he had neither the time nor the inclination.

Oberon flexed his gloved fingers, an old habit, caught himself and then headed into Philtwell. Since his mother had shooed him away from the sickroom again, he was off to take a closer look at the village. Assuming the air of a common visitor, Oberon kept his eyes and ears open as he strolled the main street, but he did not see anything out of the ordinary. The people seemed to be locals; there were no obvious foreigners or strangers.

That came as no surprise, for Philtwell appeared never to have recovered from the fire his mother had mentioned. Several blackened buildings lingered, as eyesores and possible dangers to passers-by, while the weeds and brambles that grew around them threatened to overtake the neighbouring shops.

In fact, the only place that appeared well tended was the Pump Room. From his position across the road, Oberon got a good look at the front of the building for the first time. In the bright light of day, he could see that the older structure sported a fresh coat of paint over its simple, columned façade. And a man was tending to the grounds, preparing to put in some new plantings.

It seemed that someone was going to re-open the well, or at least they were making a show of the prospect. Oberon turned, intending to cross the road to casually question the worker, when a door burst open nearby. Immediately alert, he stepped out of the way, but the man who exited swung towards him.

'Good sir, you must be new to our fine community!' he said, bowing deeply. 'As the pre-eminent physician in residence, Dr Tibold by name, I am pleased to offer my services to help you achieve complete health, no matter what your ailments.'

'Do I look like I'm ailing?' Oberon asked, with a lift of his brow. Had the fellow been watching from his rooms for potential patients? That possibility, along with his rather shabby attire, did not inspire confidence in his self-proclaimed abilities.

'Certainly not! You are the picture of health, sir.

But even those who appear robust can be suffering from some sort of inner disorder, and that is why a course of treatment is beneficial to all, even a fine specimen such as yourself.'

Tibold paused to peer at Oberon, as though assessing the worth of his clothes and the size of his purse, in order to charge accordingly. 'Have you been bled lately?'

Oberon did not deign to comment.

'But, of course, that's not always called for,' the physician said, nodding and smiling as he changed tactics. 'The waters, that is what we are famous for, and that is what you need.'

Again, Oberon lifted a brow. 'I thought the well was closed.'

The physician's face twisted, as though ill pleased by the reminder. 'Sadly, at the moment, yes, but soon we shall ply you with our famous remedy. Of course, the waters should be available at all times, for all persons, and not at the whims of a single family.' He paused to draw a deep breath before continuing in a louder voice, 'Title to such things ought to be illegal. How can a person own water? It's like taxing the very air.'

'If you feel so strongly, perhaps you should put down a new well and open your own facilities,' Oberon said.

But his suggestion was met with another scowl. 'All the prime property is owned by Miss Sutton,' he said, practically spitting out the name. 'And her tight grip is felt by all who would do good for the community.'

'*Miss* Sutton?' Oberon asked.

'Yes, a female, if you can countenance it!' Tibold said. 'Though one would hardly believe it, the way she behaves, without even the manners of a gentleman, though she mimics a man. An ape leader, to be sure.'

Oberon soon regretted his query, for Tibold proceeded to blame the woman for everything from the depressed economy to untreated boils. The physician was practically frothing at the mouth, such was his enmity, and Oberon realised he would get little solid information from the fellow. He was considering how to extricate himself when Tibold abruptly ceased his tirade and lifted a hand to point in accusation.

'There she is, right there!'

Frowning at the doctor's manner, Oberon none the less looked in the direction of his outstretched arm. From Tibold's ranting, Oberon expected to see a harridan, a crone fully capable of beating the doctor about the shoulders with her cane. But the female he saw was a plump, but decidedly dainty woman of middle age, holding a parasol, who eyed them with a vague expression of alarm.

It took Oberon a moment to realise the object of his companion's derision was not that timid-looking creature but another, a trim figure crossing the road with her back towards him. Although the length of her stride marked her as no mincing débutante, the infamous Miss Sutton did not resemble a man, at least from the rear. She wore a simple sprigged muslin gown that delineated a slender female form when caught by the breeze.

In fact, Oberon was contemplating the familiarity of those slim curves when his companion surged forwards, calling out the woman's name. Concerned for her safety, Oberon followed, ready to step in, if need be. But when she turned with a determined expression that Oberon recognised, he stepped back instead, neatly avoiding the heavy reticule that she sent swinging through the air at her pursuers. Dr Tibold, taken unawares, was struck full force in the stomach by the missile which, more than likely, contained a weight, for the physician doubled over, the wind knocked from him.

Either she didn't believe in using a more lethal weapon in public, or she hadn't the time to obtain another pistol to replace the one that was tucked away in Oberon's bureau. 'Miss Sutton, I presume?' he asked with a slight bow.

'Your Grace.' The distaste she made no attempt to hide surprised Oberon, accustomed as he was to being pursued for his company, his invitations or his influence. Even more surprising was his own, very different and well concealed, response.

At his first glimpse of her, Oberon felt a slam to the chest, just as though *he* had been on the receiving end of her reticule, his senses heightened and alert. The force of his reaction was baffling, especially since she had not stepped out of the shadows to threaten him with a gun. But perhaps the threat she posed was more subtle and her dislike stemmed from something more sinister.

For she would hardly draw his interest otherwise.

She was pretty enough; her face was a perfect oval, but her dark hair was unremarkable and her colouring was not pale enough to be fashionable. Still, it suited her, as did the green eyes that sparked with intelligence and strength of will, which had already been in evidence.

'I'll have you on charges of assault!' Tibold said, having finally recovered his breath.

'It was an act of self-defence, for you and your assassin have attacked me once and would do so again,' the young woman argued, lifting her chin.

Her fearless behaviour sent a jolt of awareness through Oberon. Although bold, she didn't appear to be brazen, and, contrary to Tibold's claims, no man in his right mind would confuse her gender. Oberon considered himself an astute judge of people; he had to be. But Miss Sutton was an intriguing piece of work. Who the devil was she?

'Ridiculous!' Tibold said. 'It is you who attacked me, as my witness can verify.'

Oberon had no intention of corroborating the mad doctor's claim and would have said so, but for the arrival of the small woman with the parasol. 'Glory, dear, whatever are you doing?' she asked, obviously uneasy.

Miss Sutton paid her no heed. 'Witness?' she said, scoffing. 'We both know that the duke is allied with you, and, indeed, is doing your dirty work!' she said, pointing a finger at Oberon.

'D-duke?' the dainty female echoed.

'Duke?' Tibold repeated.

'Westfield,' Miss Sutton said, with apparent exasperation.

Oberon could well imagine the disdainful glare she was sending his way, but he was occupied with the older woman, who had paled at the mention of his title and now swayed upon her feet. Since no one else was paying any attention to her, Oberon felt obliged to catch her as she fainted dead away.

When Tibold turned to gape at Westfield, Glory did, too, only to see that he was cradling her aunt in his arms. Horrified, she wanted to demand that he unhand her relative, but she feared he would drop Phillida to the ground. Frantically, Glory began searching past the rocks in her reticule for the hartshorn with which to revive her.

Where was Thad? Glory glanced around for her brother, but he had stopped at one of the burned buildings to urge the workers on. Though she held out little hope for his success, Glory was pleased that he was finally offering to help. Now, however, she wished they had not separated. Trying to take care of a business had made her careless, and she had walked the short distance alone. But who would have thought she'd be accosted upon the village's main thoroughfare, travelling from one property to another?

'Phillida?' Glory spoke her aunt's name sharply, though she doubted she could be heard above Tibold, who was rambling on, as usual. With her aunt prone and Thad nowhere in sight, Glory was at the mercy of the two men and she did not like turning her back on the physician, whose threatening manner had alarmed her more than once.

She felt cornered, and her hand shook as she waved the restorative under her aunt's nose. She refused to look up at the man who held Phillida, for one glance at Westfield already had robbed her of her breath. Last evening, he had been striking, but now she had clearly seen his tall form, wide shoulders and the body she once had been pressed against.

And that face. It was not beautiful in a feminine sense, for it held no softness, but Westfield might have been sculpted by one of the great artists. Indeed, he could have been carved from stone, for his expression revealed nothing. For some reason—fear, perhaps— the more Glory thought about him, the more her heart pounded.

Thankfully, Phillida snorted and blinked, and Glory eased her aunt upright while avoiding any contact with the duke. Phillida moaned in a dramatic fashion, as though eager to remain right where she was, and who could blame her? If Glory had not known the nobleman's true nature, she might have been thrilled to wake up to that handsome visage, cradled in arms that she knew were hard and strong.

Suppressing a shiver, Glory forced Phillida to her feet. 'Come, Aunt, we must be going.'

'Oh!' Phillida took one look at the duke and threatened to swoon again, but Glory was having none of it. Grabbing her aunt's arm, she pulled Phillida away from his grip. The duke said something, but it was drowned out by Tibold's speech, so they were able to make their escape. No doubt the men would have tried to detain them, if they were not in full view of passers-by.

As she dragged her aunt towards the Pump Room, Glory resisted the temptation to look over her shoulder for one last glimpse of the nobleman. Ignoring Phillida's horrified mutterings at their undignified progress, Glory did not stop even when the building's doors closed behind them, but continued on until they reached the privacy of one of the rear rooms.

There, Glory was able to deposit Phillida on a *chaise*, where she could swoon at her leisure. However, as Glory suspected, the lack of an audience speeded her recovery and she was able to fan herself as she lay prone.

'Mercy, Glory!' she said in a breathless whisper. 'I simply cannot countenance such outlandish behaviour! Whatever has come over you? It's this place, this wretched village. Oh, to be back in London. Please say that you have come to your senses and we can return to our town house.'

Since Glory heard this litany on a regular basis, she was unmoved. 'There is no reason for you to become agitated, dear,' she said, soothingly. 'Let me get you a glass of the waters.'

'No reason? Why, I have only to see my own niece in a public shouting match, in the middle of the street, mind you! And with a duke, no less!' Phillida fell back among the pillows with a shudder.

'I wasn't doing the shouting,' Glory said. 'It was that awful physician.' She paused to wonder how the shabby fellow had managed to align himself with a nobleman, but even a creature like Tibold could have connections, she supposed. She only wished they would spirit him away from Philtwell instead of trying to ruin her business.

Her business. Glory felt strengthened by the thought as she hurried to fetch her aunt a glass. Of course, Phillida did not approve, though Glory had assured her that even noblemen had run such resorts. *Noblemen*, not women, Phillida had argued, and therein lay the rub. If Glory were a man, Phillida probably would let her do what she liked.

But it was precisely because she was a woman, with few opportunities open to her, that Glory had taken an interest in the forgotten spa. Soon she would be aged twenty and firmly on the shelf in the eyes of society. Since she'd spent most of her life taking care of her younger brother after the death of their parents, Glory could not regret her unmarried status.

However, she did not care to spend the rest of her days in social calls or charity work. And she had no intention of settling quietly into a corner, tatting and sewing bonnets for her brother's future children. Although she would love to spoil babies, Glory thought with a pang, she didn't want to end up as some batty old spinster her nieces and nephews were forced to visit.

She wanted to do something with her life. But Glory could hardly use such terms to Phillida, who was an ageing spinster herself, though not quite batty. Yet. Instead, Glory had spoken of the family heritage, which was more acceptable and just as true. Queen's Well had been owned by the Suttons for generations. After the fateful fire, Glory's father, then a young man, had left Philtwell to seek his fortunes, never to return. It was only after his death that Glory discovered the legacy, rich in history, that he had left behind.

Gradually, she had found out more about Queen's Well, becoming further intrigued. She couldn't remember when the idea of reviving the spa first came to her, but it had remained at the back of her mind, a tempting possibility for the future—until Thad's wayward behaviour had forced her to action.

Although neither he nor Phillida had wanted to make the move, Glory had insisted. She had hoped the fresh air and simple pleasures of a village would change their minds, but Phillida complained of the lack of society and Thad remained sullen and uncooperative, evincing no interest in her venture.

Oddly enough, it was their encounter with Westfield that seemed to have wrought a change in him. Perhaps the presence of such an exalted personage had improved Thad's opinion of Philtwell, Glory mused. She didn't like to consider the other possibility: that Thad was simply drawn to a dangerous sort who would do him no favours.

The sound of a door slamming made Glory nearly drop the glass in her hand; for a moment she feared the duke was striding through the Pump Room, intent upon her. She turned in alarm when she heard footsteps approaching, even though she had told the workmen not to admit anyone.

But who would dare deny a duke?

Caught unprepared, Glory had no weapon except warm mineral water, but she faced the intruder with a hammering heart. She lifted her arm, only to shudder with relief when her brother burst into the room.

'Thad!' Glory admonished, lowering the vessel in her grip.

'What?' he asked. A moan from Phillida made him glance behind Glory, a questioning look on his face. 'What?' he repeated, ignoring his sister's warning grimace. 'Did something happen?'

'Yes, something happened,' Phillida said, lifting her head. 'Your sister made a spectacle of herself in the middle of the street, with a duke!' Phillida fell back, as though too overcome to continue, but she was bound to be disappointed by her nephew's reaction.

Instead of appearing shocked, Thad frowned in apparent disappointment. 'You saw Westfield? You might have waited for me,' he complained, throwing himself into a medallion-backed chair.

'It was not a social visit,' Glory said, glaring at her brother. 'He was with Dr Tibold, who approached me from behind and began shouting at me.' She did not add that she had swung at the physician in her own defence. Since Phillida had not mentioned it, Glory hoped her aunt had not seen the blow.

'The bounder! He needs a good thrashing,' Thad said, and Glory was comforted by his outrage. She had been right to share her concerns with him, for he finally was taking an interest. Or so she thought until he spoke again.

'But Westfield? I don't believe it. Why would he even be seen with such a character?'

'Perhaps they are related,' Glory suggested, though she did not need evidence of the duke's true nature. He had demonstrated it last evening, when he had put his hands upon her…

But Thad shook his head. 'That doesn't seem likely, or Tibold would have been bragging of his connections. And why didn't I see Westfield? I suppose that I wasn't paying much attention after… Well, now that I know he's out and about, I'll keep an eye out for him.'

'And why would you do that?' Glory asked, warily. She did not want her brother confronting the duke, nor did she want her brother to seek the man's company.

'Perhaps Thad can offer his Grace some kind of explanation for his sister's outlandish behaviour,' Phillida said, interrupting Glory's thoughts. 'I cannot show my face in society knowing that we will be cut by a famous nobleman. The gossip! The rumours! If only you could make amends, dear boy.' Rousing herself on to an elbow, Phillida sent her nephew a beseeching look.

Glory found the thought of making amends with Westfield disconcerting, but she did not care to admit as much to her aunt. 'It is not as though you move in the same circles,' she said.

'But aren't you always claiming that the spas are a

perfect place to mingle with all manner of people?' Phillida demanded. 'Where else might we be included in such company?'

Where else indeed? Glory thought, her own words coming back to haunt her. 'But why should we aspire to such an acquaintance? Westfield has allied himself with our enemy and proven himself unworthy of our regard.'

At Glory's words, her aunt dropped back upon the *chaise*, moaning again, seemingly unable to respond.

Ignoring the dramatics, Glory turned towards Thad. 'How did you find the work site?' she asked, eager to change the subject.

'Oh,' Thad said, looking down at the tips of his boots. 'I gave them a good talking to, and they promised to pick up the pace, as they well should.'

Although his words were reassuring, his demeanour was not and Glory bit back a sigh. More likely the men hadn't paid any more heed to Thad than they had to her, but she was grateful for his efforts.

'Thank you, Thad,' she said, trying to ignore the sinking feeling in her chest. Before new buildings could even be considered, the remains of the old needed to be torn down and cleared away. As she had many times before, Glory wondered what would convince men to avoid doing the job they were being paid to do, even at the possible forfeiture of their wages. But this time, an answer came to her.

Westfield.

Chapter Three

Trapped by the blathering physician, Oberon stood watching Miss Sutton retreat to the Pump Room, *her* Pump Room, which made last evening's story more believable. But there were still several things that didn't quite fit. The young woman seemed too well bred to be in trade and too clever to be involved with a hopeless venture like Queen's Well. Even more jarring was her array of weapons and her inclination to use them.

Her behaviour was odd, to say the least. Having disdained his help, she had raced towards the Pump Room as though fleeing his company, and it was that, most of all, that raised Oberon's suspicions. She had dragged her aunt down the road, drawing the stares of the villagers in a public display that would have her ostracised in London. Never had a female been so eager to escape him. But why? Did she have something to hide? And, if so, what made her determined to hide it from him?

Oberon's musings were interrupted by a stream of gibberish from the man at his side, which might better explain Miss Sutton's hasty exit. Having discovered Oberon's identity, the volatile physician had turned the full force of his flattery upon Oberon. No doubt he hoped for a fat purse from a noble patron, but finally his words trailed off as he realised where Oberon's gaze lingered.

'As you have seen for yourself, your Grace,' the man said, his earlier tone of condemnation returning, 'she's a bold piece, a menace to society. I'm sure everyone in our little community would be most grateful if you could use your influence to liberate our waters.'

Oberon had yet to determine if Miss Sutton was a menace, and he suppressed a startling *frisson* of interest at the prospect of finding out. However, she was hardly the low female Tibold made her out to be, and Oberon had no intention of letting the man abuse her. He flexed his fingers in an unconscious gesture, then turned to face the physician, his expression impassive.

'You will stop maligning the young woman; should I hear that you have approached within ten feet of her, I shall have you brought up on charges.' With a nod of dismissal, Oberon left the doctor sputtering in his wake and resumed his walk.

Again, he watched for anything out of the ordinary, but for the first time in years he was distracted, his thoughts unaccountably returning to Miss Sutton. He was even tempted to turn around and make sure Tibold did not follow her to the Pump Room.

Annoyed, Oberon continued on his way, strolling through a few of the shops and stopping for refreshment at a quiet tavern. Although such places were the best sources of information, the occupants were often slow to warm up to newcomers, and Oberon adopted a casual mien to keep from appearing too curious.

He asked only the most general of questions about the village and its environs, as any visitor might, resisting the urge to probe too deeply into the Suttons. However, he soon discovered that their arrival was the only significant event to have occurred recently, at least according to those to be found in the Queen's Arms.

Opinions about the Suttons themselves were less freely offered. One man praised the family for their efforts and the promise of work to be had in the future. Another grumbled about drawing the kind of sickly and infirm patrons who spent little coin and infected others with their diseases. The rest of the tavern's occupants appeared to be reserving judgement or were too tight-lipped to comment, although other, more dubious reasons, for their silence were possible.

Oberon kept his own remarks neutral, for he knew that every resident of Philtwell would soon learn of these conversations. There was no hiding the arrival of a duke and duchess, especially when his mother took such an interest in the village. And Oberon never made any secret of his identity. It was part and parcel of a reputation that was well known and carefully crafted.

The Duke of Westfield was a man with a taste for the finer things and fascinating company, a pursuer of pleasure rather than politics, though he took nothing to extremes. An intelligent conversationalist, gracious, but not too friendly, he was the perfect guest, as well as playing host to his own entertainments, where an eclectic assortment gathered. And if the crew in the tavern were not his usual companions, he did his best to appear pleasant, yet aloof enough to avoid undue scrutiny.

By the time he left, Oberon knew the names of Philtwell's most prominent citizens, the sad state of its economy and some common gossip about the residents. Having stayed longer than he intended, when he strolled away from the Queen's Arms, Oberon saw that the gardener had left the grounds of the Pump Room, meaning that he would learn no more about the owners today, unless…

Seized by a sudden urge to see if Miss Sutton was still in the building, Oberon firmly quelled the desire, yet he crossed the road in order to take the quicker path behind the building, under the trees. But no slender figure stepped out of the shadows to fix a pistol upon him, and the door to the Pump Room was firmly shut.

Oberon shook his head at his own folly, for he knew better than to court trouble. The last thing he needed was to do something reckless that endangered all that he had worked for these past years, as well as the work—and even the lives—of others. At the thought, Oberon considered returning to London, far from the intriguing young woman. But that would mean turning his back on whatever might be going on here, as well as leaving his mother behind. And he had no good reason to do either.

No matter who or what she was, Miss Sutton could hardly get the better of him. Oberon knew how to keep his head, play a part, and, most of all, maintain control.

Gossip travels fast in close environs, and Philtwell was no exception. Oberon had not yet returned to Sutton House when news reached his mother of the contretemps in front of the Pump Room. It came in through the kitchens first, a delivery boy relating the incident to the enthralled staff, and from there to the upper servants, including Randolph's valet.

While he intended to relay this information at the earliest opportunity, a couple of callers arrived to pay their respects to the visiting dowager. So it was through a Mrs Malemeyne that Letitia received the first report that her son had been seen in the village with the very young woman she had hoped he might meet.

Her initial pleasure was dimmed by the description of the encounter, which varied according to the messenger. Mrs Malemeyne, eager to ingratiate herself with the dowager, claimed that the duke was a hero for coming to the aid of a fainting woman, while the

persons he so selflessly served were ingrates who
fled the scene with undue haste. Leaning close, Mrs
Malemeyne confided that she thought little enough
of the Suttons, for the girl was too bold, by half, and
the aunt seemed in ill health, for all the swooning that
she did.

Mrs Levet was more circumspect. There appeared
to be shouting, she said, though she was sure his Grace
wasn't the one doing it. And there were reports of a
blow, though she was uncertain who struck whom.
Alarmed at this version of events, the dowager turned
to Mrs Goodhew for the truth, an elderly woman who
had once been the arbiter of the small society that
made up Philtwell.

The dowager found her old friend still residing in
a small manor house that had long been the home of
the squires that served the area. Having outlived most
of her contemporaries, Mrs Goodhew welcomed her
visitor eagerly, holding court in a chair near the fire,
despite the warmth of the day.

'It's a pleasure to see you, Letty,' she said, her
voice still strong.

'And you, Maisie,' Letitia said. 'So much has
changed since I last was here that it is a comfort to
find you and Randolph carrying on.'

Maisie snorted. 'Is that what you call it?' Then
she studied Letitia through narrowed eyes. 'And Randolph? How is he faring?'

'Oh, much better,' Letitia said, meeting the older
woman's questioning gaze head on.

Maisie snorted again, as if she was having none

of it, but she did not pursue the subject. 'I hear you brought your son along.'

'Yes,' Letitia said. 'I wanted him to see the spa where his father and I met.'

Maisie sighed and shook her head. 'It's not the same, Letty. It hasn't been since the fire.'

'Yes, that's what Randolph said.'

Maisie shook her head again. 'It was a horrible night. Frank and I were in the Assembly Rooms when it happened, all so quickly that we hadn't the sense to realise… I heard something, like a cannon ball or some sort of explosion, but I'm sure we all would have ignored it, if Sutton hadn't made us get out. Our men did the best they could, but the inn was already engulfed and it was spreading. Sutton tried to go in.'

Letitia made a sound of dismay, and Maisie frowned. 'I'm surprised more people weren't killed.' She drew a deep breath. 'But that was the end, Letty. Sutton's wife didn't have the heart for it, probably not the money, either, and something like that irrevocably damages a place's reputation.'

'Yet it might recover,' Letitia said. 'I understand the Sutton children are back.'

'Yes, but it might be too late. The village lost its heart. Damn fools haven't been very welcoming. They blame the family for everything that's happened since.'

'Yes, I heard of an odd episode today,' Letitia said carefully.

Maisie's expression grew sly. 'Involving your son.'

Letitia nodded, relieved to hear her old friend was still awake on every suit. 'I wasn't certain whether you kept yourself as informed as in the old days.'

'I do the best I can, aided by a few of my younger friends and my faithful servants, of course.'

Letitia leaned forwards. 'I would be curious to hear your version of events, for a certain Mrs Malemeyne painted Oberon in quite a heroic light, a pose that seems unlikely.'

Maisie snorted. 'Malemeyne. A trumped-up clerk's wife who tries to pass herself off as gentry.' She paused. 'I don't know your son, but I hear he was with one of the shadier characters who've invaded Philtwell in the past few years. The fellow claims to be a doctor, but who knows? Nosed around the well as though he wanted to take it over, but he has no legal right to anything.'

She paused. 'The Suttons still own all but the big house, so Randolph wrote to them, and it wasn't long before they arrived, the son, the daughter and an aunt. That didn't sit well with some people, including this doctor. From what I hear, he's been bullying the girl, who appears to be the one arranging the re-opening.'

'Ah…' Letitia sat back. She hesitated to say too much, for age obviously had not dulled Maisie's wits.

'My sources tell me that the doctor was shouting at the girl. Outrageous, if you ask me. Why, in my day, he'd have been horsewhipped. But people mind their own business now,' she said, shaking her head. 'I suspect the doctor latched on to your son as he would any well-dressed gentleman, and, not knowing who's who in our little community, the duke certainly can be forgiven for not stepping in.'

Letitia frowned at the poor excuse for her son's behaviour. 'Although I wouldn't paint him as heroic, I can't imagine he would stand aside while a young lady is abused.'

'Perhaps he did not, for no one was close enough to eavesdrop. And obviously he aided the aunt, for, by all accounts, he caught her when she fainted.'

'But then Miss Sutton dragged her away.'

'Perhaps, but it is hardly a matter of consequence,' Maisie said.

Maisie was right. In the usual course of things, the episode would quickly be forgotten, but Letitia had pinned her hopes for the future upon a felicitous meeting between her son and Miss Sutton and she saw her plans going sadly awry before they had even begun. She did not easily surrender, however, and she set her mouth in a determined line, unwilling to give up on the first decent prospect she'd had in years.

'Letty?' Maisie said, sending her a sharp glance.

'You are correct, as usual, Maisie dear, but I do so want my son to enjoy Philtwell as I have,' Maisie said, without going into details. 'Perhaps I should try to set everyone to rights, to avoid any misunderstandings.'

Such a reaction on her part would hardly be

suspect, Letitia decided, and from what she had just heard, it was clearly time for her to step in. Leery of being perceived as matchmaking, she and Randolph had hoped to let Mother Nature take its course, but that didn't seem possible now.

Unfortunately, as everyone knew, the old girl was not very reliable.

Glory lagged behind her aunt and her brother, uncharacteristically dragging her steps, for she did not share their excitement over the evening ahead. Lifting her bent head, Glory forced herself to look at the building that was their destination: Sutton House, the home of her ancestors.

By rights they should be living there, but they were comfortable enough in the smaller cottage that had remained in the family. The larger residence, set back among the sycamores, seemed rather gloomy to Glory when they had visited on previous occasions at the invitation of the current owner.

Mr Pettit seemed to be a staunch supporter of Queen's Well, but now Glory wondered about him, considering his guests. The duke and his mother must have made themselves at home, despite Mr Pettit's illness, because it was from the dowager that the invitation had come.

Normally, Glory would have been eager to gain noble approval of her plans, for a nod from a duchess would certainly be a boon to any enterprise. But her dealings with Westfield made her leery of a conversation with either of them, especially if they shared Dr Tibold's views upon the waters.

Glory might even have refused to go, if given a choice, but it was made clear that she had none. Phillida had practically swooned, with joy this time, when she received the missive. Preening over the correspondence, Glory's aunt had spent the rest of the day determining what to wear and planning detailed reports to all her London acquaintances of her new 'friendship' with the noblewoman.

Thad, too, had been eager for the outing, and since little in Philtwell interested him, Glory had kept her objections to herself, though she was determined to be on her guard. The others might be blinded by titles, but Glory knew that, beneath Westfield's elegant exterior, there was something dangerous that went beyond the power of wealth and rank.

Westfield handled himself too well. And he had handled *her* too well, Glory thought, flushing at the recollection. What other man of his position would disarm a pistol-wielding opponent, and so easily? Glory realised that she had not been a formidable foe, but, then, what gentleman would act as he had towards a woman? Westfield had no compunction against pulling her to him, twisting her arm, whispering in her ear...

Glory drew in a sharp breath. She liked to think of herself as capable, for she had held her family together since the untimely death of her father, raising her brother and making the decisions that Phillida was unwilling or unable to bother about. She managed the finances, ran the household and had chosen to revive Queen's Well, despite opposition. There was little that unnerved her.

But Westfield made her uneasy in ways that she couldn't even define. He was a threat, if nothing else, to her peace of mind, so Glory looked about warily as they entered Sutton House. But when the butler showed them into the parlour, the room was empty except for a regal-looking woman who could be none other than the dowager duchess. Approaching them with a smile, she apologised for the lack of proper introduction since Mr Pettit was indisposed.

It was not what Glory had been expecting. She had imagined a female version of Westfield—dark, aloof and threatening—and this woman seemed to be none of those things. Although Glory rarely chanced upon members of the *ton*, the social elite, she knew that often the women were spoiled, shrill and demanding, with contempt for anyone beneath them.

Yet the dowager graciously greeted each of the Suttons in turn, lastly settling her attention upon Glory. Although her eyes were blue, they held the same sharp intelligence as her son's, and she cocked her head slightly, as though to examine Glory in earnest.

'Ah, Miss Sutton,' she said. 'So you are the one.'

'The one?' Glory repeated, uncertain of the woman's meaning.

'Who would re-open Queen's Well.'

'Yes,' Glory said, lifting her chin. Having failed in their earlier intimidations, perhaps Dr Tibold and Westfield hoped to use the gentle arts of persuasion in the form of this woman. But Glory had no intention of giving in—to anyone. The more she was pushed, the more she held fast, determined to make her family's heritage a success.

Expecting her show of stubbornness to draw the duchess's displeasure, Glory was surprised at the woman's slow smile. 'Wonderful, just wonderful,' the older woman murmured. Nodding, as if in approval, she left Glory even more puzzled when she turned towards Phillida, who was asking about Mr Pettit.

'He is doing better, though he won't be able to join us tonight,' the duchess said. As she chatted with Phillida, Glory took the opportunity to study her more closely. The duchess did not much resemble her son, for she was not tall and lean, but there was something about the way she held herself that reminded Glory of the duke. And they shared the same bone structure, which made the dowager a handsome woman, if not quite as breathtaking as her son.

While Glory watched, a light came into the older woman's eyes that made her look far younger. Turning to follow her gaze, Glory was brought up short by the sight of a figure in the shadows at the end of the room. Someone had entered silently and unannounced, but there was no mistaking the tall form. It was Westfield, and Glory automatically took a step back.

Surely he would be on his best behaviour in front of his mother, Glory thought, yet she still felt a *frisson* of unease. Thus far, her dealings with the man had been unpredictable, untenable, unsavoury...

'Ah, there you are. Come join us,' the duchess said,

and Glory's heart pounded far more than was reasonable as he stepped into the light. He moved with the quiet grace of a cat, and not an ordinary pet, but one like those found in menageries…one that was stalking its prey.

Glory held her ground, but glanced away to still her racing pulse. She had learned through experiences with some of the villagers and the workmen not to let her weaknesses show, for surely her opponent, be it a vendor or an enemy, would take advantage. Unfortunately, the thought of Westfield taking advantage of her only fuelled her agitation. All too well, she recalled the feel of him pressed against her back, the warmth of his breath upon her ear…

'Miss Sutton.'

The sound of the deep voice made her jump, and Glory realised he was speaking to her. Lifting her chin, she forced herself to look into his handsome face. His dark eyes revealed little, and yet Glory suspected that there was nothing that escaped him, including the fact that she was hanging back, as far from him as possible. No doubt that's why he was making a point of offering her his arm to take her into supper.

Glory was tempted to refuse, but she did not want him to see how easily he had unnerved her. With a curt nod, she assented, but as he led her into the dining hall, she had never been so aware of another person. Her skin tingled where her fingers rested against his sleeve, and she nearly pulled away. When she took her seat, glad to be free of his touch at last, Glory felt his fingers brush against her back.

She was certain the movement had been no accident and wondered if he took liberties because of what had happened the previous night. If so, Glory had more to worry about than his designs upon the spa, and a shiver ran up her spine. She was in no position to protect herself from a powerful lord, and poor Thad had proven himself no match for Westfield. As the implications struck her, Glory was hard pressed not to leap from her chair and flee into the night.

Although she remained where she was, all the Gothic novels Glory had read came back to haunt her in the dimly lit, old-fashioned room. She told herself that even a duke could do nothing while lodged in a gentleman's home, with her family around her and his mother in attendance. And yet Glory felt as though no one else was present, the two of them existing in some kind of netherworld.

Vaguely, she heard Phillida launch into a lengthy explanation for her earlier fainting spell, including abundant praise for Westfield's fast action in coming to her rescue. Mention of the incident restored Glory to herself, and she braced herself for Westfield's comments. But he demurred, saying little and appearing uninterested, though Glory sensed that he was paying more attention than he pretended to.

'We may have arrived only recently, but I have already heard of this physician,' the duchess said. 'It seems he is a most unpleasant sort. What on earth were you doing with him, Westfield?'

Glory looked towards the duke with no little curiosity. Whatever the man was up to, his mother apparently knew nothing of it.

'The fellow accosted me, offering his dubious services, for whatever might ail me. Then he accosted Miss Sutton,' Westfield said. 'Apparently, he has designs upon her…waters.'

Glory gaped in astonishment, but she could read nothing in the duke's expression. Was he telling the truth? If so, she had misjudged him, yet she could not cast aside her suspicions so easily. There was something about the man that just didn't ring true…

'Ah, the famous waters,' the duchess said in a tone of delight. She went on to praise Queen's Well, reminiscing about her visit many years ago, in such a manner that could only be deemed genuine. Gradually, Glory's wariness receded over the course of the meal. She enjoyed hearing about the spa's past success, for she had little first-hand information about those days. Even Phillida and Thad appeared impressed by the dowager's enthusiasm.

But not the duke. Yet, even in his silence, he seemed to command Glory's attention, a dark presence at the head of the table that drew her fleeting glances. And when he finally spoke, she was jolted by the sound, deep and low and seemingly intimate. Or had it simply sparked a memory of him leaning close and whispering in her ear…?

'Why did you decide to resume operations?'

Although the question was a casual one, Glory sensed a deeper meaning behind the words. Yet she could see nothing untoward in his expression, handsome, vaguely attentive and distant. It was a polite query, nothing more.

Glory drew in a breath and wondered what on earth was happening to her. She had always been the one member of the family with common sense. It was not like her to envision Gothic scenarios or hidden mysteries, threats and dangers with no apparent substance. Stolid and determined, she was not one for fripperies or flirting. So why was her heart pounding so alarmingly?

Westfield.

When she realised that everyone was waiting expectantly for her reply, Glory forced a smile. 'It is our family's heritage and should not be allowed to languish when the well is still in good order.'

'But don't you think the time for such places has passed?' the duke asked.

'No, I think they will always be popular. Mineral springs have served as gathering spots probably since our earliest ancestors stumbled across them bubbling up from the ground,' Glory said. 'For a long time many wells were associated with saints and became the focus of pilgrimages for those who would be healed, with some people travelling great distances to partake of the waters.'

Over the years, Glory had done her research and she warmed to the history. 'Later, when shrines were frowned upon, people still sought the therapeutic waters, along with the entertainments, music, dances, cards and the like, that were added so that visitors could enjoy the pleasures of society in a relaxed and healthful setting.'

'There isn't a lovelier setting than Philtwell,' the duchess said, which made Phillida exclaim about the beauty of the area. Glory found her aunt's speech so astonishing that she had to bite back a smile as she took a sip of wine. If the dowager could convince her aunt and brother they would be happy here, Glory was not about to argue.

'But considering the current state of the village, what kind of patrons do you hope to attract?' Westfield asked.

Although he didn't elaborate, Glory assumed he envisioned only the most derelict and those who preyed upon them. She lifted her chin. 'Queen's Well has always served a fine clientele that has included royalty.'

'Queen Elizabeth?' Westfield asked, his tone wry.

'Yes,' Glory said. 'In fact, the well was rediscovered by one of her courtiers.'

'And has not changed much since.'

'It has kept the appeal of a small site, of course, but there have been many developments through the centuries,' Glory argued. 'A new well and Pump Room were constructed, and Assembly Rooms and inns were added over the years, along with plantings and gravel walks. I've already had those cleared and the trees trimmed. I'm having some flowering bushes put in around the Pump Room, but eventually I hope to add new gardens.'

'Excellent,' the dowager said. 'The spa needs plenty of tree-lined groves and secluded walks, where romance can flourish.'

Glory eyed the dowager with bemusement. 'Perhaps, but I do not want to gain a reputation for that sort of thing, which has been the ruin of many a spa. Young women will not come to visit unless they feel completely safe from importuning adventurers…or any man, for that matter,' she added, with a glance towards Westfield.

'Or any *one* for that matter,' he replied smoothly.

'But Philtwell is above reproach,' the duchess exclaimed. Unaware of any undercurrents between her son and her guests, she proceeded to assure a pale Phillida that the village was decidedly more secure than London.

'But even if Philtwell is deemed the most bucolic and picturesque site in the country, it is too far out of the way to entice any except the most determined visitor,' Westfield said.

Although Glory felt the duke's gaze upon her as he waited for her reply, she refused to look at him. Perhaps he was not allied with Dr Tibold, but he certainly seemed to be against the re-opening of Queen's Well.

'Yet in the past the spa was successful, and now the roads are better and travel more common than in those days,' Glory said. 'And revivals have occurred before. Other spas have fallen into and out of favour again and again.'

'Or opened, only to close,' the duke said.

'Don't change her mind,' his mother said. 'I do so want to see the place as it should be.'

'I am simply curious as to how she came to her decision,' Westfield said. 'The venture is a large undertaking, especially for a woman, an expensive proposition that may not repay in kind. What sort of investors have you secured?'

'Don't be rude, dear,' the duchess admonished.

Thad looked as though he would speak, but Glory sent him a warning glance. Their finances weren't anyone's business, and she was not about to discuss them.

'It is because I am a woman that you feel I am doomed to fail?' Glory asked. Reaching for a fortifying sip of wine, she eyed Westfield directly.

'Certainly not, for I am sure many females, including my own mother, are more than capable of astounding successes,' he answered, his expression bland.

'Very well put,' the duchess said. She turned towards Glory. 'And I'm sure all of us here, including Mr Pettit, wish for the triumph of what can only be an asset to the community.'

'Thank you,' Glory said, though she suspected Westfield did not share his mother's sentiments. 'I hope the spa will draw people for the simple reason that Philtwell is a lovely place to stay, with beautiful scenery and bracing air that is far more wholesome than the stench of London. If drinking or bathing in the waters proves beneficial, then that is all the better.'

'There is a bathing pool?' Westfield asked.

'No, but we have private rooms for bathing on the upper floor of the Pump Room.'

'And how soon can we look forward to seeing it all for ourselves?' the duchess asked.

'I can take you around at any time,' Thad said. The offer took Glory by surprise, though it seemed to be directed to Westfield, rather than his mother.

Not to be outdone, Phillida tendered an invitation to the cottage, as well as a trip to the Pump Room, to 'taste the waters' on the morrow.

'Delightful,' the duchess exclaimed. 'I am most anxious to see what you've done with it. And for the general public?'

'Well, I had planned to wait until the old buildings had been torn down, but I'm afraid I've had some problems with the local workers,' Glory said. Although earlier she had suspected Westfield's involvement, that appeared unlikely now. 'They seem unable to complete their work in a timely manner.'

'I've spoken to them, so we should be soon set to rights,' Thad said, and Glory wished fervently that it were so.

'Perhaps when Mr Pettit recovers, he can have a word, as well, for such behaviour reflects poorly on the community,' the duchess said. 'Although I understand that not everyone here has been enthusiastic, I'm sure they will all come around once the Pump Room is open again.'

Her words gave Glory pause, and she fell silent, which gave Phillida an opportunity to launch into a recitation of some of the supposed slights she had received since their arrival. While the duchess made soothing noises, Glory reconsidered her plans.

Perhaps it was the dowager's encouragement that moved her to make the decision. Or it might have been the duke's discouragement that made up her mind. But suddenly she was quite certain of what to do. And when Phillida finally ran out of anecdotes, Glory spoke up.

'I think we shall open next week.'

'Oh, how lovely,' the duchess said, in obvious delight.

Trying to keep a defiant expression from her face, Glory turned towards the duke, but he did not appear disappointed. In fact, he seemed only mildly curious when he spoke. 'Why the hurry?'

'I was going to wait until more work had been done, but now I think her Grace is right. If the villagers see our newly renovated Pump Room and what a wonderful addition it is to Philtwell, they will "come around" all the sooner.'

Although Glory expected the duke to raise some objection or argument, he made no further comment, and her heady sense of triumph began to fade in the face of his apparent indifference. It disappeared entirely when he began to question Thad about the activities available to young people.

Later, when they removed to the parlour, Glory tried her best to get a good look at the man's boots, but she could tell nothing except that the size of his feet were proportional to the rest of him. And, no doubt, he had an attentive valet to remove all traces of stains, including paint, from his apparel.

Glancing up from her study, Glory caught him eyeing her, one dark brow cocked in question, and she turned away, flushing. Thankfully, the duke did not comment. Nor did he say anything more about Queen's Well, but played the part of host with ease until the Suttons took their leave, yet Glory could not dismiss the notion that he was playing a part and that the Duke of Westfield was not what he seemed.

Chapter Four

It was so late by the time Letitia was able to visit Randolph's room that she wondered whether she should wait until morning to seek him out. But, eager to hear his opinion, she slipped through the door and was glad to see a candle still burning near the bed.

'Are you awake?'

'Well, if I wasn't, I am now,' Randolph grumbled, but Letitia noticed that he put aside a book, so he must have been reading. His ill mood probably was due to his continued occupation of this bedchamber, a suspicion that he soon confirmed.

'I feel like I've been cooped up here for ever.'

'You can't come out now, or Oberon will surely make plans for departure, for he has nothing to hold him here…yet.'

Randolph said nothing, but glared at her over his half-spectacles.

'Only a few more days,' Letitia promised. 'Once

we have dosed them, I will have more faith in our plans.' Without giving him the opportunity to argue, she went on. 'So, what do you think?'

'I think I'm lucky I didn't get caught sneaking around the house in my nightshirt,' he muttered. 'Your son's valet seems to have eyes in the back of his head.'

Letitia dismissed his complaint with a wave of her hand. 'Well?'

He sat back amongst the pillows and sighed. 'I do not like to discourage you, especially since I am the one responsible for your high hopes, but it does not look good to me.'

'Why?' Letitia asked.

'From what I could see, which was precious little, mind you,' Randolph said, 'they do not even like each other.'

'Well, I would be disappointed if they did,' Letitia said. 'I don't want him to befriend her. I want him to fall passionately in love with her.'

Randolph shook his head. 'I don't see how that is going to happen when they are barely civil to each other. You could have dined out on their animosity.'

'Ah, but both are strong emotions, one sometimes standing in for the other,' the duchess said. 'And I'm so pleased that he is feeling *something* that I must account it a good sign.'

Randolph shot her a questioning look, and Letitia wondered if she had said too much. She looked down at the hands in her lap. 'He was much affected by his father's death; I fear he was thrust too soon under the mantle of ducal responsibilities. He rose to the occasion admirably, of course, but he changed. I've often wondered if something happened while I was… grieving, but Oberon has kept his thoughts to himself. I worry about him, Randolph.'

He said nothing, and she sought to explain. 'He began distancing himself from his home and his family, spending more and more time at the town house in London until it has been his primary home for years now. I don't understand why he won't visit the place he so loved.' *Or his mother*, she did not add.

'It's not as though he's gambling away his inheritance,' Letitia said. 'Far from it, for he has several gentlemen overseeing everything from the farms at Westfield to foreign investments. So how does he spend his days?'

When Randolph did not answer, she went on. 'He attends social functions, frittering away his time at one ball or rout or salon after another.'

'There are worse activities,' Randolph said.

'Yes,' Letitia admitted, for she had told herself that many a time. 'But there are better ones.' And she hesitated to think what his father would say, if he knew that his heir was gadding about among a society he had held in contempt. Her husband had devoted his life to his family and public service, championing charities and improvements, so that he had left the world a better place. Letitia felt her eyes well up at the loss of her husband, far too soon, and she swallowed.

'Somehow he doesn't seem the type to be engaged in such frippery,' Randolph said, interrupting her maudlin thoughts.

'I know,' Letitia said. 'He is far too intelligent. He is well read, but beyond that he doesn't appear to have any interests.' Even worse, he didn't seem to *care*. Although she assumed that her son loved her, he was so composed that she had begun to wonder if he felt anything at all.

But tonight, there had been little hints that he was not his usual urbane self. Perhaps it was not the behaviour she had been hoping for, but it was *something*. And she was heartened by it. She rose to her feet and smiled to herself.

'I don't believe it will be too difficult to turn this passion of his in a more positive direction,' she said to Randolph. 'All we need is for Queen's Well to work its magic.'

Rain had been battering the windows since breakfast, making Oberon wonder why anyone would want to seek out more water. But he did not refuse when his mother insisted he accompany her to the Pump Room for their private tour. What he had learned the evening before only made him more curious about the Suttons and their dubious enterprise.

'It appears that Miss Sutton has rather grandiose plans for her spa,' he said casually, once they were settled in the coach for the short drive. 'I wonder where she is getting the funding for such a venture?'

'Oberon, please do not be so rude as to enquire

again,' his mother said. 'It was bad of you to do so during supper.'

'I don't see why, for it is a business, is it not? I would think they would be eager to put their case to prospective financers.' In fact, Oberon was surprised that his mother, stricken as she was with nostalgia, had not been solicited. He slanted her a glance. 'They haven't approached you, have they?'

'Certainly not,' she answered. 'Miss Sutton is too gently reared to speak of such things.'

Oberon's brows shot upwards. Miss Sutton was practically in trade, and he could think of no good reason for her silence on the subject. Although he doubted she was running a swindle, there was always the possibility that her investors wanted to keep their participation quiet. And in his experience, such secrecy meant they were up to something, whether Miss Sutton was aware of it or not.

Oberon frowned, unwilling to believe that she was a knowing participant in anything unsavoury, only to shake his head. Such thoughts led to misjudgements, mistakes or worse, no matter whether he was in London or in a remote village. And he would do well to keep that in mind, he realised, as he entered Miss Sutton's lair, the infamous Pump Room.

While his mother exclaimed in delight, Oberon assessed the place coolly. Although the main room might be light and airy on a good day, with its tall, arched windows on three sides, the rain cast a pall over the interior this afternoon. Or perhaps the dearth of patrons made it seem devoid of life. The neatly polished parquet floor was empty except for some tables and chairs clustered at the perimeter, where those who did not wish to mill around, socialising, could partake of the waters in seated comfort.

It was at one of these small tables where Miss Sutton's aunt, Miss Bamford, sat waving her hand-kerchief in their direction. An empty-headed creature who provided little beyond haphazard chaperonage, she was an odd companion for Miss Sutton. The boy was there, too, though he seemed more like a typical youth than anything else. But where was his sister?

Despite Oberon's best intentions, he felt a *frisson* of anticipation as he scanned the area, and when he saw her, his reaction was as baffling as it was difficult to disguise. He had assumed that the long evening before spent acting as host in Mr Pettit's absence would have inured him to whatever appeal Miss Sutton presented—but it had not. He felt just as he had the first time he had glimpsed her standing in the shadows behind this very building, like he had been struck by some powerful force in his gut or perhaps lower...

'Miss Sutton,' he said, with a nod.

'Your Grace,' she answered. Was there a breath-lessness to her tone? Oberon didn't flatter himself. She probably had rushed to greet the visitors. She took a seat at the table next to her aunt and Oberon joined them. They were not obliged to obtain their own waters, but were served by a robust young female in a starched apron.

'None for me, thank you,' Thad said.

'Nor I,' Oberon added.

'Drink up,' his mother urged. 'It will do you good.'

Oberon frowned as he eyed the liquid. 'So it is said of every spring in England, from the fountains of Bath to the meanest dribble coming up from a farm field that the cows refuse to taste. Each is supposed to cure everything from boils to consumption, but I don't put much faith in those claims.'

'Actually, Queen's Well has never been associated with a specific cure,' Miss Sutton said, which was hardly surprising since she seemed to argue with him at every opportunity. And yet Oberon felt, not irritated, but pleased by the byplay.

'Oh, I wouldn't say that,' his mother murmured with a sly smile. Apparently, her nostalgia for the waters knew no bounds.

However, after Oberon had downed half of the wretched brew he realised that neither his mother nor Miss Bamford had touched their glasses and he lodged a protest.

'I'm afraid I've had my share this morning,' Miss Bamford said. 'I must admit that it is rather nice to have one's own supply. No more need to buy bottles of Epsom.'

'And you?' Oberon asked his mother, lifting a brow. After all, she seemed to be the spa's chief supporter.

Smiling as though privy to some private amusement, she shook her head. 'Oh, I've no need of it,' she said. Oberon opened his mouth to enquire further until he remembered that such waters were known purgatives, so he held his tongue.

Since it appeared that the only other person drinking was Miss Sutton, Oberon lifted his glass in a toast. 'To Queen's Well,' he said, speaking words he'd never thought to utter. And somehow the noxious drink was made palatable by her surprised smile as her gaze met his own. Like the finest of emeralds, her green eyes were beautiful, rare and glowing with light, an observation that seemed to send heat surging through him.

Either that or the waters she forced on him were poisoned.

Oberon waited a long moment, but when he felt no queasiness, he allowed himself to be talked into a tour of the building. His mother claimed to have seen it all before, as did Miss Bamford, and though Thad looked eager to show off the facilities, his aunt querulously demanded his attention. That left Miss Sutton with only Oberon to guide around her domain, a prospect that obviously left her dismayed.

In fact, Oberon thought she would demur, but when he rose to his feet and gave her a curious glance, she joined him, her chin lifted. With a few words of explanation, she gestured towards what Oberon could already see: the new floor, the window seats and the curved counter behind which the drinks were dispensed.

The public displays did not interest Oberon so much as the personal, though he hardly expected to find evidence of mysterious doings. Still, he made it his business to investigate and so turned towards the stairway to the upper floor, inclining his head in question.

Although Miss Sutton seemed none too eager to accompany him up there alone, she was not one to back away from a challenge and soon was leading him up the steps to a wide hall lined with doors. For a moment, they stood in the dim, deserted corridor, silent but for the rain outside, and with no one else present, Oberon was acutely aware of his companion.

Miss Sutton, too, appeared to be unnerved, for she moved away from him and cleared her throat. 'Since the spring waters are relatively warm, we wanted to provide immersion, but right here in the Pump Room, not at a separate, more public site.'

Having been to the vast pools at Bath, where patrons of both sexes and various levels of hygiene milled about in the same unpleasant stew, fully clothed, Oberon recognised the advantages of this sort of arrangement. Obviously, Miss Sutton had done her research, and the smaller scale of the accommodations meant she would not have to build a pool in the near future, if ever.

Throwing open the nearest door, she waved towards the interior as if in dismissal, but Oberon was interested in a more thorough exploration—or perhaps a few more stolen moments alone with his guide. Brushing past her, Oberon heard her swift intake of breath and felt his own, swift reaction. In the ensuing silence, the sound of his boots were loud upon the tiled floor, which would serve well against spills. A neat fireplace against one wall would ensure the desired warmth in the room itself, while a window could be opened to let in the summer breezes.

'We will have servants to fetch the waters, of course, but eventually hope to install shower baths and piped water,' Miss Sutton said, following him into the small space. 'For complete privacy.'

Oberon turned to look at the low bathing tub with its sloping sides that would provide easy access to patrons. 'So the bather can totally disrobe,' Oberon said, pausing to glance at her.

She flushed. 'Well, yes, in order to receive more direct benefits of the spring waters.'

Oberon could see other benefits as well, as he eyed his companion. Although not given to whimsy, he could imagine steam rising from the waters, moisture thick in the heated air, and the corresponding slick skin of a certain spa owner, naked, her dark hair falling loose and damp...

Despite Oberon's practised mask, something must have shown in his face, for Miss Sutton flushed and looked away. A pulse pounded in her throat that Oberon would have liked to examine more closely, and he felt the temptation rise, swift and unwelcome. Thankfully, before he could act upon it, his quarry turned and hurried from the room, as if the devil himself was after her. And perhaps he was.

Or maybe the waters had had an adverse effect, after all.

* * *

Oberon stood to let Pearson help him on with his coat, having risen early for the opening of the Pump Room later this morning. Although normally he would have taken little heed of such an event, he was curious to see who might be in attendance, including the elusive investors. Despite spending more time in their company, he was still uncertain about the Suttons and their motives in reviving Queen's Well.

For a name so tied to Philtwell, they remained an enigma. After the fire that had closed the spa, all traces of the family had disappeared, or at least no one was telling Oberon anything. Accustomed to coaxing even the most close-mouthed to speak, he was growing frustrated.

'Did you find out anything from the servants?' he asked over his shoulder.

'I'm afraid not, your Grace,' Pearson said.

After an earlier servant had proven to be a liability, Oberon had made certain he would be better served in the future. Pearson was not only discreet and loyal, but was useful as an extra pair of eyes and ears, making Oberon entrust far more to the man than his grooming.

'The Sutton staff is all newly hired and knows nothing more of their employers than one might expect,' Pearson said.

'No late night meetings? No secretive visitors?' Oberon asked. The revival of a spa could provide a convenient excuse for certain forces to gather, and the remote location guaranteed no notice would be paid to such assemblies—at least not by any official authorities. Dissidents, traitors, and spies, including the changing faces of enemies and allies over the course of the country's long wars with France, could be hatching plans and no one would be the wiser.

But Pearson shook his head and Oberon realised he needed another source of information. Although he rarely used the post, especially for anything sensitive, he might have to send out some enquiries, couched in the most casual terms. 'I fear I'm forced to write to London.'

'I could deliver your correspondence, your Grace,' Pearson offered.

'Yes, but that would look odd, and by the time you returned, we might be on our own way back to London anyway,' Oberon said. His mother had not spoken of departing, but she would not tarry here indefinitely, and Oberon had no reason to linger unless he found something worthy of his interest.

'Perhaps you should speak with Mr Pettit,' Pearson said. 'He does not appear to be as ill as reports would claim.'

Occupied in the careful tying of his neckcloth, Oberon did not turn his head, but slanted a glance at the man who was brushing the back of his coat. 'What makes you say that?'

'I have seen him.'

'And how did you manage that?' Oberon asked. Whenever he tried to meet the man in whose home he was residing, he was fobbed off by his mother, who claimed her cousin was not yet ready for visitors. 'My mother hovers over his room like a hawk.'

'He was not in his room,' Pearson said, 'but sneaking around the lower floor.'

Accustomed as he was to the sort of intrigues to be discovered in London, for one startling moment Oberon wondered whether his mother and her so-called relative were conducting a liaison. The dowager's sudden visit to a cousin he did not recall had been curious from the start and even more so since their arrival.

'It was last night during supper,' Pearson added, when his employer stiffened.

Since his mother had not left the table, a tryst was unlikely, and Oberon loosed a low breath of relief. Should his mother be entertaining any gentleman, he did not care to be on the premises.

But Pearson's sighting proved one thing: Pettit existed. Oberon was beginning to wonder if the man was a figment of his mother's imagination. And perhaps their strange behaviour could be explained by Pettit's illness. He could be suffering from fevers that influenced his mind, or worse, an advanced case of the clap, which would explain both his seclusion and his wandering.

Oberon frowned, less than eager to interview such a subject, especially when there were more promising prospects. 'Perhaps I can pry the boy or the aunt away from Miss Sutton long enough to question them,' he said.

'Very good, your Grace,' Pearson said as he gave

Oberon's coat a final brush and stepped back. 'And might I suggest that, in this case, there is the possibility that the family is just what they seem.'

Oberon turned to eye Pearson closely, for the valet did not comment without reason. 'You think I am looking for something that isn't there?'

Pearson did not nod, but inclined his head formally, as if acknowledging the likelihood. 'Hardly an unusual pursuit for someone in your position, your Grace.'

Oberon frowned. He could not discount Pearson's opinion, for the man was a good judge of character. And Oberon had enough sense to realise that he might be using the Suttons to occupy himself, instead of kicking his heels until he could return to London.

And yet questions about the family remained, not the least of which was his own response to the young woman. Although it had been some time since Oberon had parted from his last mistress, that did not explain Miss Sutton's disturbing effect upon him, a detail that he had not shared with anyone, including his valet.

He had never been prey to feminine wiles, nor was he the type whose head was turned by a pretty face, an indifference that had served him well in his work. When he indulged, his preferences were for polished blondes who moved in the best circles and were well practised in discretion.

Since Miss Sutton was a far cry from those women, Oberon was at a loss to explain his reaction. And Pearson, who was not in possession of all the facts, could not make an accurate judgment. So Oberon thanked him with a nod, shot his cuffs and turned to go, his determination unwavering.

He was going to find out all he could about Miss Sutton—and then put an end to his fascination with her.

Glory hurried ahead of Thad and Phillida, anxious to reach the Pump Room. After her unsettling experience the other evening, she had insisted on keeping the keys to the building in her possession, so she would have to let the servants in when they arrived, before admitting the public.

The suddenness of the opening meant that few would attend beyond residents of the area, but Glory was determined to gain their approval. And she had posted notices to newspapers as far away as London with the hope that word would spread and Queen's Well would again become a destination for travellers.

Although she refused to let her expectations run away with her, Glory was thrilled at the prospect of her dream finally coming to fruition. From the looks of the pale sky, she couldn't have asked for a better day. Drawing in a deep breath of the still-crisp air, Glory wondered how anyone could prefer the choking haze of London to this peaceful village, empty at this hour except for a couple of other early risers.

Abruptly, Glory's admiration of the scenery turned to wariness, for she realised that one of those early risers was striding right towards her. Hoping that it was not Dr Tibold, intent upon more trouble, she now wished there were more people about.

'Miss Sutton!' At the hail, Glory paused, uncertain, only to realise the man approaching was not wearing a frock-coat, so likely was not the physician. However, her relief at recognising Mr Goodger, the butcher, was tempered by the man's sombre expression.

'Miss Sutton, I'm glad you're here,' he said. 'I was just going to send my Bob for you. I saw it first thing on my way back from my cousin's house.'

Saw what? Glory wondered. At her blank expression, the man inclined his head towards the Pump Room and Glory glanced towards the white-painted building and the neat grounds, with a surge of pride. But as she looked closer, she realised that the hastily erected sign announcing the opening was no longer on its post.

And the entrance… Glory felt her heart trip as she saw that the main doors were askew.

She picked up her skirts and ran. Ignoring Thad and Phillida's exclamations from behind her, Glory didn't stop until she reached the post. But the missing sign was not on the ground, and she was forced to look elsewhere, finally spying something poking out of the newly planted lilacs. There she found the painted notice broken into pieces. As she stared numbly at the symbol of the spa's resurrection, Glory heard Thad's voice ring out in the stillness.

'What the devil?' he said. 'How could it fall this far? Was it blown off its hooks?'

'It didn't fall or blow down,' Glory said. 'Someone did this deliberately.'

'Oh, my.' Phillida sounded breathless when she reached them and Glory hoped she wasn't about to faint. 'This is dreadful! Dreadful!'

'But why would anyone smash the sign?' Thad asked.

Phillida's shaky voice rose to a high-pitched wail. 'Maybe it's a warning not to open the well.'

'What?' Glory turned to face her aunt.

Phillida paled and clutched at Thad's arm. 'I simply... I didn't want to say anything, but I've heard some rumours...'

'From whom? I thought you decried the lack of society here,' Glory said.

'Well, it's certainly not London—' Phillida began, but a glance from Glory stopped her from arguing that point further. Instead she eyed her niece grimly. 'Some of the older people, those who were here for the...fire have implied that the spa is...is ill luck for the village.' Faltering, she looked at Thad. 'I thought you were going to tell her.'

Thad grunted. 'It seemed a load of nonsense, so I wasn't going to repeat it.'

But Phillida, always superstitious, ignored his scorn and looked at Glory, her eyes wide. 'You don't suppose it's cursed, do you?'

Glory swallowed the sharp retort that came to her lips and drew in a deep breath. 'The only curse would be that of villagers who are out to ruin Queen's Well.'

Unreliable workers and shadowy trespassers were one thing, but this was a blatant act of destruction.

The thought made her glance towards the building itself, and she realised that the sign was of little consequence when compared to all the other work that had been done. Leaving Thad to gather up what remnants he could, Glory hurried towards the entrance, fearful of what else she might find.

The doors were open, not wide enough to draw attention, but enough to bode ill, and Glory steeled herself as she pushed on the heavy wood. Vaguely, she was aware of Thad's warning behind her to be careful, but she was too stunned to heed him.

Just a few days ago, the interior of the Pump Room, restored to its former glory, had dazzled the Duchess of Westfield. Now, the tables and chairs that had lined the main room were overturned, some of them broken. A heavy pier glass had been shattered, its shards littering the new parquet floor.

Behind her, Glory heard footsteps approaching, but she was frozen to the spot. Only the sound of Phillida's wail made her move, and she turned to see Thad catch their swooning aunt. For an instant, Glory wished for someone strong to lean on herself, and a certain tall, dark figure came to mind, but she pushed the vision away and forced herself to keep going. Passing by the main stairway, Glory headed towards the rear rooms that were closed to the public, just to make sure…

'Careful!' Thad called out again, his voice revealing just how shaken he was.

In response, Glory slowed her pace, though she suspected that whoever had been here was long gone. Still, the thought of meeting the person responsible in one of the shadowy back rooms gave her pause. It was not that long ago that she had stood alone in the darkened structure, sensing another presence, and she halted her steps to listen intently.

When she heard something coming from a room ahead, Glory was tempted to call Thad, but she knew he had his hands full with Phillida. Again, she cursed her lack of a pistol and wondered whether she ought to step outside and call for help. But who would respond?

It seemed, as always, that the Suttons were on their own. Reaching down to pick up a broken chair leg, Glory held it like a cudgel and inched forwards until she could hear the sound more clearly. Unless someone was tapping on the walls, it was too rhythmic to signal a presence, so she continued on, her makeshift weapon at the ready.

The doors to the rooms stood open and Glory carefully moved towards the one from which the noise emanated. Peeking around the door frame, she slumped against it, for though nobody stood inside, they had left their mark. Cupboards were flung wide, their contents of cups and glasses strewn upon the floor. The *chaise* where Phillida so often reclined lay upon its side, a curtain flapping against it, caught by the breeze from an open window.

Glory nearly sank to her feet and wept, but she heard a scratching noise and turned, heading into the other room. Although armed with the chair leg, she gripped it, frozen with terror, when she saw a flash of something in the dimness. Her low cry sent it racing past her, and she stepped back, teetering off balance as a cat leapt to the window and bounded away.

Although Glory would have liked to blame the creature, she knew that no animal had been responsible for such destruction. She leaned shakily against the door frame, unable to summon the wits to move, until she saw that the rear entrance was open as well. The door stood askew and a shadow moved across her line of sight.

The thought of the perpetrator standing outside, gloating over his handiwork, spurred Glory's flagging courage. Lifting her broken piece of wood, she pushed at the door with her foot, ready to bring down her club upon whoever lurked outside. But she only gasped in shock when she saw the figure standing there.

Westfield.

Glory blinked in astonishment, unsure whether to thump the man roundly with her cudgel or drop her weapon and throw herself into his arms. But the latter impulse was so unnerving that she simply stood where she was, gaping at him.

Handsome and elegant, he didn't seem at all embarrassed to be discovered. He lifted one dark brow as his gaze swept over her. 'Does everyone receive this kind of greeting, or am I privy to special treatment?'

When Glory didn't answer, his brows drew together, and his manner changed. 'What is it?' he asked, and for a moment, she thought she glimpsed something other than indifference in those dark eyes. The urge to go to him was nearly overpowering and he stepped forwards, as if in response. But a shout from Thad halted him.

'Glory? What the devil are you doing with the broken furniture?' Thad asked. He took the chair leg from her numb grasp and would have pulled her back inside, but then he saw Westfield.

'Your Grace! What the...uh, how do you happen to be here?' her brother sputtered. Apparently, even Thad was surprised by the duke's appearance at the scene of the crime, and as Glory's scattered wits returned, she waited to see just how the nobleman would explain his presence.

'I was summoned by young Bob here,' Westfield said. He gestured behind him, and a ginger-haired lad stepped out from behind the trees.

'Mr Goodger sent me,' the boy explained. 'To fetch the magistrate—seeing as how something looked to have gone wrong at the Pump Room.'

'Mr Pettit, the magistrate, being indisposed, I came in his stead,' Westfield said. He lifted both brows as though questioning whether the Suttons objected.

Glory might have, but she couldn't seem to summon the words, and Thad welcomed him heartily. 'Oh, yes, thank you for coming, your Grace. We're most grateful to have your help.'

Were they? Glory wondered, for her own feelings were decidedly mixed. The duke had seemed to be against them, which made it hard for her to trust his offer of aid—or trust him at all. But somehow the sight of him acted as a restorative, and Glory's despair began to give way to a slow, steady resolution that this would not be the end of Queen's Well. And no one was going to stop her.

Not even Westfield.

Chapter Five

Oberon wasn't sure what he was expecting, when summoned by the boy, but not Miss Sutton, looking pale and drawn, her green eyes oddly lifeless. She was a formidable woman, always ready with a crushing comment, if not a pistol, and Oberon struggled to hide his reaction as emotions he hadn't felt in years threatened to burst through his very skin. Had she been assaulted? *If so, he would surely do murder.*

'What happened?' he asked, too sharply.

'Someone broke into the Pump Room,' Thad said.

'Just now?' Unable to stop himself, Oberon reached out to grasp Miss Sutton's arm. 'Are you all right?'

'No one's here now, as far as I can tell, and I checked upstairs,' Thad said. 'They must have come during the night when the place was empty.'

Oberon followed the boy's gaze to where his gloved

fingers gripped Miss Sutton, and he dropped his hand. But not yet satisfied, he turned to face her. 'You are unharmed?'

When she nodded, Oberon felt a measure of relief and flexed his fingers against an urge to touch her again, as if to reassure himself that she was…herself. Without pausing to consider when that had become important to him, Oberon turned away long enough to dismiss the boy named Bob and gather his composure. When he turned back around, his mask was once again firmly in place.

'Now, let us see what is missing,' he said, pushing the door aside for Miss Sutton and shutting it behind him. Oberon was not sure what could have occurred in order to so change Miss Sutton, but he had only had to step inside to receive his answer.

'What the devil?' Oberon's aplomb faltered again as he viewed the destruction. He had come out of curiosity more than anything else, wondering what could have been taken from a well, especially since no wealthy patrons were in attendance to lose their jewels or their pocket watches.

But this was no petty theft.

As he walked through the rooms, Oberon felt the kind of anger that he hadn't known in years. He'd dealt with duplicitous characters and weak men who would sell anything for money, people with no thought of what they had wrought, no honour or loyalty. But this was different. This was personal.

Surveying the damage, Oberon realised that someone had gone to a lot of trouble, but for what purpose?

He didn't want to consider the more unsavoury possibilities, or worse, that his own presence in Philtwell might be responsible. But he could not ignore them.

'Was anything stolen?' he asked, turning to eye the Suttons closely.

'What would they take?' Miss Sutton countered, with a gesture towards the mess.

Oberon flexed his fingers even as he tried not to be swayed from an impartial investigation. 'I don't know,' he said. 'You tell me.'

At his tone, Miss Sutton lifted her head, a flash of the old spark in her emerald eyes. 'It's a Pump Room! What on earth could they want besides the waters?'

Either she was a consummate actress or she was telling the truth, and it was a measure of his own peculiar state that Oberon was simply glad to see her returned to some semblance of her usual self.

'Maybe they were looking for something?' Thad suggested.

'Amongst the drinking glasses?' Miss Sutton countered.

The boy shrugged.

Why break the glasses and the chairs? Oberon wondered…unless you were enraged or were trying to prove a point. Despite her seeming innocence, Miss Sutton might be involved up to her neck in something dangerous, perhaps without being aware of the fact.

'Do you have any enemies?' Oberon asked.

For a moment, she looked at him blankly, then her eyes widened. 'Doctor Tibold.'

'*That b*—bounder,' Thad said, though Oberon thought he'd intended a more forceful appellation.

The physician might be lunatic enough to wreak this sort of havoc, but why? 'I thought he was anxious for the waters to be available.'

'Free of charge,' Miss Sutton said.

Although Oberon did not see how destroying the Pump Room would bring that about, the good doctor didn't seem particularly reasonable. Making his way into the main room, Oberon chose his steps carefully, looking for any signs that would confirm the man's involvement.

'Oh, your Grace!' Miss Bamford's wail led him to where she reclined upon a window seat. 'Thank heaven you are here to aid us. Do you think the place is cursed?' She lifted a handkerchief to her face and moaned. 'Oh, if only we could return to London.'

'Cursed?' Oberon echoed.

'This vicious attack upon the property,' she said, with wave of her handkerchief. 'I fear it is a sign that Queen's Well should remain closed. Oh, I knew we should never have come here!'

Oberon frowned. He didn't believe in signs or curses—unless they were deliberately laid by someone with ill intent, whether Dr Tibold or someone else. 'Perhaps it *is* meant to prevent the re-opening,' he said. Again, he eyed the siblings closely, but he could see only concern in Thad's open expression and resolve in Miss Sutton's.

She crossed her arms in front of her in a stubborn stance, and Oberon felt a rush of something indefinable at her apparent recovery. Struggling to ignore it, he turned to scan the room. While the destruction was dismaying, it could be righted without too much trouble. Thankfully, the building itself had not been damaged; the windows and doors and new paint were as pristine as before. A broom and removal of the debris would soon return it to working order, minus the broken furniture.

He swung round to face Miss Sutton. 'So I suggest you do just that.'

'What, close it?' she asked, green eyes flashing.

'No, open it,' Oberon said. He inclined his head towards the front entrance. 'The day looks to be a fine one. So while the interior is cleared, why not move on to the lawn?'

As Glory watched the people milling in the grounds, chatting and drinking the waters of Queen's Well in borrowed glasses, she loosed a sigh of relief. This morning it had seemed as though the grand re-opening would have to be postponed, but against all odds, the day had been a success—thanks to the most unexpected of heroes.

The man she had thought more adversary than ally had come to her rescue, and Glory found herself glancing his way more often than she should. Although she told herself she only wanted to see what he was doing, her gaze lingered longer than required, more often than not.

'I see you're no longer at daggers drawn.'

The sound of Thad's voice startled Glory from her

thoughts, and she turned to find her brother standing beside her, eyeing the duke. 'You two will have to work together now that he's acting magistrate,' he said, turning towards her.

The idea of working with Westfield made Glory's heart flutter, a helpless reaction that made her frown. 'We were never at daggers drawn.'

Her brother snorted. 'You've been finding fault with a fat goose ever since you met him.'

Glory shook her head. If she'd been wary of Westfield, she'd had good reason. 'You have to admit that his behaviour at first was suspicious: sneaking around the empty Pump Room, consorting with Dr Tibold, maligning the spa…' His whole attitude had been prickly, just as though they *were* at daggers' drawn, Glory realised.

But Thad simply snorted again.

'And what of his skills with his fists and weapons, his eerie composure in the face of anything, his… stealth?' Glory sought for the words to express her feeling that the duke was, if not suspicious, then certainly unusual. 'He's not a typical nobleman.'

'And how many nobleman do you know?' Thad asked. 'He's bang up to the mark.'

Glory did not argue with Thad's assessment, especially since her brother recently had been taken with far less suitable characters. She had to admit that Thad could do worse than to admire and emulate the duke, despite his…peculiarities.

'Maybe you've been up in the boughs because you fancy the man,' Thad said.

'What?' Glory flushed to the roots of her hair. 'Don't be ridiculous.'

'Methinks the lady doth protest too much.'

'Very amusing,' Glory said, refusing to glance at her brother. 'Though I'm glad that you remember some of your tutor's assignments.'

While Thad protested that he was well read, even though he rarely opened a book these days, Glory gathered her composure. When she spoke again, it was in a light, but firm tone meant to convey her views without 'protesting too much'.

'While you may yet turn out to be a scholar, there is no possibility that a man of Westfield's standing would be interested in me,' Glory said. And before Thad could argue, she gave him a serious look. 'For you know as well as I that, for the sake of his title, a duke must make a good match with a noble young lady whose relations and connections will serve him well.'

Thad frowned. Perhaps he'd had hopes for a closer relationship with the man he thought 'bang up to the mark', but Glory had no intention of letting him foster that notion.

'However, you were right about Westfield,' she conceded. 'I vow not to be suspicious of the man any longer.' *No matter what curious skills he might display.* 'And to work with him as magistrate.'

Slightly mollified, Thad nodded. He might have said more, but he was hailed by one of the local young people and soon disappeared into the crowd. Glory loosed her breath, relieved that the conversation was over, yet her brother's words lingered.

Was he right? If Westfield wasn't dangerous, then why did her pulse pick up its pace whenever he was near? Glory frowned, for she was too old to become breathless at the sight of a pair of broad shoulders and dark eyes. But maybe now that Thad was grown up and no longer needed her attention, she had succumbed belatedly to the girlish nonsense she had not known when younger.

However unpalatable the thought, Glory told herself that any handsome man would then have the same effect upon her. She just hadn't seen any others in Philtwell—or at least any to rival Westfield. But who could? Glory swallowed a snort of her own. Even disregarding his looks, his presence, his power, what he had done today was enough to gain any woman's attention.

Glory liked to think that, after recovering from her initial shock at the condition of the Pump Room, she would have come up with the same idea as Westfield. But the duke had reacted swiftly and surely. He had sent to Sutton House for glasses and directed the arriving servants to clear a path to the waters, so they could serve patrons outside. The duchess brought additional servants, and others, hearing of their troubles, loaned items and helping hands.

In fact, Glory had been astonished at the outpouring of kindness. Before, she had heard only rumblings of displeasure from the villagers. Now, she realised that many of the area residents were welcoming.

When the boy, Bob, returned with Mr Goodger, he was heartily thanked. And the owner of the bake shop set up a stand and sold biscuits and sweets.

Yet, even as Glory mulled over her good fortune, a cloud passed over the sun as if acting as a portent to darken the day. And whether it was coincidence or because she had been too distracted to notice before, Glory felt the familiar sensation of eyes upon her. Glancing around the group milling around the lawn, she could find no one staring her way, but it was too strong to dismiss.

With a shiver, Glory realised that among the people she had thought so welcoming stood someone who was not. And whoever had vandalised the Pump Room could not be pleased by the success of the opening. In fact, Glory felt their enmity, like an eerie presence, dark and dangerous. Fighting against the panic that threatened, Glory slowly began to turn, as though to divine the source through sensation alone.

And then she saw Tibold.

He was not looking in her direction. In fact, his back was turned, but there was no mistaking that frock-coat, and Glory heard him loudly order waters for two fat, wheezy fellows he claimed were his patients. Although they were paying customers, Glory was tempted to have them barred from the property. Eyes narrowing, she studied the strangers and wondered whether they were responsible for breaking into her business.

Westfield must have wondered the same, for he soon approached the men, and Glory inched towards them to listen. 'I told you to stay away from Miss Sutton,' the duke said to the doctor. Although he spoke in his usual smooth tone, there was no denying the underlying threat, and Glory felt suffused with a certain warmth at Westfield's implied protection.

'I am allowed to partake of the waters, the same as anyone else,' Tibold argued, 'as are my patients.'

'Only when she's not nearby,' Westfield said. 'But since you're here, I'd like to talk to you.' He manoeuvred Tibold away from the others, so Glory could not hear what was said, but the physician did not look happy. In fact, the normally red-faced charlatan turned as pale as a ghost.

Westfield's back was to her, but Glory knew he needed no rock-filled reticule or pistol to intimidate. And the physician who had so often shouted at her kept quiet, shaking his head and muttering. Finally, after bowing several times, he slunk away like a whipped dog.

But such animals had a habit of returning, and Glory looked towards Westfield in question. Trying to ignore the sudden leap of her pulse as he turned towards her, she assumed an expectant expression until he reached her side. After all, she was only curious as to the exchange between the two men.

'Miss Sutton,' the duke said, acknowledging her with a slight nod, and Glory realised he still was dangerous, only in a different way. For the girlish nonsense that she had always dismissed took hold of her, making her not only enamoured of his handsome face, but of the man himself. She swallowed.

'Thad tells me you've had a change of heart.'

Glory felt her jaw drop open. 'What?'

'Apparently, you've been suspecting me of all sorts of nefarious doings just because I happened to be in the wrong place at the wrong time. Or the right place at the right time.'

Glory actually sputtered, unable to believe that Thad had spoken so freely to this man, who was little more than a stranger to them. As glad as she was that her brother's choice of companions had improved, she was still going to murder him.

And to add insult to injury, Westfield was enjoying her discomfiture in a way that a true gentleman would not. However, there was nothing suspicious about that. It was something Thad would do, if he were still alive, which he wouldn't be when she got hold of him.

Westfield was waiting, a dark brow cocked in question, and Glory struggled to come up with a polite reply. But his taunt was eroding the good will she had been feeling towards him for his help today. 'I beg your pardon,' she said stiffly. 'But you have some remarkable abilities that hardly seem typical of your peers.'

Westfield inclined his head. 'I'll take that as a compliment, however it was intended.'

Glory was torn between irritation at the man and a giddy response to his closeness.

'I admit that I wasn't too sure about you, either,' he said, jolting Glory from her girlish nonsense.

Uncertain of his meaning, Glory eyed him warily. 'What?'

'Being held at gunpoint has a tendency to rouse my suspicions.'

Glory flushed. 'I told you—' she began, but West-field held up a hand to silence her.

'Since I find myself in the position of acting magistrate, and you find yourself in need of my services, it appears we must work together. So let us simply agree to a cessation of hostilities, a private treaty, if you will.'

Glory thought his choice of words odd for someone who was not a politician—she would hardly describe their mutual mistrust as hostilities. But she nodded and some of the tension left her body, only to be replaced by a different kind as she wondered just how closely he expected them to work.

Pushing that apprehension aside for now, Glory cleared her throat. 'And I would like to thank you for all that you've done here today,' she began, prepared to give a gracious speech. She really was grateful, but the duke shook his head, dismissing her words. Piqued, Glory frowned until she realised that although he appeared to be focused solely upon her, Westfield was somehow keeping an eye on Tibold's cohorts, as well.

Surprised, Glory turned to look at the two men, who were stuffing themselves with pastries and loudly asking about available entertainments. Now that they weren't with the fanatical physician, they looked more like gouty patrons than villains.

'The good doctor denies his involvement, of course,' Westfield said in a low voice. 'He claims that he was eager for the Pump Room to open because his livelihood is tied to the waters, which makes sense. However, I'd like to speak to his patients before they disappear from view.'

Nodding, Glory nevertheless felt a certain disappointment at his departure, which gave her pause. She might have put her doubts about the duke behind her, but she should not be as eager to abandon her wariness. It was all well and good to like the man—just as long as she didn't like him too much.

It wasn't until the last customer had left the grounds that Glory returned to the Pump Room, and the changes that had been wrought in her absence were startling. All the debris had been cleared away and the undamaged furniture restored to its place. In fact, the duchess waved her over to the table where she sat with Phillida and Glory gratefully sank into a solid chair.

'I can't thank you enough, your Grace,' Glory said, for the noblewoman had been tirelessly gracious, moving among the patrons and drawing more in to make the day a success.

'Nonsense. I was just doing my part for Queen's Well, and you, too, my dear,' she said with a smile as one of the servants placed some glasses in front of them. Having seen enough of the waters for one day, Glory pushed hers aside and reached up to rub the back of her neck, stopping when she saw Thad approaching, along with Westfield.

Dropping her hand, she sat up straighter, her weariness seeming to fade at the sight of him. When she felt herself flush, Glory glanced away to focus on her brother, who seemed so much more adult in the duke's company that she could only shake her head in bemusement.

'Westfield doesn't seem to think Tibold is behind this business, but who else could it be?' Thad asked, his brows furrowed.

'Not who, but what,' Phillida said, dramatically. She waited until she had everyone's attention before continuing in a breathless whisper, 'It's the curse.'

Glory stifled a groan, while the duchess looked confused. 'Curse?'

'Several of the residents told me that the well is blighted. It has long been associated with ill luck,' Phillida said.

'Nonsense,' the duchess said, briskly. 'Nothing could be further from the truth, for the waters have always been the cause of good fortune, not bad.'

'I doubt if all the owners would agree,' Westfield said drily.

The duchess frowned at her son. 'There is a difference between outside events and the effects of the waters, which are steeped in legend.'

'But Miss Sutton claims her waters were never associated with miraculous cures,' Westfield said, turning towards Glory, as if for confirmation.

'And I spoke the truth, as far as I can tell,' Glory

said, hesitant to contradict the duchess. 'Although discovered by the Romans, the waters appear to have fallen out of use after their departure, so Queen's Well was never a shrine or holy site during the great age of such cures.'

'All mineral waters are known for their healing,' the duchess said with a wave of dismissal. 'But those from Queen's Well are unique in their benefits.'

'And what might they be?' Westfield asked.

The duchess smiled slyly. 'The waters here have a certain propensity for bringing about unions.'

Glory blinked in surprise, while Westfield looked dubious. 'Unions?' he asked.

'Romance, dear, romance,' the duchess said. 'How do you think I met your father?'

'You were introduced to him,' Westfield said. 'Whether this happened in a Pump Room, rather than somewhere else, does not make the place enchanted.'

'Enchantment gone awry,' Phillida muttered loudly. 'Perhaps that is what led to the curse or is a part of it.'

Dead silence followed her pronouncement, though Glory doubted it was Phillida's nonsense that had struck everyone dumb. Glory and Thad, at least, were accustomed to their aunt spouting rubbish. But the duchess was a different sort altogether, which made her claim all the more astonishing.

Westfield lifted a dark brow. 'If such are its properties, I'm surprised every randy buck from London isn't here drinking his fill.'

His mother frowned. 'The waters do not incite lust, but true love.'

'Then why hasn't word of this spread throughout the *female* populace?' Westfield asked, making light of her argument.

But his mother gave him a jaundiced look. 'Because it is not widely known. Those who are affected do not suspect that they have been brought together by anything other than their own appeal. And the waters only work upon two suitable parties. They are not a love potion, but a stimulus for romance between those ripe for it.'

Thad turned towards Glory in obvious confusion. 'Do you know anything about this?'

Glory shook her head. She had read some strange, old references to the 'powers' of Queen's Well, but she had assumed they were curative. And she had never seen anything alluding to matters of the heart, unless… She drew in a sharp breath. 'Wait! I'd forgotten that the old Roman site was known as Aquae Philtri.'

'The spa of the philter, especially of love,' Thad translated aloud. He glanced down at the glass before him as if it were filled with poison and slowly pushed it away.

Glory laughed at his reaction, only to swallow her amusement as she realised just who had been drinking those very waters a few days before. Flushing, she tried to recall whether anyone except Westfield had joined her, but all she remembered was their shared toast. Against her better judgement, Glory glanced up at him and saw that infernal brow was cocked. That and the smile playing about his lips told her, in no uncertain terms, that he had not forgotten.

'Well, then,' he said, his dark gaze meeting hers, 'it's a good thing I'm not a superstitious man.'

Oberon felt like he was working blind—or with his hands tied behind him. Because he had no contacts in the area, he could not summon anyone to follow Tibold or the doctor's patients. But Oberon's main concern was Miss Sutton, who, by all appearances, was an innocent victim of vandalism—or worse.

Oberon frowned. It was the violence of the destruction at the Pump Room that disturbed him, and while Thad seemed to be a devoted sibling, the boy had already proven himself incapable of protecting his sister. That left Oberon to choose between watching over her or pursuing an investigation that had become official.

Whatever his own vague suspicions about the revival of Queen's Well, there was no denying that a crime had been committed there. And although Oberon had no idea what Randolph Pettit might have done, as acting magistrate he intended to find the perpetrator and prevent any further harm—especially to Miss Sutton.

Not wanting to leave her unguarded, Oberon headed out early, determined to find out what he could before she left the safety of her cottage. Something she had said while dining at Sutton House sent him to one of the burned-out buildings that was being dismantled.

There he found two men employed for that task lounging in the grass, which certainly confirmed her complaints about their progress. But did it have anything to do with the vandalism at the Pump Room? When questioned, one fellow simply shrugged. The other, named Jeremy, gave Oberon a surly look.

'We're working as fast as Jeb wants us to,' he said. Apparently, the noticeably absent Jeb, whether he existed or not, was in charge.

'Well, tell him he's been replaced,' Oberon said, as he handed both men some pound notes. 'You are now in charge,' he told Jeremy. 'And if Jeb has any questions about his employment, he is to see me, not Miss Sutton. Do you understand?'

Although Jeremy appeared suspicious of such largesse, he pocketed the money, while the other fellow scratched his head in wonder.

'And the faster you work, the more money you'll receive. From me,' Oberon added. 'So there's no reason to mention our little arrangement to the Suttons.'

After the two men nodded their agreement, Oberon remained where he was, one eyebrow cocked expectantly, until they began their labours. When he was satisfied with what he saw, Oberon turned towards the Pump Room. A glance at the front of the structure showed nothing amiss, so he walked by, only to duck into the trees behind the building. Although nothing moved except the leaves above him, Oberon was aware of a presence in the shadows.

'All quiet?'

'Aye, your Grace,' the figure said, keeping to his position off the path. 'Not a soul's been around since the place was closed up last night.'

'Very good,' Oberon said. 'You can go now, but I'll expect you back this evening.'

'Yes, your Grace,' the fellow said. 'I'll be here.'

Without any associates of his own, Oberon had to make do with those he had chosen yesterday from the crowd at the opening. Forced to trust his instincts, he had hired Finn, the butcher's brother, to secure the building against any further disturbances.

But there was no one he trusted to guard Miss Sutton, and so he took the path that led to the family's cottage while trying to ignore an insidious sense of anticipation. However, despite his best efforts, he felt something indefinable when she appeared, exiting the small house.

She glanced towards him, and Oberon was lighter somehow, as though the weight of the last years was lifting from his shoulders. The thought gave him pause, for his life had not become a burden. His existence was what he had made it, what he had needed to make it. Wasn't it?

'Your Grace!' Thad's hail drew Oberon's attention from Miss Sutton to her brother, who was following behind her. The boy brushed past his sister, far more eager to see Oberon than she had been, or at least more willing to show it.

'Where are you headed this morning?' Thad asked, like an eager pup.

'I was going to ask your sister to accompany me upon a visit that my mother recommended,' Oberon said. 'I'm hoping that the local matriarch, Mrs Good-hew, might be able to give us more information on the local residents and who might be responsible for your vandalism.'

Oberon saw a flash of indecision cross Miss Sutton's face before she nodded and turned to hand her brother a set a keys. In a low voice, she instructed him about the servants and the hours of the Pump Room, information that made Thad frown impatiently before he hurried off.

'You should let your brother handle things himself,' Oberon said as he gave her his arm.

To his surprise, she nodded. 'I know, but he was so against the spa to begin with that it is taking me a while to become accustomed to this new attitude, which is very welcome, mind you, just unexpected.'

'He was against the spa?' Oberon asked.

'Oh, you know that any young man would prefer the enticements of London,' she said, brushing off his question.

Oberon sensed there was more she wasn't telling, and he wondered whether to pursue the subject or let it drop. Instead he said nothing, for sometimes the urge to fill a silence made people speak. And she was obviously uneasy, her gaze resolutely fixed on the distance as she drew a deep breath.

'Your Grace, I…uh…want to make it quite clear

that I was unaware of the…legend that the duchess mentioned yesterday.'

Oberon bit back a laugh at her confession. Perhaps Pearson was right, and he had been immersed in his work for so long that he saw shadows everywhere. However, his amusement fled at the thought that he might not be able to conduct a normal conversation, and the vaguely alarming notion made him determined to do so.

'Really?' Oberon asked, and he took a moment to enjoy Miss Sutton's discomfiture. 'I would think you'd know all there is to know about your family's spa.'

She lifted her chin, in preparation for dressing him down, no doubt, and Oberon decided to avoid any arguments. 'I assure you that I do not believe in such nonsense and I apologise for my mother, who has succumbed to a nostalgia that seems to have robbed her of her usual wits.'

Although she nodded, Miss Sutton appeared ill at ease and drew another deep breath. 'While I appreciate her support, I do hope that she won't revive that old fustian about the waters acting as some sort of matchmaker,' she said. 'It's just not the kind of thing I'd like Queen's Well to be known for, you understand. Of course, we want to draw genteel visitors and I'm afraid that wouldn't be the case if patrons came for…romance. A spa survives or fails on its reputation, you know.'

'I doubt whether she has been spreading the tale, for yesterday was the first time she made mention of it,' Oberon said. Then again, his mother might have had good reason to keep quiet about her magic brew.

Although Pearson claimed he was overly suspicious, now Oberon wondered whether she had arranged for him to share a drink with Miss Sutton. In her younger days, his mother would never have left the ducal succession up to a glass of mineral water, but she had changed after his father's death. As had they all, Oberon thought grimly.

But surely she could have found a better prospect than Miss Sutton, who did not seem a likely duchess. Oberon could understand his mother trying to throw him together with the daughter of one of her friends, such as Lady Oxbridge or Lady Eppington, young women who could move seamlessly within the requisite social circles. But only a week ago he had questioned whether Miss Sutton was using her real name, and he knew little of her antecedents, except that her forebears were associated with the spa.

Slanting a glance at her averted profile, Oberon reminded himself that her suitability for such a position was irrelevant. For no matter what faith his mother might place in a glass of foul-tasting liquid, he had no intention of making anyone his wife, not even Miss Sutton.

'I hope you are right,' she said, looking worried still. And Oberon realised that she certainly had experience in the running of a venture on the scale of a noble household. The spa was a huge undertaking for one woman, with only a boy and a goosecap to aid her, and again, he wondered who else might be involved.

But he forced himself to put such concerns aside and conduct an exchange in which he sought no information except that which might please himself. It would be a good exercise should he one day retire, Oberon thought, only to pause in his steps, for he had never considered the possibility.

Miss Sutton glanced up at him curiously; to explain his sudden halt, Oberon turned to point out some bright red blossoms that lined the walkway ahead.

'Oh, they are beautiful, aren't they?' she said and the smile that lit her face transformed her from merely lovely to beautiful. 'I adore flowers, but I would never have guessed that you would hold such an interest.'

She eyed him askance, and Oberon, who had spent most of the past several years inside amongst society, nevertheless took exception to her scepticism. 'But of course,' he said. 'There are extensive gardens at Westfield.'

And though they resumed walking, their steps were slower and their conversation decidedly normal.

Chapter Six

Glory had seen Mrs Goodhew before, but not often, for the older woman rarely left her home. It was not until a servant showed the visitors into a cosy room with a crackling fire that Glory realised she should have brought some of her famous waters.

'I'm sorry I didn't think to bring you a bit of Queen's Well,' she said. 'I'll be sure to have some sent over.'

'Thank you, my dear, but I had a servant fetch me some yesterday, although I wasn't quite up to an outing myself. I'm so glad that the Pump Room is open again, though I understand there was some trouble?'

'Yes,' Glory said. As she explained about the attack upon the building, the older woman's expression turned grim.

'It makes me ashamed to live here,' Mrs

Goodhew said, shaking her head. 'What has the world come to?'

She sank into silence then, as if in contemplation, until Westfield spoke. 'My mother said that you might be able to tell us who could have a grudge against the Suttons or the well.'

'You are asking that of a woman who rarely leaves her house?' Mrs Goodhew asked, but then she smiled. 'I have been around a while, as they say, and I do try to keep up as best I can. Of course, I know all the old families. But I can't say the same of a few of the interlopers, like that new doctor, who earns no favour.'

Although they talked for some time, Mrs Goodhew refused to suggest any particular person was responsible. 'I can name you some who aren't among the best people, disgruntled residents who might blame the Suttons for the decline of the village, but I don't see what damaging the Pump Room would prove.'

She shifted in her chair and eyed the duke. 'Have you considered that some of the boys might have had too much to drink and decided to smash up the place on a whim?'

He nodded. 'But for all the damage, the perpetrators were quiet and contained. They didn't break any windows, for instance.'

Glory sucked in a breath at the thought of the cost of replacing the glass, as well as the danger the elements would pose to freshly painted walls and parqueted floors. And she was thankful there hadn't been more damage.

'How much did your father tell you about Queen's Well?' Mrs Goodhew asked, fixing Glory with her sharp gaze.

'Nothing,' Glory murmured automatically, only to recognise how odd her answer must sound. 'He died some years ago.'

'Yet, while he was alive, he didn't speak of your family's heritage?' Mrs Goodhew looked puzzled.

Glory had never given much thought to her father's reticence. After all, he had not been a man of leisure and had spent most of his time building his businesses. He had told Glory and Thad stories, but mostly about his life in London or with their mother. Now, Glory realized, with no little wonder, that his past, as well as his wife's, had never been discussed.

Mrs Goodhew sighed. 'Well, I suppose it's not surprising, considering the circumstances when he left. The fire, you see.'

While Glory listened, rapt, the elderly woman spoke about the spa's final night and how Glory's heroic grandfather had saved lives at the expense of his own, how Sutton House was sold, the cottage shut up and the family gone. 'No wonder your father never returned,' Mrs Goodhew said.

Glory drew in a shaky breath at the first-hand account. 'Perhaps the past was simply too painful for him to share,' she said.

'Obviously, the tragedy impacted the village, since the major source of revenue was abruptly cut off,' Westfield said. 'Perhaps the revival has opened old wounds.'

Mrs Goodhew shook her head, as though mysti-fied. 'It's not as though the Suttons set fire to their own livelihood. They gained nothing, but lost a hus-band and father.'

'Does anyone know what started the blaze?' West-field asked.

Again, Mrs Goodhew shook her head.

'But the buildings that were destroyed were all owned by the Suttons?' the duke said.

The elderly woman nodded.

Westfield leaned back in his chair. 'Miss Sutton's aunt mentioned a curse?'

'A curse?' Mrs Goodhew echoed.

Glory shook her head, embarrassed. 'My aunt is rather fanciful. She says she's heard rumours that Queen's Well brings misfortune.'

'Well, perhaps such things are being said now, but I certainly never heard them before the tragedy, and the well had a long and reasonably successful history, one that you can take pride in,' Mrs Goodhew added, eyeing Glory directly.

'Thank you,' Glory said. 'I'm afraid my aunt is the superstitious sort. And I'm sure that many odd stories have grown up over the years, including romances attributed to the waters.' Glory instantly wanted to recall her words when she realised that Westfield was seated next to her, and she flushed in anticipation of a sardonic comment.

But it was Mrs Goodhew who spoke. 'Well, now, that I have heard about,' she said with a sly smile.

Glory blinked in surprise. 'But it's…absurd.'

Mrs Goodhew laughed. 'Whether you believe in them or not, the powers are part of the well's legend, an open secret among those of us who remember the old days, just like the Queen's Gift.'

'The Queen's Gift,' Westfield echoed. 'What is that?'

'I don't know,' Mrs Goodhew said, shaking her head. 'No one does, I suspect. The tale is that Queen Elizabeth was so taken with the spa that she presented something to the well, or perhaps its owners, probably some fancy bauble that was sold long ago.'

The elderly woman paused to study Glory. 'Unless you know, Miss Sutton.'

Glory shook her head. 'I haven't been able to learn much about the history of the spa, so this is the first I've heard of it. And we certainly don't own anything that would qualify as a royal treasure or trinket.'

'Have you looked through the cottage?' Mrs Goodhew asked. 'Unlike the house, it remained in the family, so there might be old records, ledgers, letters or the like tucked away in the cellar or attic.'

Glory blinked in surprise. She had been so focused on the Pump Room and other renovations that she had not bothered to search the cottage thoroughly. What little she knew about the spa had come from her father's papers in London, but they had been few. A place that had operated for centuries must have generated more records, if they had not gone missing over the years.

Lost in thought, Glory did not become aware of the silence until Westfield caught her eye and put a finger

to his lips. For an instant, all she could do was stare,
enthralled by the sight of the long digit pressed against
his mouth. But then he inclined his head toward their
hostess and Glory followed his gaze, only to see that
Mrs Goodhew had nodded off.

Rising to their feet as quietly as possible, they
took their leave under the watchful eyes of the housekeeper; Glory was glad to step from the close room
into the fresh air. A brisk breeze heralded rainclouds,
which would do little for business at the Pump Room,
especially since most of the villagers had partaken
yesterday. But Glory was not disappointed, for the
weather gave her an excuse to pursue Mrs Goodhew's
suggestion rather than join Thad there.

Instead of strolling languidly in the sun as they
had earlier, she and Westfield hurried into the gust-
ing wind and cut short the discussion of their visit,
which was just as well. Earlier, Glory had seen a side
of Westfield so charming and witty that she could
well believe his reputation as an excellent host and
favoured guest. And never in her sheltered life had
she accompanied such a man, let alone been the focus
of his attention.

Obviously, working with the duke was far preferable to working against him. But Glory was still wary,
if not of the man then of herself, especially since her
attacks of girlish giddiness seemed to be increasing.
If that's what they were. Glory was afraid to consider
any other explanation for the heart palpitations and
blushes that struck her without warning.

It was with some relief that Glory stopped at the

cottage gate and thanked the duke again for his escort. 'I think I shall heed your advice and let Thad manage for a while longer,' she said, turning towards the house. 'And I have much that I must do here.' That was true enough. She had bills, ledgers and correspondence that required her attention sooner or later.

But she was more likely to get to them later. And she had the feeling that Westfield knew full well what she intended because that dark brow of his shot upwards in query. For a moment Glory thought he might invite himself in or ask to join her, and the notion of spending more time with the man, perhaps cooped up together looking through the attic, brought on another bout of heat and pounding pulses.

But, to her relief, Westfield did not dispute her claim. 'You plan on staying in the rest of the day, I take it?' he asked.

When she nodded, he bowed his head and Glory took the opportunity to escape into the cottage. Shutting the door behind her, she removed her bonnet with shaking fingers, half-expecting the duke to follow, thrusting aside the heavy wood to fill the doorway behind her.

With a sigh, Glory shook her head at such fancies. Whatever she had once imagined, Westfield was a decent man who was acting as magistrate in order to elp her. He was not about to break down the door ravish her in her own home. Drawing in a sharp , Glory flushed at the memory of their first meeting, when he had forced her against his hard body…

The appearance of their maid, Cassie, brought Glory from her thoughts and she handed her hat to the girl. 'How is my aunt?' she said, returning to more mundane matters.

'She went out, miss.'

'What? Where?' Glory asked, for Phillida had taken to bed earlier with a sick headache.

'She didn't say, miss.'

Glory frowned. More than likely, having no audience to listen to her woes, she had taken herself off to the Pump Room to bother Thad. Glory nearly put her bonnet back on to head back out, but she remembered Westfield's words. *Let him handle it himself.*

Perhaps she should, Glory thought, for she was anxious to see what she could find in the cottage and could do it far better without any interruptions. Unlike Westfield, Glory doubted that she would discover any clues to the recent attack upon Queen's Well. But she hoped to learn more about the spa's history and mysteries, including this supposed gift from Elizabeth.

Climbing the stairs to the upper storey, Glory soon found the narrow steps that led up under the eaves. At the top, she pushed open the door, only to choke on a whirl of dust. It seemed that the caretakers who had looked after the property over the years had not bothered to venture here.

A loud crack of thunder made Glory jump, and she realised that she should have brought a lantern. The few windows were dark and grimy, and rain began to pelt against them loudly. Glory called down the steps for Cassie, but she was not surprised that the girl did not respond. She was probably in the kitchen, chatting with the cook.

Thad had complained that they should have more servants, but the cottage was so small that Glory thought it would be too crowded. Now she wasn't so sure. She turned, intending to fetch a lantern herself, along with an apron to keep her skirts clean, but an opened crate caught her eye.

Who had left the lid ajar—and when? Glory glanced around, relieved to see that a thick carpet of dust appeared to cover everything, apparently undisturbed. But she wondered how much of the original contents remained. After what had happened to the Pump Room, she considered herself lucky that the place had not been rifled long ago.

Stepping towards the crate, Glory knelt and peered inside, but it was too dark to see what lay there. She pushed at the heavy lid, the noise loud and grating in the stillness of the space. Still unable to tell what lay within the shadows, she lifted a hand to reach inside only to pause, uncertain. There might be rodents or remnants of…what?

Frowning at her own temerity, Glory lifted her hand only to pause again at a low sound. Had she heard the creak of a step? 'Cassie?' she called out. But there was no answer. Suddenly, the cosy space under the eaves took on a more sinister cast, the linens that ̄red some of the items looming large enough to ̄ intruder.

Glory swallowed hard and wished she had fetched the lantern, if only to check for footprints in the dust. She told herself that she was perfectly safe in her own home, with two servants as company, but another creak made her duck behind the crate.

It was probably just the old structure, full of quirks, or the rain and wind that lashed at the roof. Perhaps even a leak might be responsible for what she was hearing. But still Glory wished she had her pistol and vowed to get it back from Westfield. There was no reason for him to keep the weapon from her, especially after what had happened at the Pump Room.

'Hello?'

Loosing a strangled cry at the sound of a voice, Glory fell backwards, bumping against something that rattled precariously before crashing to the floor. As she scrambled to her feet, Glory heard a high-pitched scream, followed by a wail and a thump coming from the stairway. Snatching up the first thing that she could, she hurried towards the door where she found Phillida lying in a heap. Apparently, her aunt truly had fainted this time.

'Did you kill her?' A shocked voice rose from below, and Glory looked down the steps to see Cassie standing at the bottom, a horrified expression upon her face. 'I didn't see anything, miss, not a thing,' the girl said as she backed away.

It took Glory a good minute to realise she was standing at the top of the steps, holding a cricket bat over her head, while the prone body of her aunt lay at her feet.

* * *

'It's the curse, I tell you,' Phillida whimpered. She was tucked into bed, a dish of tea in her hands and a plate of her favourite biscuits nearby. The wary maid finally had been convinced to fetch the hartshorn, and between the two of them they had managed to get Phillida settled, with no apparent injuries. Glory was thankful Cassie had not fled her employment—or sent for the magistrate. She had no desire to explain the incident to Westfield, who might never return her pistol if he thought she was assaulting her relatives.

Already the day seemed a long one, and Glory reached up to rub the tension from the back of her neck. 'There is no curse, Aunt,' she said.

'Then how do you explain my tumble?' Phillida demanded in a wavering voice.

'You scared me, and I scared you,' Glory answered succinctly.

'You keep telling me how much better this place is than London, but I never took a fall there,' Phillida said, with a sniff. 'I was never frightened in my own home.'

Personally, Glory thought it was a miracle that Phillida had not been hurt before, considering her penchant for swooning. But having been the cause of this accident, she was not about to argue.

'It's all my fault,' Glory said. 'I was startled, that's all.' *And frightened in my own home.*

Phillida sniffed again. 'Perhaps there's a reason your father never returned here.'

'Nonsense,' Glory said. 'He was too busy with his London businesses to resume the spa's operations.'

'Was he?' Phillida gave her a tremulous look. 'He could have sent someone, hired a man of business, yet he never did. He never wanted a thing to do with this well. How do you explain that?'

'Is that what he told you?' Glory asked in surprise.

Phillida glanced away and shook her head. 'He never spoke of it.'

Glory frowned at the confirmation of her own suspicions. 'What of Mother? Did she tell you anything?' Surely he would have discussed his past with his wife.

Phillida shook her head. 'He was probably trying to protect her.'

'Nonsense,' Glory said. 'If there was anything to fear at Queen's Well, you can be sure Father would have warned us against it.'

'Perhaps he intended to, but did not have the time,' Phillida said. 'The man could hardly expect to be struck down so quickly, in the prime of life.'

But their father knew how capricious fate could be after the death of their mother. If it was important, he would have taken the time, Glory thought. Hadn't he taught her how to defend herself? Suddenly that simple act took on ominous overtones, but Glory dismissed them as foolish. London was far more dangerous than Philtwell, and her father was the sort of man who put his affairs in order. If there was a threat associated with the well, he would have left something behind, a note among his papers or a letter with his solicitor.

'No doubt, he feared to talk of it because of…the curse,' Phillida whispered, as though some nameless, formless entity would strike if she spoke too loudly.

'Father didn't discuss Queen's Well because his history here was too painful, and that's probably why he didn't return either—to the scene of his father's death and his mother's despair.'

When Phillida looked as though she would argue, Glory cut her off. 'There is no curse,' she said. 'Westfield and I spoke with one of the residents who is quite conversant in the lore of the waters, and she has never heard of such a thing. It's just another ploy to drive us away.'

As soon as she spoke the words, Glory realised they might well be true. The attack upon the Pump Room, the slow workers who impeded her progress, and the rumours, untraceable to any source, all seemed to point to one thing.

Someone didn't want Queen's Well to re-open.

The next day dawned cloudy and dreary; Glory was not as enthusiastic about going to the Pump Room as she should have been. She was more eager to return to the attic, but she didn't want to send Thad alone again, and Phillida, having recovered from her mishap, was off to visit the duchess.

They were all heading out of the cottage when Westfield appeared at the gate, and Glory's heart began to pound accordingly. She wondered whether he intended to come by every morning, a prospect that was both delightful and disturbing. Just how often did he plan on working with her? And what possible work could they do?

Glory flushed at the notions that ran through her head; while Thad and Phillida greeted the nobleman, she hung back, uncomfortable under the sweep of a dark gaze that missed nothing. Did he know the effect he had upon her? Glory tried her best to appear indifferent, but she could not stop the flush that stole over her cheeks.

Although she suspected the duke was well used to adoration, Glory had thought herself above such nonsense. However, despite all her accomplishments, it seemed she was just as giddy as any other female, a discovery that brought a frown to her lips.

'Your Grace, what a surprise,' Phillida exclaimed. 'Dare I hope that you have come to escort me to call upon your dear mother?'

'Actually, I was hoping to accompany Miss Sutton about her business this morning,' Westfield answered, though he was more than gracious to Phillida.

'Oh, Thad is taking her to the Pump Room, so if you would be so kind, it would save me a walk and Thad a trip as well,' Phillida said, waving a hand in dismissal of Westfield's wishes. She leaned in close to speak, as if in confidence. 'I won't go anywhere alone, you see, not after the shocking attack upon our property... Well, I simply don't feel safe.'

Unable to escape his fate, Westfield nodded and Glory ducked to hide her smile. Perhaps such unwelcome duties would put a stop to his visits. The idea, which ought to have given rise to relief, instead caused Glory a sharp pang of disappointment. And as if in anticipation of the loss, her gaze lingered longer than it should have, while she noted how elegant he looked in a midnight coat and doeskin breeches tucked into tall boots.

In fact, the image stayed with Glory long after they had parted and she resumed her place at the Pump Room. Trying to drive Oberon from her mind, Glory spoke with a carpenter about salvaging some of the broken furniture, but then there was not much for her to do except supervise the servants, who were occupied with few a patrons.

Thad was standing by one of the tall windows, staring out, but apparently content, and Glory wondered why she remained in the near-empty building when she could be looking through the attic. Finally, she told Thad she was heading home and would send him back something in the way of luncheon.

'All right,' he said, without even turning round. 'Do you need me to go with you?' he asked, over his shoulder. Having fully expected him to beg to leave, too, Glory wondered whether he had actually taken a liking to the Pump Room. If so, she was not about to discourage it by drawing him away.

'No, I'll be all right,' she said. 'I am not afraid to make the short walk in broad daylight.' In London a genteel female would not go out without a maid to attend her, at the very least. But in the country,

such strictures were relaxed and Glory had come to
appreciate her relative freedom.

Thad turned, a frown upon his face, as if considering her safety. 'I suppose Tibold has no excuse to
harass you any longer.'

'No, he does not,' Glory agreed and, before her
brother could change his mind, she donned her bonnet
and exited the rear of the building. The trees outside
greeted her rather ominously, their leaves rustling
in a manner that presaged another storm, and Glory
ducked her head against the wind. Intent upon her
goal, she drew her cloak tight and hurried towards
the cottage, without glancing about.

It wasn't until she reached the gate that Glory
looked up, but the area was deserted, hardly surprising considering the weather. Once inside, she shut the
door against the elements, the sound echoing throughout the small house. Then the sturdy old structure fell
pleasantly quiet, a welcome refuge from a day that
had turned so blustery.

Untying her bonnet, Glory laid it on the nearby
table and started to remove her cloak, only to halt at
the sight of something on the floor. Walking towards
the small parlour room, she frowned, for someone
must have left the window ajar, scattering papers.
But when she stepped through the doorway, she saw
that the secretary she used was standing open as well,
receipts and notes and records lying everywhere.

Glancing around in confusion, Glory called for the
maid. But there was no answer. Perhaps the girl was
upstairs and had not heard the door, Glory thought.

More likely she was in the kitchen, gossiping with the cook, and Glory walked through the small dining room and down the narrow passage that led to Mrs Dawber's domain.

But when Glory stepped into the room, it was silent and empty, dim except for the light shining through the small windows. There was no cook, no maid and no signs of the usual activity, such as baking bread or bubbling stew. For a long moment, Glory stood there, too puzzled to react, but a creaking sound jolted her from her thoughts. She looked up to see the door into the garden standing open, swinging wide with the rhythms of the wind.

Suddenly, Glory's confusion turned into something else as a chill ran up her spine. She told herself that, just like yesterday's experience in the attic, she was liable to find nothing amiss. Perhaps Mrs Dawber had sent the maid out to pick some herbs and then followed. Still, Glory warily approached the doorway.

Outside, the wind lashed the leaves overhead and sent blossoms swirling into the air above the neat and well-tended beds. The effect made the small, homely spot seem desolate, especially since there were no signs of occupation, past or present. And yet... Tugging at her billowing cloak, Glory felt the eerie sensation of being watched.

But who? Where? The cottage sat back from the road and looked over empty acres that had been let go during the long years it had been uninhabited. Unnerved, Glory wished again for her pistol, though it would do her no good against phantoms. Abruptly, she turned, intending to duck away from the prying eyes, but then she realised she didn't know whether the presence was outside—or in.

She stood for a moment, uncertain of what to do. Unless she wanted to clamber over the stone wall that edged the garden, she would have to go back inside and out the front door in order to hail someone or go to the nearest neighbour's house. Hopefully, someone could then run to fetch Thad, so she would not have to leave the cottage unattended.

A gust of wind snatched at her hair, loosening the strands, and Glory reached up for a bonnet that wasn't there. Frowning, she ducked into the kitchen, snatched up cook's heavy rolling pin and made her way to the front of the building as quickly and silently as possible.

But in the dining room, she paused at a sound ahead. Had she heard a thump or a knock? Refusing to quail in her own home, Glory drew a deep breath and continued on. Although she heard nothing else, when she approached the door, the heavy wood began to inch open slowly and she lifted her weapon high.

Chapter Seven

When his knock received no answer, Oberon felt a flash of panic and reached for the door. But as his fingers closed over the handle, he stopped short of throwing it open. Just because he was in Philtwell did not mean he could let his guard down, and his concern for Miss Sutton was no reason to become careless.

With the stealth of long practice, Oberon inched the portal open and then stepped back, out of the way. He waited a moment in silence before tipping it further with the toe of his boot, an action that served him well, for as it swung inwards he caught a glimpse of something coming towards him.

In an instant, he thrust himself through the narrow opening, one hand closing over the threatening object, while the other reached for his assailant. The heavy weapon thudded to the floor and rolled away, just as he realised that his opponent was no villain.

In fact, it seemed they recognised each other at the very same moment, for the woman in his arms stopped struggling abruptly, her breath coming fast and heavy. And just as abruptly, Oberon became aware of the soft female form pressed to him—so like the night they met. And his own breath came quickly, too.

Although he loosed his grip, Oberon remained where he was with Miss Sutton's back against him. Her hair had come loose somehow, and he felt like burying his face against the silky strands. Had he thought them plain? The thick, dark mass was shot with traces of auburn, as fiery as its owner.

Temptation such as he'd never known rose up, threatening to undo years of discipline. He had only to drop his head to gain access to her slender neck, and the arm that crossed her shoulders need only slip slightly lower to find the curve of her breasts. The knowledge caused an uncontrollable reaction, and he groaned.

Whether prompted by the sound or by the evidence of his body, Miss Sutton finally moved, slipping from his grasp to turn towards him. Her emerald eyes were wide, her chest rising and falling with either the effects of their tussle or the other struggle they now faced.

For Oberon had only to reach out to pull her to him, and at this moment, he wanted nothing more than to assuage the bone-deep yearning that coursed through him. But then what? There were servants, perhaps even relatives, about who might object to his ignoble behaviour. Miss Sutton was no lightskirt to be taken advantage of in an afternoon and left behind. And he could do nothing else.

Oberon didn't know how long they had been standing facing each other, their gazes locked, the tension between them running high, but that reminder of his duty brought him to his senses. He took a step back, away from temptation, and bent to retrieve the fallen weapon.

'A rolling pin?' he asked, eyeing Miss Sutton curiously as he held it up.

She appeared so dazed and flushed that Oberon nearly threw aside the utensil and took her in his arms. But then she focused on the heavy wood, and the sultry expression left her face. Oberon had only an instant to regret the loss before her gaze flew to his.

'Someone was here,' she said.

Oberon glanced around and spied a few papers that fluttered across the floor from a nearby room. Moving towards them, he paused to scan the small space where more were littered and saw an open window.

'Perhaps the wind is only to blame,' he said, with a gesture towards the disarray. 'Did you question the servants?'

Miss Sutton shook her head. 'The house is empty.'

'What?' Oberon asked sharply.

'I returned from the Pump Room to find this, as well as the back door standing open, with no sign of the cook or the maid,' she said. 'I was trying to leave the way I had come when you opened the door.'

Although Oberon could find no fault with her actions, he was seized by a helpless rage at the dangerous situation. Miss Sutton was resourceful, but she was no match against a determined man. Had he been intent upon harm, he was damn sure a rolling pin wouldn't have stopped him. *And it hadn't.*

'I need my pistol back,' she said, as though aware of his thoughts, and Oberon nodded. But would a pistol be enough? Just what was going on here?

A noise from the rear of the cottage made Oberon stiffen. Motioning for Miss Sutton to get behind him, he moved through a dining room and into a narrow hall. He didn't have a pistol, but he had his hands, a knife tucked into his boot and the skill to use them. Hearing a low muttering ahead, he pulled out the dagger and grasped it tightly, ready to throw or wield in close quarters.

Slipping around the doorway, he called out a warning, but the only person in the room was a plump older woman, who promptly shrieked in terror. And then Miss Sutton hurried past him, heedless of any danger, to comfort her.

'It's Cook,' she said as she went by.

While Miss Sutton tried to calm the frightened servant, Oberon made his way through the rest of the small house, but he found no signs of anyone else or other disturbances. When he returned, the older woman was seated by the hearth, with a cup in her hand. Crouched before her, Miss Sutton looked up when he entered.

'Mrs Dawber said a boy came to tell her that her cousin had need of her immediately.'

'A boy? You didn't know him?' Oberon asked.

Mrs Dawber shook her head. 'I thought Lucy, my cousin, had sent him. She lives a fair walk away,' the servant explained. 'I gathered up my things and hurried over there, but she said she hadn't sent anyone for me.' She shook her head in bewilderment. 'I turned around and headed right back, lucky to get a seat on a farm cart, or I'd still be trudging along.'

'And what of Cassie?' Miss Sutton asked. 'She's our maid of all work,' she explained to Oberon.

'I told Cassie that I had been called away and would return as soon as I could,' the cook said. 'Didn't she tell you?'

Miss Sutton shook her head. 'When I came home, you were both gone.'

The cook glanced around in alarm, but Miss Sutton reached out to soothe her, urging her to take another drink of whatever was in the cup. And Oberon found himself wishing he were in the servant's place, receiving the ministrations of Miss Sutton, who acted like no woman he had ever known.

Instead of crying or fainting, she had the wherewithal to face down an intruder, whether with a pistol or a makeshift weapon. She was intelligent enough to ask the right questions of the cook and determined yet compassionate enough to get a reply. Oberon couldn't help wondering whether someone that resourceful could prove to be an asset, rather than a hindrance…

Frowning, Oberon dismissed such thoughts just as the door rattled. The two women froze and he moved forwards, putting himself between them and the entrance. But since a high-pitched giggling presaged the new arrival, Oberon doubted that he would need his knife. And he was proved right when a mop-headed girl wearing a twisted apron entered, only to stop and stare at the occupants of the kitchen. Her amusement ceased and she began smoothing out her skirts with one hand.

'You're back,' she said to the cook before turning guiltily towards her employer. 'Um…I just stepped out into the garden for a moment.' She gestured towards the door, apparently hoping that her absence had just now been discovered.

While the cook muttered something about bird-witted girls, Miss Sutton rose to her feet, all gracious kindness. 'It's all right, Cassie,' she said. 'Just tell us where you were.'

It took some doing, but Miss Sutton finally rangled a tearful confession from the girl. It seemed that one Edward Plummer had come knocking at the door. Long an object of the girl's affections, he had never so much as glanced her way before, so how could she refuse him? How indeed? Oberon wondered. And why go 'walking' when they had an empty cottage at their disposal? Oberon vowed to have a talk with the young man, just as soon as he could.

But first he needed to speak privately to Miss

Sutton. Drawing her away from the servants and into
the narrow hall, Oberon turned to face her. 'Have the
girl pack up some of your things to send on to Sutton
House.'

'What?' She looked so startled that Oberon hastened to explain.

'Obviously, you are not safe here, but you will
be with my mother,' he said. 'There's a larger staff
to prevent this sort of thing and to see to your every
need.'

'I can't stay with you,' she said, as though alarmed
by the prospect.

'Thad and your aunt are welcome, as well,' Oberon
said. 'I know she will feel more secure there.'

'That's completely unnecessary. I'll hire additional
servants, more reliable ones,' she added, 'in order to
keep out intruders.'

Her words reminded Oberon that along with all her
admirable qualities came stubbornness, independence
and a tendency to argue with everything he said. 'Is
there some reason you need to remain here, something you are not divulging?' he asked, his patience
wearing thin. 'Because I need to know everything if
I'm going to protect you.'

She glanced away, her cheeks flushing, and
Oberon's dormant suspicions roared to life. 'I thought
we agreed to work together,' he said, more sharply
than necessary.

'Work together, not live together!'

Oberon lowered his voice. 'Someone has broken
into the Pump Room and your own residence,

someone who went to a lot of trouble to make sure the house was empty,' he said. 'What if you had stumbled upon whoever was rifling through your things?'

Miss Sutton refused to meet his gaze. 'I'll take better precautions,' she said. 'It won't happen again.'

It certainly wouldn't, for Oberon would make sure of that, with or without her cooperation. He eyed her directly. 'As magistrate, I'm ordering you under my protection.'

It was the wrong thing to say, as evidenced by the abrupt lift of her chin. 'I hardly think that's within your authority,' she said. With a stiff incline of her head, she took her leave and all Oberon could do was let her go.

She was right, of course. His concern had gone beyond all bounds and, short of tossing her over his shoulder, he could not force her to obey his wishes. But he was not accustomed to failure and he wasn't finished yet.

By the time the sun set this evening, Miss Sutton would be under his roof.

Glory paused at the entrance of the dining room and peered in. When she saw that only Thad sat at the long table, she loosed a low sigh of relief. However, she did not head towards the sideboard, where a variety of meats and egg dishes, jams and pastries were arrayed. She was too unsettled to eat and began restlessly walking around the room, its gloomy atmosphere ensured by the heavy curtains that covered the narrow windows.

'These need to be torn down or opened,' she said. 'It's far too dark in here to be comfortable.'

Thad scoffed. 'Well, I'm very comfortable, thank you,' he said, pushing aside a copy of the *Post* to look up at her. 'Dem, Glory, you know that cottage is too small for us. Leaving all our servants behind, hiring day girls and such, is all right for a brief visit, but not for a long stay. Why keep us cooped up in such small quarters?'

'Because the cottage is ours, handed down over centuries. We don't belong here,' Glory said, though her arguments yesterday had fallen on deaf ears. When approached by the duchess, Phillida had accepted the invitation to remove to Sutton House with glee and Thad had been just as enthusiastic. Although Glory had tried to convince them otherwise, she was swiftly overruled, as familial allegiance fell sway to the duke's wishes.

Westfield. She could hardly tell her relatives the real reason for her refusal: that the man was dangerous, perhaps not in the way she had originally thought, but in a more personal fashion. Twice now he had held her tight against him, and though she could not blame him in light of the circumstances, in neither case did he behave as a gentleman should.

And in neither case did she behave as she ought. In fact, yesterday it was all she could do to step away from his hard body, taut with strength, yet capable of gentleness... Shivering at the memory, Glory ran a

finger over the dingy mural that took up most of one
wall, pausing as a wild thought struck her.

'You don't think there's anything to that old legend
about Queen's Well, do you?' she asked, She had
dismissed the notion, for no reasonable person could
believe the waters acted as some kind of love potion.
But the closer she was to the duke, the closer she
wanted to be, which explained her reluctance to join
him in his household. She had pushed a heavy chair
in front of her door last night, unsure whether she
was keeping him out or herself in. And the pistol she
found lying on her bureau did little to reassure her,
for it meant he had been there…in her room.

'Why?' Thad asked, suddenly at her elbow, and
Glory started. He stood beside her, cocking his head
to one side, as if to study the painting. 'Do you see
something?'

Glory blinked, confused, until she realised her
brother was talking about the story of the Queen's
Gift, which she had passed on from Mrs Goodhew.
Too embarrassed to pursue her enquiry, Glory followed Thad's gaze to the mural, where the figure of
a woman dressed in a magnificent costume stood
holding out her hands.

'Dem,' Thad muttered. 'Do you suppose that's
Queen Elizabeth herself?'

Glory chided his language, but she was inclined
to agree with him. Although the background was
too dark to see clearly, there appeared to be the outline of a building that might well be Sutton House.

Was the monarch actually giving its residents a precious gift?

'I wonder what she's got,' Thad said, echoing Glory's thoughts. He stepped closer to squint at the wall, lifting a hand as though to remove a smudge there.

'Don't touch it; you might wipe away something.'

The sound of that voice, deep and rich and compelling, made Glory swing around too quickly. At least that's how she explained her sudden dizziness. It certainly wasn't the memory of the man's arms around her that made her giddy. Still, it was probably best not to focus on his tall form, Glory decided, glancing towards her brother.

'Oh, right,' Thad muttered, letting his hand fall. 'I was just trying to see what the woman's holding. Do you know?'

Westfield stepped forwards to eye the mural, his mother close behind him. 'Her hands appear to be empty,' he said.

'Perhaps she has already given the Suttons her gift,' the duchess said.

Glory scanned the background, but could not recognise anything except the outline of the house.

'Or someone could have rubbed it away, as I was about to do,' Thad said, glumly.

'The lighter area might be a symbol of her approval or patronage,' Glory suggested. 'Maybe that's all the gift ever was.'

'Perhaps,' the duchess said. 'But I think it high

time Randolph arranged to have an expert work on the mural before it fades away for ever. I must admit that I hadn't paid any attention to the painting before, but, naturally, it would have to do with the well. This is Sutton House, after all, and was in the family for generations.'

She paused to smile at Glory. 'And how well you look back here again. It is so good to have you,' she said before heading towards the sideboard to fill a plate.

Glory felt churlish at her reluctance to come, but she could not tell the duchess the truth either. The fact that Westfield had held her to him, making her even more wary of him, did not seem like something to share with the man's mother.

'Ah, the *Post*,' the duchess said, taking a seat at the table near Thad's abandoned paper. 'Is there anything of interest in it?'

'Just news of the war,' Thad said, looking a bit sheepish.

'But I thought Napoleon had been forced to abdicate, and we shall soon see an end to it all, for good this time,' Glory said. England had been battling France during most of her lifetime, and she glanced towards the duke, who was likely to be more knowledgeable than the rest of them, but he did not comment.

Instead, it was the duchess who spoke. 'What's this?' she asked as she scanned the open page.

Thad lurched towards the table as though he would snatch the paper from her very hands, if Glory had not reached out to restrain him. She frowned in dismay at his behaviour, but the duchess paid him no heed.

'Foul Waters?' she said.

Thad fell back, looking uncomfortable, and Glory realised why when the duchess began reading bits of the article aloud. The re-opening of Queen's Well was announced, but what followed was hardly a recommendation to visit. 'Consumptives were drawn to the spa…? Many deaths in the past…? Lack of decent lodging…? A fearsome, murderous blaze?'

The duchess pushed aside the paper in disgust. 'They make it sound as though the fire killed all of the guests when it was your grandfather who saved them,' she said. 'And the rest of the piece is a pack of lies. I shall write to the editor at once with the information that I am at Queen's Well with a host of friends, enjoying the new facilities.'

'Thank you, your Grace,' Glory said, too shaken to say more. She could understand why Thad hadn't wanted her to see the notice. It seemed that her plans to revive her family's heritage were met with trouble at every turn. What began as a labour of love had become a frustrating struggle that forced her to take refuge with strangers. And rather than face their pity, Glory headed towards the sideboard and began picking over the delicacies, despite her lack of appetite.

'Someone is trying very hard to drive away your business,' Westfield said, and Glory heard Thad's murmured assent.

'Perhaps you should have another chat with that horrible doctor, dear,' the duchess suggested.

'Perhaps I will,' Westfield said. 'But who would benefit most from the closing of the well?'

'I don't see how Tibold would benefit at all,' Thad said. 'If the spa closes, he loses access to the waters and whatever patients he has managed to acquire.'

'Unless he—or someone else—took my advice, presumably before I gave it,' Westfield said.

Glory turned in surprise to see the duke wearing a thoughtful expression.

'Whatever are you talking about?' the duchess asked.

Westfield turned to address his mother, and Glory tried to concentrate on what he was saying, instead of the curve of his lips. 'When I first met Dr Tibold, he complained about the Suttons having a monopoly on the waters and I asked him why he didn't put down a new well himself.'

Thad snorted. 'He can't even afford a new frock-coat.'

'Yes, he denied having the necessary funds to launch such a venture, but that doesn't mean there isn't someone out there doing just that,' Westfield said.

Thad snorted again. 'Here? We're as far from anywhere as you can get and the spa has been closed for years. Why would anyone else be interested in starting up a new one?'

'Competition has been the death of many,' Glory said, returning to the table. 'It happened at Epsom, once New Wells was established. And I believe Mr Pettit originally wrote to me because someone was nosing about our buildings.'

'But Philtwell is so small, I can't imagine something like that happening without it becoming common knowledge,' the duchess said.

'Maybe someone has tapped the same source of waters in a nearby field or the next village and is keeping it quiet,' Westfield said. 'I'll send Pearson out to see what he can discover.'

'Your *valet*?' the duchess asked.

'No one knows him, yet he has a common touch that should serve us well in dealings with residents of the area,' Westfield said, rising to his feet and putting an end to the discussion. 'I have some questioning of my own to do, including a visit with the good doctor.'

He paused to eye Thad. 'You will stay with your sister at all times?'

Thad looked reluctant, for he could hardly be eager for such a task, but when the duke lifted a brow, he nodded. And when Glory opened her mouth to protest that she needed no bodyguard, least of all her brother, Westfield turned that dark gaze upon her. A silent contest of wills ensued before Glory finally glanced away, for fear her thundering heart could be heard by all.

The man was trying to protect her, she told herself, and she should be grateful for his efforts. So why did it feel like he was a tyrant, manipulating her at every turn?

* * *

As soon as Letitia stepped into the dim bedroom, she was tempted to turn around and exit. It was as stifling as a tomb and nearly as dark. Walking to the windows, she pulled aside the heavy curtains and lifted the sash. The suite had long needed renovation, but perhaps soon it would be bright and airy and filled with love…

'What's that? The sun? I'm blinded,' Randolph said in a mocking tone. 'A fresh breeze? I might choke.'

'I think it is time to set you free.'

'Hallelujah,' Randolph said. 'If I lie here any more, I'm sure to have a relapse.' He paused to turn a sharp eye on Letitia. 'What prompted my release? A betrothal, perhaps?'

Letitia shook her head. 'Nothing quite so dramatic, but I think we've made enough progress to allow for your recovery. If Oberon shows signs of bolting, you can always worsen.'

'No, thank you,' Randolph said, sourly. 'Or I'm the one who's liable to bolt.'

Letitia eyed him askance. 'Not after all our work.'

'*Our* work?' Randolph said. 'It is I who have been cooped up here, regretting my every correspondence with you.'

Ignoring his complaints, Letitia walked towards the bed to take up her usual chair nearby. 'Of course, you won't be up to your magistrate duties, so Oberon can continue in that role. But I think our success is such that he would do so, anyway. He has been most determined in his investigation.'

Randolph frowned, as though mulling over that statement. 'I'm not sure I care to face your son when he is determined. I don't want him asking me questions that I'd rather not answer.'

'Nonsense,' Letitia said. 'It is the doings with the spa that has his attention.'

Randolph slanted her a glance. 'Letty, you haven't had a hand in that, have you?'

'Of course not,' Letitia answered. 'Do you think me capable of vandalism, home breaking and the like? Besides, I didn't need to do anything other than put those two together and watch the waters do their magic. You will soon see, Randolph. When they are near each other, the air fairly crackles with it.'

'I hope so,' Randolph said. 'I don't want to return to this bed, but the last time I saw them together, the crackling was due to antagonism more than anything else.'

'Electricity, Randolph,' Letitia said, with a smile. 'It is a force of nature.'

Randolph frowned, his enthusiasm for their scheme having been dampened, either by recent developments or his enforced idleness. But Letitia knew it would revive once he was up and about and could see the results for himself, especially with Miss Sutton living under their very roof. And so she ignored the dark look he sent her, as well as his warning.

'Lightning is dangerous, Letty,' he said. 'Someone might get hurt.'

Chapter Eight

❦☙❧

As Oberon expected, Pearson accepted the assignment with his usual alacrity, changing into clothes that would help him blend in among the residents of the area. A man of medium height and build with receding brown hair, the valet was unremarkable and could adopt nearly any speech required of him.

'I don't think you'll be in any danger, but take one of the pistols as a precaution,' Oberon said.

Pearson eyed him askance. 'Surely you don't expect a rival well digger to shoot should I ask… probing questions?'

Oberon ignored the pun. 'It can't hurt to be prepared. We still don't know what is going on here; she could be up to her pretty neck in something.'

At his words, Pearson eyed him once more. 'Surely you do not refer to Miss Sutton? I assumed you had abandoned your suspicions of the young woman.'

Oberon bristled at being questioned by his valet, but he forced himself to answer reasonably. 'Although Miss Sutton is the victim of we-know-not-what, she might have brought it upon herself, unwittingly. She wouldn't be the first to be duped into aiding and abetting others, less innocent, in some shady scheme.'

Although Pearson said nothing, Oberon sensed the man's scepticism. 'What?' he asked, more sharply than necessary.

'I beg your pardon, your Grace, but we are in a sleepy village far from London or any known hotbed of foreign activity. Might I suggest you more closely examine your…feelings about the young woman.'

Oberon paused in the act of slipping his knife into his boot and glared at his valet, who bowed serenely and turned to go. Muttering a few choice curses about meddling servants and ill-advised confidences, Oberon was tempted to dismiss the man's words. But he did not need his observant valet to tell him what he already knew. He had only to remember his behaviour yesterday to realise his interest in Miss Sutton went beyond mere duty.

In the course of an afternoon, the cool demeanour he had so carefully cultivated for years had nearly been undone by a slew of emotions: fear, protectiveness, passion… Although not that long ago Oberon had vowed to uncover all of Miss Sutton's secrets and purge himself of his unwelcome attraction to her, it only seemed to grow stronger.

Rising to his feet, Oberon revised his original plan to focus on fulfilling his responsibilities as magistrate, for the sooner he discovered whatever threatened Miss Sutton, the sooner he could do away with it. And then, perhaps, he would be rid of his fascination with her, as well.

With Miss Sutton under his roof, Oberon was free to resume his investigation, and he headed into the village without a backward glance.

However, throughout the day Oberon was aware of a certain tension, which expressed itself in the clenching of his fingers and repeated glances in the direction of the Pump Room. It wasn't until he was back at Sutton House, stripping off his gloves, that the sensation receded, driven away by the sight of her.

Miss Sutton was safe, and that accounted for the relief that surged through him. But as he stood watching her talk to her aunt, he was struck by something else, too: a sense of rightness. Miss Sutton simply looked *right* standing in the doorway to the parlour. And it felt right to be returning to her.

Oberon ought to have been alarmed at such nonsense, but he could not work up any indignation. Instead, he wondered what it would be like to return to her after *every* journey, after any hours spent away. It had been a while since he had been home to Westfield, even longer since he'd felt any anticipation upon travelling to the family seat.

But he pictured her waiting for him there, a greeting upon her lips, an emerald spark in her eyes. And in that instant, she turned to look towards him. Their gazes met across the space of Sutton House and

Oberon felt a sudden jolt that could not be denied. Was he still imagining things, or did he really see his own strange yearning reflected back at him?

'Oh, your Grace, you have returned!'

Miss Bamford's shrill voice put an end to the moment. Miss Sutton looked away and Oberon was reminded of the circumstances in which he found himself. Miss Sutton made her home in this remote village, running a business, while he had resided for years in the London town house, where his life had no place in it for a waiting woman—this one or any other.

Assuming an impassive countenance, Oberon answered Miss Bamford's hail and listened to her chatter. But his attention was caught by Miss Sutton's hair, tied neatly in a knot at the back of her head. Simple. Utilitarian. Perhaps even prim. But he remembered when the thick strands had fallen loose and flexed his fingers at the thought.

'Oh, I believe her Grace is calling us in to supper,' Miss Bamford said, before turning to head towards the dining room.

Left behind, Oberon fell into step beside Miss Sutton, which gave him a chance to remind himself of her scent, some kind of rosewater perhaps, deceptively light but intoxicating.

'Did you speak with Dr Tibold?' she asked.

Oberon nodded. 'I did, but I'm afraid I did not learn anything new.' In fact, the normally disgruntled physician seemed eager to entice new patients to Philtwell, not drive them away. And as for the possibility of taking his business to another well, the man seemed far too volatile to be entrusted with such secrets.

'However, he did direct me to your maid's young man,' Oberon said. 'It seems that Edward Plummer has quite a reputation with the ladies, but his interest in Cassie came on suddenly, thanks to a boy who offered him good coin to woo her away from the cottage.'

'What?' Miss Sutton glanced up at him sharply. 'Do you suppose it was the same boy who gave the cook her message?'

Having wondered that very thing, Oberon inclined his head. He had even returned to Miss Sutton's work site, where much progress had been made in the absence of the former overseer, who had not returned. If questioned, would the missing man, too, mention a boy?

Miss Sutton appeared thoughtful. 'But surely someone must know this youth?'

'One would think so, if he is a local resident,' Oberon said. And he had gone straight to those who would know, offering a reward to a group of Philtwell youngsters for any information on the lad. 'However, there is always the possibility that he is an outsider, in the employ of a resident or someone unknown in the area.'

They had reached the dining room, so Oberon said no more. In fact, he was surprised into silence at the sight of his mother on the arm of a stranger. A slender gentleman of middle age, the fellow had

light brown hair and a wary air about him that invited
suspicion.

'Mr Pettit!' The chorus of greetings told Oberon
that he was meeting the owner of Sutton House at
last. After introductions were made and many queries
tendered about his health, Mr Pettit took a seat at the
head of the table and began accepting large portions
of all that was offered him.

'You don't want to overdo it,' the duchess warned.
'Remember, that you are still a recovering invalid.'

'Oh…uh…yes, of course,' Pettit said with a bleak
expression. He took no more, but seemed to heartily
enjoy his food when no one was looking, making
Oberon wonder whether the duchess was running
roughshod over his sickroom. As if to confirm his
suspicions, she soon announced that Mr Pettit was
not well enough to assume his magistrate duties as
yet.

'Yes, your Grace, but I am most grateful to you for
stepping in,' Pettit said, nodding to Oberon. 'I scarce
can believe what I've been hearing.'

'Tell us, Mr Pettit, what do you think about these
happenings?' Miss Bamford asked. 'Should Glory
close the spa?'

'Of course not,' the duchess said. Her sharp answer
made Oberon wonder whether nostalgia had completely overtaken her wits.

'But what of the well's…curse?' Miss Bamford
asked in a dramatic whisper.

'I've never heard anything about a curse, and

I've been living here for... How low long has it been now?' Pettit asked.

He looked to Oberon's mother, who shook her head rather vehemently. 'I'm sure I don't know.'

Oberon tried not to read anything into the behaviour of those at the table, but, as Pearson said, his habits were ingrained, and he watched carefully as they discussed the events of the past few days. He had hoped that a different perspective, that of someone who knew the village and its inhabitants well, might provide new insights into the troubles. But Pettit could add little to the conversation and expressed his bafflement as to the culprit or the cause.

They lapsed into silence then, everyone seemingly deep in thought, but Oberon noticed that Thad was staring at the mural. Apparently, Pettit noticed as well.

'We wrote to London this very morning to find someone who can restore it,' the man said, nodding towards the painting that covered one wall of the dim room.

But young men like Thad were not known for their patience, and he did not seem keen upon waiting for expert advice. 'Yet you must know... Does it show Queen Elizabeth presenting a gift?'

Pettit shrugged. 'I've never paid any heed to it until now, seeing as how I was not to make any changes to the...' His words trailed off and he reached for his wine, taking a big gulp.

Oberon slanted the man a glance, for he was unsure what to make of Randolph Pettit. In another situation the fellow's demeanour would be cause for interest, but Pettit had been ill and it might have affected his behaviour. And, as Pearson reminded him, they were not in London. Yet there appeared to be plenty of intrigues in tiny Philtwell. Gesturing to the serving maid, Oberon made a quiet request and she bobbed a curtsy before heading off.

'But you have heard of the Queen's Gift?' Thad asked his host.

'Yes, there have always been rumours of that nature,' Pettit said. 'I cannot tell you whether the legend is based upon fact, but I am hardly a scholar of either the spa or the period in question. However, if you are interested, there is much in the Sutton House library upon Elizabeth, quite a collection, in fact. Perhaps you should take a look.'

Thad frowned, apparently none too eager to delve into historical study. 'But do you think the gift, if there really is such a thing, could be somewhere here at Sutton House?' he asked. 'The mural seems to show the queen standing on the grounds.'

Pettit shook his head. 'I catalogued everything when I moved in and there was nothing that would qualify, unless it was artwork or the like. Perhaps that's all it was and the tale grew in the telling, as they say. In those days, people imagined treasure everywhere for the taking, especially after Elizabeth's father dissolved the Catholic church, with its hoard of relics and riches. Religious sites became a favourite spot for excavating, but even old mounds and ruins did not escape the shovel.'

Thad brightened. 'So you think it's buried outside?'

Pettit laughed. 'No, my boy.'

'But if the queen is standing in front of—' Thad began, only to be cut off by his sister.

'Thad, you are not to start digging up Mr Pettit's property,' Miss Sutton said in an admonishing tone. 'The mural might have been painted long after the fact, simply to depict the queen visiting the house, especially since she doesn't appear to have a gift in her hand.'

'Perhaps it is hidden away,' Miss Bamford said, looking over her shoulder as though something might suddenly leap out at her. 'These old houses are riddled with priest's holes and the like.'

Like an eager pup, Thad seized on that notion and glanced at Pettit, who gave the boy his blessing. 'I have found none, but you are welcome to search all you like. This is Sutton House, after all.'

'I don't know whether you should, Thad,' Miss Bamford said ominously. 'If there is a curse, perhaps you had better leave well enough alone.'

Oberon's reservations were more pragmatic, for if the boy should find a prize, it would belong, not to him, but to the owner of the residence. However, Oberon said nothing; when the maid returned with the requested items, he rose to his feet.

'I've some experience with delicate documents and the like,' Oberon said, not going into detail. 'So with your leave, I shall see if I can remove the dust, without harming the painting.'

'Of course,' Pettit said.

'Do you really think you ought to?' Miss Bamford said, eyeing the mural warily. 'Meddling with such things might simply call more troubles down upon us.'

'Nonsense,' Oberon's mother said briskly.

Ignoring their aunt's warning, the Suttons took up the candelabras from the table and brought them over to the wall. The brightness illuminated new details, although the background remained dark and impenetrable.

'What have you there?' asked Thad.

'A soft paintbrush,' Oberon said. Positioning the brush over the outstretched hands of the female figure, he carefully dusted away what he could. And after several strokes, the area between the queen's fingers grew brighter, as if radiating light.

'Maybe it's a crown,' Thad said. 'Do you know how much something like that would be worth?'

Oberon shook his head and glanced towards the boy, whose face was shining with excitement. But his sister was not as enthusiastic. 'It's probably only a symbol for her reign,' she said.

'You might find out more in the library,' Pettit reminded Thad.

'Or in the cottage,' Oberon said, slanting Miss Sutton a glance.

She refused to look at him, but acknowledged his suggestion with a nod. 'Yes, Thad, perhaps we can have a look there.'

'Why don't you two go?' Thad said. 'I'm no good at reading through old papers.'

'Yes, I would be interested,' Oberon said. 'There might be some hint to the current troubles amongst the past records.'

Still not meeting his gaze, Miss Sutton turned to Miss Bamford. 'Aunt? Will you join us?'

'Oh, heavens, no,' Miss Bamford said, with a shudder. 'I refuse to have anything to do with that mural or whatever might invoke the curse. And you shouldn't either.'

Miss Sutton did not bother to respond, but eyed Oberon warily, 'Very well, then, your Grace,' she said, inclining her head. 'Let us see what we can discover.'

Oberon felt a surge of anticipation, which he firmly dismissed. This was an opportunity to further his investigation, not an assignation. And thankfully, there would be no chance of temptation. Along with the burly characters he had hired to watch the cottage, the additional servants would make for a full, rather than empty, house.

The two of them would not be alone again.

Oberon frowned at just how wrong he had been, a rare occurrence theses days. His instincts were strong, his judgements astute, but in this instance, he had miscalculated. So he ducked under old beams under the eaves with Miss Sutton. And the assurances he had given himself were for naught because there weren't any servants up here. Hell, there wouldn't be any room for them.

Mercifully, the dismal space with its shrouded objects and aged crates did not invite intimacy. Dark and stuffy and crowded with forgotten items covered with a thick layer of dust, it did not even invite exploration.

'Perhaps you should have one of the maids tidy up here before you begin searching,' Oberon said.

'I didn't think of that,' Miss Sutton admitted as she knelt before a crate. 'When I was up here before, I left…rather abruptly. Can you move this lid?' she asked, setting down her lantern.

Obviously, she was not bothered by the state of her surroundings, a trait that Oberon could only admire. Now he could add gritty work to the long list of things that Miss Sutton did not fear. Her only concession was to wear an apron over her sprigged muslin gown, which somehow managed to make her look even more appealing.

Drawing in a sharp breath, Oberon wondered whether he should leave Miss Sutton to her searching, for she was in no danger up here from anyone— except perhaps himself. But he took a seat upon a wooden box on the chance that she might need him, if only to move heavy items, and told himself he could prove useful. He was not prepared to admit how much he craved her company.

Leaning back against the wall, he watched her pull various pieces of clothing from the crate, dust motes drifting about her in the lantern light. And despite the peculiar circumstances, Oberon again felt that sense of *rightness*, just as though she was right where she ought to be—and so was he.

Even though he shook his head at such nonsense, Oberon took the opportunity to study his subject more carefully than ever before. There, in the quiet confines of the attic, he noted the tempting expanse of her throat, the quirk of her mouth as she examined a new object and the excited murmur she made when she found something of interest.

She chatted amiably over her discoveries, speculating on their past histories or possible uses, and Oberon was content to listen. There was something soothing about her voice, and yet, when it dropped to a husky whisper, he was stirred in a way that had little to do with comfort. In those instances, his gaze lingered on the slender curves he well remembered until he shifted uncomfortably and looked away.

'What's this?' she asked, recapturing his attention as she bent down to shine her lantern deep under the eaves. 'It looks like an old trunk that has been pushed out of sight.'

Her enthusiasm was refreshing and Oberon decided that was part of her attraction. When he returned to town, he would set his sights upon a different diversion from his usual mistress, cool and jaded. But as he got to his feet, carefully avoiding the beam overhead, Oberon suspected Miss Sutton would not be replaced that easily. And he felt a certain uneasiness at the prospect.

He had barely dragged the trunk forwards when

she reached out to lift the lid, so Oberon crouched beside her to place the lantern close. The dark interior was soon flooded with light, revealing a stack of thick record books or ledgers, as well as loose papers.

'At last,' Miss Sutton said, her voice low and breathless, and Oberon felt anything but soothed. When she turned to him, her face glowing, temptation rose, swift and fierce. And despite his best efforts, she must have seen something in his face, for she stilled and stared at him in silence, her green eyes wide.

Heat stained her cheeks and Oberon saw that a smudge of dirt marred her flawless skin. Lifting a hand to cup her chin, Oberon wiped it away with his thumb, a simple gesture that was far too intimate. It seemed even more personal than when he had held her in his arms, perhaps because this was no accidental encounter. He could make no excuses for his behaviour now.

And though Oberon was well aware that he had no business touching her, he couldn't seem to pull his hand away. Instead, he lowered his thumb to her lips, running the pad over the silken surface and parting them. He paused, expecting her protest, but she only stared at him with eyes bright and feverish, so he leaned close to brush his mouth against hers.

The contact sent heat surging through him and Oberon deepened the kiss, revelling in the sweet, fresh taste of her. When she made a low sound of pleasure, he reached for her, his vaunted restraint slipping further with every breath. He needed her nearer, in his arms, wrapped up in him, and all the reasons why he dared not act upon that need faded away.

But the close quarters that were his undoing were also his saving grace. For as he pulled her to him, the lid to the trunk fell from its precarious position, brushing against them on its way down. The resulting thud raised a cloud of dust and Miss Sutton turned away to cough against her hand.

That ingenuous response brought Oberon to his senses at last, and he wondered what the devil he was doing. Pulling out a handkerchief, he handed it to Miss Sutton, an apology upon his lips. But the sight of her, wide-eyed and flushed, only made him want to capture her face in his hands and begin again, to take her right there upon one of the dusty sheets that had fallen to the floor.

'Hello? Are you up there?'

The sound of his mother's voice sent Oberon shooting to his feet and he stepped in front of Miss Sutton just as the duchess appeared in the doorway. She blinked at the sight of them, then turned to go with amazing speed.

'I'm afraid it's too crowded up here already,' she called over her shoulder.

'No!' Miss Sutton said. 'That is, the attic has become quite stuffy in the heat of the day, so I shall go with you. I crave some fresh air.' She scurried towards Oberon's mother as if the duchess were a lifeline, leaving her precious finds behind without a second glance.

'I'll have the trunk sent to Sutton House, where you

can examine the contents at your leisure,' Oberon said, but Miss Sutton made no reply. His mother reached out to brush dust from her back as she slipped by, and then the duchess, too, disappeared down the stairs, leaving Oberon alone to compose himself.

Flexing his fingers repeatedly, he tried to make sense of what had just happened. There could be no excuses this time, for he had not disarmed an assailant. He had known full well whom he was dealing with and yet he had acted anyway, against all the dictates of propriety, jeopardising years of hard work in a single instant.

Yet even now the longing lingered, making him feel rather like Darcy of Miss Austen's popular tale, struggling against a passion that could come to nothing. But unlike his fictional counterpart, Oberon could not resolve the situation with tender words and fine deeds.

Miss Sutton's place was here, with the spa that she loved, while he belonged back in London, where his duty lay.

Letitia found Randolph in the garden, sitting on a stone bench that stood in the sun, and she made no effort to curb her steps as she hurried to join him. He glanced up, a greeting dying on his lips when he saw her agitation.

'What is it? Has something else happened?' he asked with an expression of alarm.

Letitia nodded. 'I have made a dreadful muddle of things, Randolph!'

'Letty, you didn't do something to Queen's Well, did you?' he asked, paling.

'No, of course not, you old fool,' Letitia said. 'I imagined the two of them cooped up with a pile of mouldy papers, surrounded by the servants to fetch whatever they cared to investigate. How was I to know that they would go into the attic themselves?'

'What are you talking about?' Randolph asked, looking bewildered.

'What do you think?' Letitia asked, tempted to smack him, if only she had a fan. 'Oberon and Miss Sutton! Our very purpose, Randolph.'

'What of them?'

Letitia sighed. 'I had hoped to throw them together upon a long walk by having them attend me only to conveniently fall behind.'

'Of course,' Randolph said, wryly.

Ignoring his sour tone, Letitia leaned close and lowered her voice to a whisper. 'Instead, I interrupted what can only have been a tête-à-tête.'

'*What?*'

Letitia nodded, her elation at the discovery tempered by the disappointment of her blunder. 'I stumbled across the two of them alone in a place where they were certain to be undisturbed.'

'The attic?'

At her nod, Randolph wrinkled his nose. 'It hardly sounds like the ideal location for romance.'

Letitia frowned at him. 'Well, to the young anywhere serves as a possible rendezvous.'

'I suppose,' Randolph said, doubtfully. 'But how

do you know that they were doing anything other than exploring the place?'

'I know for a fact they were exploring each other because Miss Sutton sported a dusty handprint on the back of her gown.'

Randolph's brows shot upwards. 'If that is the case, why didn't you have a talk with the boy about his responsibilities to his gender and to his name?'

Letitia waved away the suggestion. 'Should I try to prod him to do the right thing, he will only dig in his heels. I have seen it many times before when I have put forward a suitable candidate for marriage. This is my main chance, and I am not going to risk it by interfering.'

'Well, what will you do, then?'

Letitia frowned thoughtfully. 'I will simply have to try again tomorrow, weather permitting.' Feeling better now that she had decided to implement her original plan, though later than she would have wished, the duchess sat back and smiled. She did not see Randolph roll his eyes heavenwards.

'I'm not sure what you're calling it,' he muttered, 'but to me that sounds like interfering.'

Chapter Nine

It had been an awkward trek back to Sutton House, with Glory trying to hide her distress while the duchess prattled on as though rattled, making Glory wonder just what the older woman had seen when she'd entered the attic. Her face flaming, Glory had been unable to look at the duchess and responded to her chatter with monosyllables.

Once inside the residence, Glory was relieved to part with the older woman, who hurried off in search of Mr Pettit, while she secluded herself in the library. Earlier, Glory had been studying some of the materials to be found there and she opened a thick volume, hoping to gain an escape from her own thoughts.

But she could not so easily forget that she had been kissed—and by whom. Glory bent her face over the pages, unseeing, as she attempted to sort it all out. When had she gone from fearing the duke as a powerful adversary to welcoming his...advances? Glory shook her head. Lately, she had come to admire the man; their conversations, whether over supper or upon walks or in the attic, had become less antagonistic and more congenial. But that hardly explained her shocking lapse in behaviour.

Glory lifted both hands to her cheeks as she remembered the way he had looked at her, something sparking in his unfathomable dark eyes, and then the thrill of his touch and his mouth upon her own... *Girlish nonsense.* That's all it was, Glory told herself. She had been taken with Westfield's good looks from the very first sight of him; later, she was dazzled by his manners, when they were in evidence, a heady combination for someone who had never known any man's attentions.

Perhaps a more experienced young woman would have been able to avoid the situation, Glory thought, wishing for some feminine advice. But she dared not write to friends in London, and here there was only her family.

Glory shook her head again. Thad's increasing devotion to all things ducal might lead him to excuse the nobleman's behaviour, but should he take offence, Glory did not want another bout of fisticuffs—or worse—between the two males. And though Glory longed to confide in another woman, if she told Phillida about the incident, her aunt would start planning the nuptials.

Glory choked back a laugh at the very thought, for the man certainly was not courting her. And why would he? She was not a suitable match for a duke and needed to remember that, as well as the tenuous position of an unwed female of any rank. The thought was a sobering one and enough to make Glory rue her lapse, no matter how much she might secretly long for a re-occurrence.

Dropping her hands from her face, Glory frowned. Today she had played with fire and escaped without being burned, but she could not be as reckless again. What had she once told herself? It was well and good to like Westfield, as long as she did not like him too much.

Kissing the man was definitely too much.

Oberon stood by the window in the library at Sutton House, looking blindly out upon the afternoon and trying to quell his restlessness. In London he spent most of his time indoors, so there was no reason for his sudden ennui, but he was accomplishing nothing here except keeping watch over Miss Sutton, who was safe enough in Pettit's home. Yet he could not seem to bring himself to leave.

'There are a lot of references to Dr Dee in here.'

At the sound of her voice, Oberon turned towards Miss Sutton's dark head, bent over the books and papers that littered the table. 'That old mystic?' he said.

'What do you know of him?'

'A scholar, a visionary, a genius, a fool,' Oberon said. 'I believe that all could be applied, for while his accomplishments were many, he was drawn to the occult.'

'He was one of Elizabeth's advisers and attended her here,' Miss Sutton said.

'Interesting,' Oberon said, though he did not see how that information was going to help him solve the problems that plagued Queen's Well. And since Pearson had found no evidence of plans for a rival spa, he was fresh out of ideas. Perhaps it was that knowledge that irked him, but Oberon suspected his frustration sprang from something far more insidious.

As if to prove his theory, Oberon watched Miss Sutton reach for a thick volume, his attention drawn to the slender length of her fingers, and he was immediately struck with a fierce yearning for her touch. Loosing a harsh breath, Oberon wondered if the famed air outside would do him good, though he assumed there was only one way to assuage his restlessness. Frowning, he glanced away from Miss Sutton towards the doorway, only to see his mother appear.

'Come, you two,' she said, pulling on her gloves. 'You have been working in the library far too much and cannot be expected to remain inside on such a beautiful day. I insist that you join me for a walk.'

'Take Miss Bamford with you,' Oberon suggested.

'She is not here. Neither is Thad, and Mr Pettit is unfit. So I shall brook no refusals,' she said.

Since he was not accomplishing anything here but an excess of brooding, Oberon inclined his head in agreement, then, inevitably, he looked to Miss Sutton.

'Perhaps you could walk me to the Pump Room,' she said, stirring from her chair.

'Nonsense,' the duchess said. 'You have done enough work for one day; this afternoon we are headed elsewhere.'

In the face of his mother's formidable resolve, even Miss Sutton could do little, and they were soon following her along paths that led above the village, part of the spa regimen to improve one's health and appreciate nature.

'There is nothing to compare with the crags in summer. Your father and I used to take this very route,' his mother said. With a misty smile, she waved them on. 'I'll catch up with you in a moment.'

Although Miss Sutton looked as though she would rather remain with his mother, Oberon shook his head subtly. 'I think she is sunk deep in nostalgia,' he said, once they were out of his mother's hearing, 'and memories of her younger days.'

Miss Sutton nodded. 'How long has your father been gone?'

'Too long,' Oberon said. Although he always cut short any such discussions, he found himself speaking haltingly of the man whose life had ended too soon. And as they climbed higher, he was reminded of the walks they had taken, not here, but at home.

'We used to go on rambles around Westfield for hours,' Oberon said. He shook his head at a sudden realisation. 'I don't think I've walked the land there since.' It made him feel ashamed somehow, although the estate, and all the family properties, ran well without him, and his duty lay in London.

'Why is that?' Miss Sutton asked. 'Are the memories too painful?'

'At first,' Oberon admitted, though he had spoken of that time to no one. He paused. 'I was young and heartbroken and easy prey for those who would use me and my rank for their own ends.'

Miss Sutton appeared shocked and Oberon gave her a tight smile. 'There are always those who seek the influence of the titled to gain their own power or positions.' Even now, he could not go into the details, but for a while he had felt lost, betrayed, alone. And then Portland had approached him, offering him the chance to take advantage of his situation, to encourage those who would curry favor and others, far worse. To do his part...

It had been a godsend at the time, and Oberon had accepted both the work and the persona gratefully. And if the cost was what was left of his family, Oberon had been more than willing to shut down all emotion and function without the distractions—and pain—that came with them. But now, as he took in the stricken look on Miss Sutton's expression, he wondered how much of himself was left.

As if to shake off the odd mood, Oberon hurried round a bend in the path, only to halt at the striking vista ahead. This was rugged country, far different than the rolling hills to be found at Westfield, yet with its own appeal. Below stretched lush pastures, wooded dales and moorlands of heather and peat, and above, the ground rose into rocky peaks.

'It's beautiful, isn't it?' Miss Sutton whispered from beside him. 'If prospective guests could see this, we would surely be inundated.'

Small copper-coloured butterflies flashed by, searching out clumps of bright pink flowers. The quiet was broken only by the faint rustle of bracken in the wind and the scurrying of a mountain hare. How long had it been since he'd noticed such things? Oberon wondered. For years, his observations had been limited to people, ferreting out their secrets, gauging their words, testing their loyalties. Now he considered how much he had missed—and not only scenery.

Although they had stopped to admire the view, Oberon soon found himself admiring his companion. Her cheeks were flushed and wisps of dark hair had escaped to caress her face in a way that invited him to do the same. Oberon felt a familiar jolt, and the memory of that moment in the cottage attic came rushing back.

Oberon didn't know whether his contemplation drew her attention, but Miss Sutton turned towards him. And, as if she, too, recalled their kiss, her eyes widened, her lips parting, perhaps in anticipation of another.

A full minute stretched by while they stood silent and still, Oberon struggling against a temptation that he knew well not to indulge. When a puff of breeze sent a stray bit of heather towards him, Miss Sutton

finally moved, stepping forwards to brush it away—
along with the last vestiges of his restraint. Despite
his best intentions, Oberon covered her hand with his
own, his heart pounding beneath her fingers.

But above that rapid beating, he heard the cackle
of a grouse, a warning to intruders that meant the
bird had been disturbed by animal or man. Loosing Miss Sutton's hand, Oberon turned the way they
had come, expecting to see his mother, yet the path
remained empty. And before he could swing back
around, Oberon felt Miss Sutton slam into him, sending them both sprawling into a patch of Jacob's ladder
to the tune of a thundering too loud to be his heart.

Realising the noise was that of falling rock, Oberon
rolled Miss Sutton beneath him and wedged them
under a small outcropping. There they lay while a
boulder of some size, followed by smaller ones, struck
the place where they had stood. Only now did he
realise how far out they had been on one of the edges,
as the locals called them, that dropped away into the
valley below.

Oberon's heart slammed again, this time with
the thought of what might have been: Miss Sutton
injured, or worse, falling to her death. He held her
more tightly, fear for her knifing through him, along
with rage that he could do nothing except lie prone
as silence descended once more—for he was certain
that this was no accident.

Was their attacker lying in wait further up the path,
or had he scrambled up on to the crags above to send
stones raining down upon them? Had he dislodged

the rocks and fled, or was he, even now, searching them out to complete his work? Oberon had a clear view of their immediate area, but he did not know these paths. Nor could he leave Miss Sutton in order to give chase.

'Do you have your pistol?' Oberon whispered against her ear. She nodded. Oberon had the knife in his boot, but if there was more than one assailant, he wanted Miss Sutton armed.

'Good girl,' he said. 'Can you reach it?'

Again she nodded, wiggling a bit in order to access her reticule. Then they both lay still, barely breathing as the long, tense minutes dragged by, until, finally, Oberon heard light footfalls. Perhaps their foe had come to view his handiwork. Oberon reached for his knife.

'Oberon? I thought I heard something...'

The sound of his mother's voice forced Oberon to move. If he warned her away, she might well meet some mishap herself, so they would have to chance their escape. 'Duck, Mother, and watch for falling rocks,' Oberon said as he rolled from his position. She paled when she saw him appear from beneath the outcropping, dragging Miss Sutton along with him.

Although he could discern nothing from above, Oberon did not linger. 'Hurry,' he said, urging them around the bend in the path and down, away from the precipitous edges that now seemed more deadly than picturesque. And all the while, he was alert for any sounds other than their own progress as they stumbled, hunched over and clinging to the growth that lined their way.

When they finally reached an open area, Oberon looked in all directions, but saw no one behind or ahead. Whoever was responsible had either fled earlier or remained well hidden, a possibility that prevented them from lingering any longer than to catch their breath. In fact, his mother was gasping and clutching her side after their race to safety, but she waved him away when he expressed concern. In her own way, she was as formidable as Miss Sutton.

Oberon turned towards the woman whose quick actions had made all the difference. 'How did you know?'

She turned her head, her gaze travelling upwards, as if searching for signs of life among the cliffs. 'I felt them as I so often have since coming here. Eyes upon me. Watching,' she whispered, and Oberon heard his mother's gasp.

'What happened?' she asked, in a voice pitched higher than normal.

Miss Sutton did not answer, but looked down at the pistol she was still clutching and slipped it back into her reticule, making his mother eye him in alarm.

'Miss Sutton saved my life,' Oberon said, though he was sure he was not the intended victim.

'*What?*' His mother clutched at her throat.

With a nod, Oberon grimly scanned the area once more. 'It seems that our villain has upped the stakes of the game,' he said. 'From vandalism and house breaking to attempted murder.'

* * *

Dazed, Glory let the duke and his mother lead her to Sutton House and deposit her in a comfortable chair in the library. A maid brought some wine and the duke urged Glory and his mother to take some, but Glory knew that no drink could cure what ailed her. In fact, she was too stunned to do much except blink, and it was not the attempt upon her life that was responsible for her confusion.

Her deadly encounter was shocking enough, but more startling was the realisation that came to her in that moment. For when she heard the rumbling, her first thought was not for herself, but the man beside her. The suspicions she had once had, as well as her mixed feelings about working with him—his tendency to run roughshod over her wishes, and his unwelcome effect upon her—were all gone in an instant. And Glory realised the truth.

She was in love with Westfield.

It was ridiculous, of course. Glory had never even believed in love, at least not the kind of romantic nonsense that the poets wrote about. In her younger years she might have harboured hopes for a nice, companionable union with a gentleman of similar means and a houseful of children. But as she grew older, Glory realised that she did not care to cede control of everything—herself, her fortunes, her family— to just anyone, not that anyone was interested.

And she had been interested in no one—until Westfield. She had dismissed her pulse-pounding reactions to the man as the awakening of passions that had long been neglected. She was female, after all, and just as susceptible to a handsome and elegant nobleman as any other. The kiss she could not dismiss as easily, but surely there could be no harm in just a taste of what she would never know? However, it was not ardour that made her throw herself at the man, knocking him out of the path of whatever was coming towards them.

She was in love with Westfield.

'Here, dear, drink some more brandy,' the duchess urged, putting another glass into her hand. But Glory did not want to cloud her errant thoughts, and she put the glass aside. She looked up at the duke, only to glance away, afraid that her feelings might show. Then she reached again for the wine, took a large swallow and tried to regain her composure.

Phillida and Mr Pettit arrived, and for once, Glory's aunt did not swoon at the ill news of this latest calamity. She sank into a chair, fanning herself, presumably in an effort not to faint, but she seemed more concerned about her niece than her own health.

'And what of Thad? Where is Thad?' Phillida asked, her voice rising in alarm.

'He was not with us,' the duchess said.

'I sent a servant to find him,' Westfield said. 'If he is at the Pump Room, he will arrive shortly.'

Indeed, the duke had barely spoken when Thad appeared in the doorway. 'What is so important that I must leave our customers?' he asked, glaring sullenly at Glory.

Glory might have scolded him for his attitude, but

for the bruise on his face. 'What happened to you?' Glory asked, imagining the worst. Had Thad been set upon, as well?

He shrugged off the question. 'Just a little disagreement with another fellow.'

'Over what?'

'His manners,' Thad muttered.

Glory didn't know what to say to that. The past year had brought radical changes in the boy she had raised as he faced all the challenges of growing into a man. But an argument over manners? Glory couldn't help wondering if he was hiding something from her.

'You're sure the incident had nothing to do with Queen's Well?' she asked.

'Not everything has to do with your precious spa,' Thad answered in a tone with which Glory was familiar. However, the duke and duchess had not been treated to it before, and Westfield did not look pleased.

'Perhaps you will forgive us for our interest,' the duke said. 'Your sister and I were just nearly killed in what cannot be deemed an accident.'

Thad's face flamed, and his eyes widened as Westfield related their deadly encounter.

'The locals warned us to be careful where we went,' Thad said. 'They claimed the walks around here can be dangerous and that some who went out to view the crags never come back.'

'I think perhaps they were being overly dramatic,' Mr Pettit said. 'All newcomers are advised to watch what they are about when treading those paths, but there is a difference between a misstep and murder.'

The word hung in the air, casting a pall over the company, and Glory summoned the will to say the words she'd never thought to utter. 'Perhaps we should close the Pump Room, temporarily.'

'Oh, surely not,' the duchess said.

'That's what they want, isn't it?' Thad said. 'You'd be playing right into their hands.'

'We are assuming that's the motive behind these incidents, but I'm more worried about keeping your sister safe,' Westfield said. He turned towards Glory. 'I would advise you not to go out until we know more.'

Glory blinked at this pronouncement. Once, she would have protested on the grounds that he had no right to order her life and that she would not be locked into Sutton House. Now, she had other concerns. 'What about you?'

Westfield shook his head. 'I think we can all agree that you were the intended victim.'

'But what if they would be rid of the magistrate, as well?' Glory asked, worry for him making her grip her glass tightly.

'I can take care of myself, should the need arise,' Westfield said, dismissing her concern as he rose to his feet. 'But perhaps I'll brush up my boxing skills upon you, Thad, if you would be so kind as to oblige me.'

Thad sputtered his eager assent. 'Uh, of course! I'll just go and change.'

Her brother rushed from the library, as though to avoid any objections from Glory, and she swallowed her protests. She still thought fisticuffs a dangerous activity, but if it would give Thad an advantage over their enemies, she would not stand in his way. After all those years raising a boy, Glory sometimes forgot that Thad now was a young man.

As though sharing her thoughts, Phillida sighed deeply. 'I hope he has not got himself into any more trouble.'

'Trouble?' Westfield asked.

'Just the usual temptations every young man in London faces,' Glory said. Since she had been careful to keep Thad's escapades from their aunt, she wasn't quite sure what Phillida was talking about. Nor did she care to discuss her brother's past in public.

But Phillida had no such qualms. 'I did not like the look of his friends,' she said, with a sniff. 'Low sorts, who did not seem trustworthy. And, make no mistake, they were leading him astray!'

'Thankfully, there are none like that here in Philtwell,' Glory said. In an effort to put an end to the conversation, she rose to her feet and walked towards the table littered with the journals they had found, along with various references. 'I'll return to looking for something among these records that may prove useful.'

'Of course,' the duchess said. 'Shall we repair to the parlour?'

Soon, everyone had filed out of the library, except for Westfield, which wasn't quite what Glory had in mind. The last thing she wanted right now was to converse privately with him. What if he could see just how she felt? She deliberately eyed the book before her.

'It is your decision whether or not to keep the Pump Room open, but I worry about the waters,' he said.

Glory looked up at him blankly, unable to form a thought except for the terrifying knowledge that she loved him. It coursed through her blood, sending warmth and life to every part of her body.

'If someone would manage to put something into the well itself or the pump or even into some of the glasses, you might be faced with real illness or death, rather than rumoured ones, as the newspaper story implied,' he said.

Glory's heart skipped a beat that had nothing to do with her feelings for the duke. 'You don't think someone would…poison the waters?'

Westfield stepped forwards, as though to reach out for her, but then turned aside. 'I think after what happened today, we should take every precaution.'

Glory didn't want to disappoint Thad, who finally had shown an interest in the Pump Room, but she could not endanger her patrons. And even the slightest outbreak of illness could spell their ruin. 'Perhaps it would be best to shut its doors for a while.'

'I think that would be wise,' Westfield said. He inclined his head politely, then turned to go.

For a moment, Glory wanted to call him back. But what would she do? Or say? The only thing that had changed between them was her own feelings. He was still Westfield, a duke of the realm, and there was little chance of him pursuing her for anything except a dalliance.

Glory flushed, but it was a truth she would do well to remember. These feelings of hers could only lead to more trouble, and she had enough problems with Queen's Well. She drew in a deep breath at the thought of her beloved spa, which would still be here when Westfield was long gone. It was all she had ever wanted.

And it would have to be enough.

Lifting her chin, Glory took her seat at the table and reached for the books in front of her. Earlier, she had been reading an old manuscript, in hopes of discovering more about the Queen's Gift in order to satisfy Thad's curiosity. But instead of trying to make her way through the difficult, old-fashioned language, she put it aside to study the most recent ledgers that they had found in the trunk.

Although Westfield had suggested such records might hold a clue as to 'past enmities', Glory hadn't paid him much heed. After all, Queen's Well had been closed for a generation and had been successful for much of its history, operating for centuries until the fire… Glory paused as a sudden, dark suspicion seized her and she wondered whether the spa's ultimate destruction was deliberate, an act of arson.

Frowning, Glory shook her head. Even had someone set the fire, it was unlikely that the same person could be responsible for the problems that plagued the Suttons now. Too many years had passed. And yet Glory knew that some of the villagers had not welcomed the family's return. She remembered the sensation of being watched by unfriendly eyes and shivered. Then she bent over the books.

But it was tedious work, and soon a noise from outside drew her attention away from the pages. Setting aside the heavy volume, she rose to her feet and wandered to the tall doors that faced the rear of the property. She could see nothing except the old walled garden, but she heard a shout, and concern drove her out on to the gravel path. She hurried around the corner, to where the formal gardens began, only to halt in her tracks.

She'd forgotten that Westfield had planned to box with her brother. But even if she had remembered, Glory certainly wouldn't have expected this. The two males were facing each other, shifting from foot to foot, their fists poised in front of them. But it wasn't what they were doing that made Glory gape; it was the way they were dressed.

Apparently, they had become too warm from their exertions and had stripped off their shirts. Glory might had scolded Thad for that unseemly behaviour, especially when he was not at home, but she could not find her voice. The sight of Westfield robbed her of even her breath.

Wide shoulders and a solid chest two shades darker than Thad's pale back glistened in the sun, strong muscles undulating beneath the smooth surface. He sported no bruises or scars or imperfections of any kind, the only interruption in the expanse of skin being a patch of dark hair that narrowed until it disappeared into the waistband of his breeches.

Glory swallowed hard and forced her gaze upwards to where his dark hair fell across a throat free of high collar and neckcloth. Moving with a lithe and silent grace, the man kicked out suddenly, then smiled as Thad dodged his foot. Glory realised that for once Westfield was not wearing his usual impenetrable expression. His handsome features hinted at concentration, but also a kind of joy, perhaps of his physical freedom.

Her heart thundering, Glory knew she should turn and go, but she couldn't wrest her attention away from him. Then, as though aware of her scrutiny, he glanced in her direction and she saw something in his face that made her sway upon her feet. Passion flickered in his dark gaze, so heated that Glory felt as though he had stripped away her own clothing with one look, leaving both of them naked and wanting.

Gasping at her wayward thoughts, Glory turned and fled, back into the house and the relative safety of the library, where she pressed hands to her burning cheeks and took great gulps of breath. *Dangerous*. Westfield was dangerous, just as she always suspected, for the giddiness she had dismissed as romantic nonsense had turned into something else entirely. And like a smouldering ash, all it needed was one spark to flare and burn out of control.

Chapter Ten

Although Glory tried to return to her research, she found it hard to concentrate, and when she heard footsteps approaching the library, she looked up warily, her heart thudding. But it was not Westfield who entered, only Thad, now fully dressed and eager to share the excitement of his first boxing lesson.

Her mind still filled with the image of a half-naked duke, Glory was slow to comprehend what Thad was rattling on about. But eventually, she was induced to stand up, so he could demonstrate. And after her initial reluctance, Glory realised that she might learn something, if she listened.

In fact, she learned to keep her thumbs down when forming a fist and to keep her hands up to avoid a facer. Blows to various other parts of the body were termed bodiers, doublers and the like, but Glory was not so much concerned with the terminology as the technique.

'A moving target is harder to hit,' Thad advised, hopping about in a sort of a jig that looked more like dancing than fighting. Glory thought it nonsense until Thad proved just how easily it would be to land a flush hit upon a stationary opponent.

'Westfield says if you're not in a proper mill, but a rough and tumble, then you do anything you can to floor your adversary,' Thad told her. He showed her how to strike a 'chopper' with the back of the hand and how to kick out suddenly, a manoeuvre that would be hampered by the typical female garments.

In truth, Glory was more interested in the simple right-handed swing to the jaw, as well as the left-handed 'dig' that sneaked under an adversary's guard. She practised both until Thad grew weary of the game and set off to change before supper.

But after he had left, Glory continued, going over her steps and throwing tentative punches in the air in front of the long mirror between the windows.

Later, when Thad returned to take her to the dining room, she proudly exhibited her improvement.

'Uh…maybe you had better not say anything about my, uh, demonstration,' Thad said, frowning. Apparently, his excitement had waned through his *toilette*, and he realised that teaching his sister to box probably wasn't something of which Westfield, let alone Aunt Phillida, would approve.

'Of course,' Glory said, taking his arm. 'And I hope you won't use your newfound skills to get into any more mills with the locals.'

'What? Oh, of course not,' Thad said.

As they approached the dining room, Glory's pulse picked up its pace in anticipation of seeing Westfield. She told herself he might not be there, but she soon saw that he was examining the mural with Mr Pettit. At least his back was turned. *And at least he was dressed.*

Her face flushing, Glory was happy to take her seat and avoid looking his way. But, eventually, she needed to speak to him, if only to share her discovery. So as soon as the usual pleasantries over the meal had subsided, Glory took the opportunity.

'I've found something in the recent ledgers that you might find interesting,' she said, daring to glance at the man. But when his gaze met hers, she swiftly turned towards his mother and Mr Pettit. 'Do you know anything about a possible investor in Queen's Well, someone outside of the family?'

'What? When?' the duchess asked, looking confused.

'Before the fire, when the spa was last open.'

'I don't recall anyone else ever being involved in the spa, at least during my time. It was always a family enterprise,' Mr Pettit said firmly. He reached for his wine glass. 'Was it a local fellow?'

'I don't know,' Glory answered. 'But there's a nota-tion in the margin of the final ledger reporting *Thorpe paid in full.* And when I looked further back, I found an influx of capital attributed to the same name.'

Mr Pettit frowned. 'I understand that the spa was

not doing as well in those final years. Perhaps Mr Sutton was forced to seek additional funding.'

'But who is this Thorpe?' the duchess asked. 'And why didn't anyone know of him?'

'He could have been a silent partner, a secret investor,' the duke said, in an odd tone.

'Then you think this Thorpe is the one causing all the troubles?' Mr Pettit asked.

Glory shook her head. 'He would be quite elderly, wouldn't he? And the notation shows that he was paid, probably through the sale of this house, so I don't see what grievance he would have.'

'Still, it's something that wasn't common knowledge and anything involving money is worth pursuing,' Westfield said. 'I'll call upon Mrs Goodhew again and see if she knows the name or can recommend someone else who might.'

Thad did not seem to share the others' interest in Glory's revelation. 'I thought you were trying to find out information about the Queen's Gift,' he said, frowning. 'I don't suppose you've got anything to report about that?'

'Actually, I have,' Glory said, with a smile.

'What? Why didn't you tell me?' Thad asked, leaning forwards eagerly.

'I have nothing definite, but I became curious after coming across several mentions of Dr Dee,' Glory said.

'Dr Dee? Is he one of the spa's physicians?' Phillida asked.

'No, he was one of Queen Elizabeth's advisers,

among other things,' Glory said. 'Since his name cropped up so often in the older records, I did some investigating of my own and discovered he was quite an unusual character.'

'Yes, Dr Dee was ahead of his time in many fields, including mathematics, astronomy, map making, and cryptography,' Mr Pettit said. His knowledge surprised Glory until she realised that he would hardly be unfamiliar with the works in his own library, which he had recommended to her.

'Cryptography?' Phillida asked in a voice that suggested graves might be involved.

'The study of ciphers and codes,' Mr Pettit explained.

'For secret messages?' Thad asked, showing a sudden interest.

Mr Pettit nodded. 'For political uses, mostly. Such communications were Queen Mary's undoing by order of Elizabeth herself.'

'Dee was also a mystic, dabbling in astrology and the occult,' the duke said, in a dismissive tone.

'His interests were many and varied. Some say he was more than an adviser to the queen, serving at times as a spy for his sovereign,' Mr Pettit said.

'Really?' Glory asked, for she had not discovered that bit of information. 'How intriguing.'

However, Westfield was not impressed. 'I fail to see what Dee has to do with Queen's Well, unless you are suggesting that he used a divining rod of his own design to discover the source of the waters.'

'Obviously, you are too literal minded to appreciate

the romance of the tale,' Glory said, though she might have said the same of herself not that long ago.

'But if this Dee is famous for hidden messages, maybe he left some clue to the location of the Queen's Gift,' Thad said.

Glory smiled at her brother's enthusiasm. 'I think that is doubtful, but I did find some references to rumours that he was involved. So perhaps he had a hand in choosing or presenting the gift or made an offering in the queen's stead.'

Thad sat back, frowning in apparent disappointment. 'So you're saying the Queen's Gift could just be some old manuscript about mathematics?'

'It might be a mystical object,' Phillida said, ominously. 'Perhaps one that is responsible for the curse.'

'There is no curse,' Glory said. 'Whether there was a gift or not, Elizabeth's patronage made Queen's Well a success for many years.'

'And when I met my husband here, although on the wane, the spa was still a lovely place to visit,' the duchess added. 'And it will soon be so again.'

Once Glory would have agreed automatically, but now she had her doubts. 'I hope so, but not yet, I'm afraid. Until we can be assured of the safety of our patrons, the Pump Room will have to close.'

'What?' Thad sputtered. 'You can't mean to give in to them!'

Glory shook her head. 'I would hardly call it that, but I will not be responsible for anything happening that could cause more harm and ruin us for ever.'

Thad looked as though he would say more, but the duchess stepped in. 'It is a loss for everyone, young man,' she said. 'Why, we all have a stake in the success of the waters, don't we?'

Mr Pettit appeared to choke upon his wine, while Phillida looked unconvinced. The duke scowled as he reached for his own glass, and Thad, who had brightened after his boxing bout, now visibly sulked.

It was enough to make even Glory suspect a curse—of more recent vintage than any Dr Dee could have conjured.

Oberon waited until long after supper to pursue the nugget he had heard let slip at the table. Experience had taught him it was best to wait until the person he planned to question was completely at ease, unconcerned with watching his tongue. It was a technique he had honed on foreign ministers, visitors and politicians, but that he never had expected to use upon his own mother.

He found her in her favourite spot in the parlour, relaxed by wine and a friendly game of cards with her cousin, who was well into his cups by now. 'Ah, Oberon, come join us,' she urged.

'If you don't mind,' Oberon said, with a nod towards his host.

'Of course not,' Pettit said, waving his arm in an expansive fashion. 'Have a seat wherever you wish. After all, it's your house.'

Oberon's mother laughed shrilly. 'I'm sure we've

all come to think of Sutton House as home because of your generous hospitality, Randolph.'

Oberon could not help but notice the look that she sent her companion, but it seemed that Pettit was a little slow on the receiving end.

'Oh, of course, yes,' the man finally said, gesturing towards Oberon. 'We're all family here.'

Were they? Oberon wondered, but he nodded. 'Then you won't mind if I have a little chat with my mother.'

Apparently, Pettit was not that foxed, for he eyed Oberon warily and shifted in his seat.

'No, please, stay,' Oberon said when the fellow looked like he might bolt. 'You might be able to clarify some things for me.'

This time there was no mistaking Pettit's panicked expression, but the duchess stepped in. 'What is it that you want, Oberon?' she asked. 'I warn you that I can spare you only a moment because I am trouncing Randolph quite soundly and do not wish to lose my edge.'

That was unlikely. No matter what Pettit was, the Dowager Duchess of Westfield was no fool, and Oberon knew it. 'Oh, it won't take long,' he said. 'I was just wondering how much you've sunk in the spa?'

'What?' His mother had the grace to look bewildered.

Oberon leaned back and crossed his legs. 'I've always wondered who Miss Sutton convinced to funnel money into an abandoned spa, and for a long time I thought those unknown investors were responsible for the problems plaguing the enterprise. So you can imagine my relief to discover that no usurers or shady characters were involved, only my mother.'

The duchess blinked at him. 'Have you been drinking?'

'At supper, you admitted you had a stake in the well,' Oberon said.

His mother laughed. 'A stake is an interest, dear,' she said. 'Don't take everything so seriously.'

'So you are saying you have not put a penny into Queen's Well?' Oberon asked, eyeing her directly.

'I have not put a penny into the spa,' she said, but Oberon noticed that Mr Pettit looked pale. Had the fellow consumed too much alcohol, or was the course of the questioning responsible for his ashen hue?

'So how is Miss Sutton paying for all these improvements when she has, so far, taken in very little?' Oberon asked.

His mother smiled coyly. 'Why, didn't you know? Miss Sutton is funding the spa's revival herself. Her father was quite successful in business, once well away from Philtwell, and that was before he wed.' She laid down a card as if trumping her son, not her opponent. '*Lady Ormesby* brought her own money to the marriage, though, as I understand it, her father did not approve, forcing his sister, Miss Bamford, to side with his daughter.'

Oberon wasn't quite sure why his mother practically crowed with this news, but he was grateful that none of his family's money had been sunk into the spa, at least none of his *immediate* family. He turned abruptly towards his host. 'And what, exactly, is your stake in the waters?'

'Oh, uh, well…' Pettit's stammering was interrupted by the duchess, but Oberon held up his hand to silence her.

'Well, uh, of course, we have a stake in the waters, in the house and in you two young people,' the man finally said, looking pleased with his vague reply.

It was the latter part of it that garnered Oberon's attention, for he well remembered the day he had been forced to drink the well's swill, along with Miss Sutton, while everyone else abstained.

'Surely you were not hoping to snare me into… marriage with some fanciful legend about the well's romantic powers?' Oberon asked.

Pettit nodded and then shook his head violently. 'Of course. Not.'

'I am not in the market for a wife,' Oberon said.

'Who said—' his mother began.

'Why ever not?' Pettit asked.

'That, sir, is none of your concern,' Oberon said. 'Are you even related to me by blood?'

Pettit looked sheepish.

'I thought not,' Oberon said, ignoring his mother's protests and explanations. 'And to whom does this residence belong?'

The expression on Pettit's face might have been comical, but Oberon was not amused when the fellow inclined his head towards the duchess.

'What the devil?' Oberon said, swinging round to face her.

'Oh, there is no need to get excited, dear,' she said. 'When the house came up for sale, I instructed Randolph to buy it for me, so that…I would have a place here should I ever wish to return.'

Oberon sensed she wasn't telling him everything, but were her hidden motives a product of nostalgia or this nonsense about the waters? Either way, it appeared that she had lost her wits. And after years of uncovering deceit, he had been duped by a madwoman and a drunken fool.

'You dragged me here under false pretences, away from important commitments in London,' Oberon said, without bothering to hide his annoyance. 'Is that the extent of it, or are you responsible for these attacks upon the spa as well? Were you tossing about boulders this afternoon?'

'Oberon Makepeace!' His mother threw down her cards. 'How could you think such a thing?'

'I don't know what to think,' Oberon said, rising to his feet. 'Tell me that you have involved no one else in this scheme of yours, who might have taken it further than you intended.'

For a moment, he thought his mother would refuse to speak, but she finally turned towards him, her expression one of rebuke. 'There is no scheme, Oberon, and if you feel so strongly, perhaps you should run back to your *commitments* in London, for I would not want your *family* or anything else to interfere with them.'

Although his mother had made no mention of his father, it was there in her face, a silent accusation that he was not the man the duke had been. And how could he dispute it? Oberon turned on his heel and strode from the room, not even pausing when he heard the sound of Pettit's voice from the parlour behind, calling drunkenly after him.

'You can't fight the waters!'

Clenching his fingers, Oberon stalked through the house, pausing when he reached the shaft of light that fell from the library. Although he had guarded his privacy for years, revealing nothing to anyone, right now he wanted nothing more than to go inside and unburden himself to Miss Sutton. But he could hardly discuss such personal matters with her, and while they once might have shared a laugh over his mother's machinations, that, too, could prove an awkward topic, considering that he had kissed her.

That had changed everything.

It did not convince him that the swill he'd been forced to drink had any magic properties, but it prevented him from making light of such things to Miss Sutton. Oberon halted his steps, uncomfortably aware of his misbehaviour in connection with the well owner. A gentleman did not press his attentions upon a genteel young lady, and Oberon could just imagine what his mother's response would be, if she knew.

She would expect him to do the right thing. In fact, she seemed to think that her revelation about Miss Sutton's connections would prompt him to propose.

Oberon shook his head, for she had only proven how little she knew her son. If he placed value in such things, he would still dismiss Miss Sutton as being in trade, despite her noble relations. But the young woman's connections or lack thereof didn't matter to him.

He simply was not in the market for a wife.

And knowing that, he had no business pursuing his acquaintance with Miss Sutton. He might be required to work with her, to aid her in his role as magistrate, but that's not what drove him towards the beckoning glow of the doorway. And if he stepped inside, it would not have anything to do with duty, but the sudden selfish desire to take her face in his hands or bury his own in the smooth, scented expanse of her throat, seeking solace, if nothing else.

You are not the man your father was.

Clenching his hand, Oberon turned away from the shaft of light and headed to his room, where Pearson might provide him with company, though not confidences. It was ironic that a man famous for his social life should have no real friends, but Oberon's work prevented such close associations. And, at one time, he had been glad to dispense with the demands of emotional attachments.

Only now did he feel the lack.

Letitia gathered up the cards and put them away, for her luck was at an end. She had been caught out and all her elaborate plans were for naught. She shook her head, for she had hoped that something here, if not the waters, then the air and the countryside far from London, would work upon her son as they had upon his father. But they had not, and now she felt foolish for pinning her hopes upon an old legend.

She had been deluding herself, Letitia realised, about Queen's Well and about her son, who had been as lost to her as her husband for years now, distancing himself from her after his father's death until he was her offspring in name only. And although that was not uncommon among *ton* society, where marriages were often contracts and children born of affairs, it was not what she and her husband had planned when they had set family above all else.

'He might, even now, be preparing to leave,' Letitia whispered, her throat thick.

'He has *commitments*,' Randolph said, waving his glass in the air.

'Commitments to social functions,' she murmured.

'I don't know,' Randolph said, his words slurring, for in his remorse, he had hit the bottle in earnest. 'He seems far too serious a fellow...' Randolph paused to hiccup loudly '...to be so devoted to mindless gadding about.'

Swallowing her automatic reply, Letitia glanced at her dear friend thoughtfully. For years, she had bemoaned her son's increasingly aimless existence, but now it struck her that Randolph had a point. When Oberon was away in London, she knew little about his behaviour except what she heard through her own acquaintances, but after spending so much time with him here, she saw the truth in Randolph's words.

Oberon was not the type of man to have no other interests beyond the drawing rooms of London. Why, even the Prince Regent himself fit some good works into his round of elaborate parties. Architecture. Travel. Art. Books. Oberon could talk knowledgeably of all those things, but he didn't collect or build or take tours. He didn't gamble or drink to excess or scandalise the *ton* with his affairs.

'Then what, exactly, does he do?' She mused aloud.

'That is the question, isn't it?' Randolph said. 'Perhaps he has a wife and ten children tucked away in Surrey.'

'Randolph!' Letitia scolded, snatching away his empty glass. But a faint spark of hope kindled inside her, and she leaned forwards. 'Perhaps we should do some sleuthing. Do you know anyone in London who is discreet?'

Randolph shook his head. 'Forget about London—and Surrey,' he said. 'Any sleuthing you do should be concerned with what's happening right here.' He punctuated his words by pointing in the general direction of the floor.

'Why?' Letitia asked.

'Because of what happened on the crags,' Randolph answered. 'If your son and Miss Sutton should be killed, then that is the end of all your plans for any grandchildren.'

Letitia looked at him in startlement, both horrified

by such a prospect and cheered that Randolph thought there was still a chance for success. His optimism fuelled her own, but cautiously, for there were many obstacles, not the least of which he had just pointed out.

'Yes,' she said. 'Now that we've done all that we can to throw the two together, perhaps it's time we turned our attention to finding out just who is trying to do them in.'

Chapter Eleven

Glory was bent over a pile of books when the duchess burst into the library and urged her to catch up with the duke, who was headed out to speak with Mrs Goodhew. If she'd had time to consider, Glory might have refused, rather than spend more time than necessary with the man, but her first reaction was a surge of delight at the prospect. And it was that which urged her on, as well as the desire for a much-needed escape from what had become her prison.

Snatching up her bonnet, Glory found him at the door, a tall, handsome figure superbly dressed in elegant clothes. And she tried not to imagine him without his midnight coat. Or his pale waistcoat. Or his white shirt. And when her face flushed from the effort, Glory began to question the wisdom of rushing to meet him, but with her hat in hand, it was too late to change her mind.

'I'm coming with you,' she said. 'I'm going blind from looking over ledgers and mad from being cooped inside,' Glory said, the admission making her more determined.

'No.'

'Your Grace, you can hardly keep me locked up at will,' Glory said, a challenge in her tone.

But something flashed in his dark eyes that spoke of Westfield's power, especially over her, and Glory glanced away, lest he see more than she wished.

'I am only concerned for your safety,' he said, which seemed to be his continual excuse for controlling behaviour. But this time he gave her his arm, and Glory bit back a smile at the small victory. Her pleasure was short-lived, however, as he soon issued a warning.

'Keep alert,' he said. 'Not just to those nearby who might bump into us, but for anyone in the distance, even movement among the trees.'

Glory glanced around warily as the open grounds of Sutton House took on an ominous cast. A strong breeze rustled the leaves of the tall elms and she realised how many places there were to hide even in the familiar environs around Philtwell.

She had thought Westfield more than capable of subduing any opponent, and there were no rocks to send crashing down upon them, but the duke obviously was concerned with other possibilities. 'You don't think someone will try to…shoot at us, do you?' Glory asked.

'I'm not ruling out anything,' he said. 'So far the

efforts against you have all been clumsy, but failures breed desperation.'

Glory blanched, and, for once, she tried to tell whether she was being watched. But she was aware only of Westfield at her side and her feelings for him, which made her efforts at conversation difficult. Thankfully, the duke was unaffected and asked her what she was learning in the library. Precious little, she thought, but she managed to report upon what she had been reading; before she realised it, they were standing in front of Mrs Goodhew's home.

There, they were shown into the same cosy room, though Glory could have done without the fire today. It was warm outside and even more so inside. And she wasn't taking into account the unwelcome heat that came from Westfield's nearness.

'Thank you for meeting with us again,' he said.

Mrs Goodhew inclined her head. 'Of course, your Grace.' She paused to study them with a sharp eye. 'I understand that you two have been busy.'

Her shrewd look suggested something of a personal nature, and Glory flushed once more.

But Westfield showed no sign of discomfiture. 'Apparently, not busy enough to thwart whoever is out to close down Queen's Well.'

'Now that they have succeeded, perhaps they will cease their meddling,' Mrs Goodhew said, settling back into her upholstered chair.

'That's what I'm afraid of,' Westfield said.

Glory was surprised by the statement, but quickly recognised the truth of it. For if her nemesis disappeared, how was Westfield, or anyone else, to snare the villain and normal activities resume? She realised, with sudden dismay, that Queen's Well might be closed indefinitely.

'I don't understand it,' Mrs Goodhew said, shaking her head. 'Times certainly have changed when neighbours turn against neighbours.'

'We don't know that anyone from Philtwell is behind our troubles,' Glory said in an effort to soothe the elderly resident.

But Mrs Goodhew was not placated. 'Who, then?'

Glory leaned forwards. 'Have you heard of anyone named Thorpe, who might have invested in the spa?'

Mrs Goodhew's eyes narrowed. 'When was this?'

'Right before the fire.'

She looked pensive. 'I never heard of any investor, though there was no denying the spa wasn't as successful then as in past years. In those days, travel was more difficult, and we were far away, with fewer entertainments than some other resorts that were more popular.'

Mrs Goodhew paused to fix Westfield with a stare. 'I know your mother would argue, for she has cherished memories of Queen's Well, and rightly so, but it was not what it had been in my mother's day or my grandmother's. Sutton had closed one of the inns, leaving the place to stand empty, and the grounds just weren't kept up the way they used to be. Not that it wasn't still a lovely place.'

She frowned suddenly. 'If this fellow was some kind of outside partner, have you no address for him?'

Glory shook her head. 'Of course, I haven't looked through all the materials yet, but I found no contract or legal documents, just a notation by hand and a name. Thorpe.'

Mrs Goodhew paused, as if in thought. 'It seems as though I met someone by that name. He wasn't from Philtwell, I can tell you that much. He was here with his wife and baby, but they were just visiting. In fact, I thought them guests just like any others, and that was some time before the end. I never saw them again.'

She shot Glory a sharp look. 'Did you check the guestbooks?'

'Guestbooks?'

'All the visitors signed them,' Mrs Goodhew said. 'If they weren't lost in the fire, you might be able to find a record of the family.'

Glory nodded, though she was not eager to go through more old tomes. Once, she had longed for information about Queen's Well and had revelled in discovering it. But after so much time in the library at Sutton House, she did not look forward to searching for more needles among the haystacks, a reluctance she shared with Westfield after they left Mrs Goodhew's home.

'But what else have we right now?' he asked. 'Let

us not dismiss this Thorpe until we've done all we can to find out more about him.'

Glory bit back a sigh. 'But I don't know where the guestbooks are or if they even survived.'

'Which is why we are stopping at the cottage,' Westfield said.

He paused to open the gate with a flourish and Glory blinked at it in surprise. She had not returned since Westfield had kissed her under the eaves, and she flushed as the memory came flooding back.

Unable to look at him, Glory shook her head. 'But we've already been through most of the attic,' she said, her heart thundering at the thought of being lodged again in that small space with the duke.

'Yes, but what of the cellar?' he asked, gesturing for her to precede him.

Glory could do little except comply, even as her pulse raced in a mixture of anticipation and trepidation. She told herself she was being foolish, for Westfield could hardly be planning an assignation below ground. In fact, she doubted he was thinking of anything of the kind and dismissed the kiss in the attic as an accident, a product of curiosity, spontaneity and proximity.

Or so she hoped.

Anything else did not bear considering because Glory did not trust herself to behave as she should, her feelings for Westfield tending to erode all of her good sense and scatter her wits. So when he opened the door that led beneath the cottage, Glory greeted the musty blackness with a sense of relief. It was even more unappealing than the attic.

Drawing a deep breath, Glory made her way down the narrow stairway into the darkness, as the light from the lantern struck cobwebs and revealed indistinct shapes ahead. The further down she descended, the more she wrinkled her nose at the air, rife with damp and the faint smell of rot, as though some animal might have crawled in long ago, never to find its way out.

Glory did not find the thought comforting.

When they reached the bottom of the steps, she squinted into the shadows at hulking crates and the outlines of abandoned implements. It seemed that the cottage's caretaker had neglected anything above or below the main rooms, but the attic was a cosy retreat compared to this chill area, with its dirt floor and ancient stone walls.

As Glory stood still, unnerved, Westfield moved past her, intent upon the nearest crates. 'Surely, anything down here will be decayed,' she said, imagining mould and damp and…rodents? Hearing a rustling sound, Glory inched nearer to the duke.

She glanced around, but the pool of light from the lantern faded away into blackness, where anything—or anyone—could lurk. Shuddering, Glory told herself that no one else could have entered the cellar, with the cottage now guarded by an army of servants. The only threat here was Westfield, who did not appear to have any designs upon her person, romantic or otherwise.

In fact, he was already lifting the lid off an old container, and Glory stepped closer to marvel over the candelabras carefully packed inside. It soon became apparent that much of what was left of Queen's Well had been put away here, rather than at Sutton House, which must have already been sold. They came across linens that had turned grey and glasses that had once held the famous waters, which meant that the guest-books might be here somewhere, as well.

In fact, in the next crate, Glory caught a glimpse of some kind of ledgers lining the bottom. But when she leaned over to reach inside, a stray draught tickled her neck, and then the lantern went out, plunging them into near blackness. Glory froze where she was, her heart thundering at the possibility that they were being assailed once more, this time not by falling rocks, but by assassins in the dark. *Where had she put her reticule?*

'Westfield?' she whispered.

'Right here.' The sound of his voice, low and deep and close, made Glory shiver more than the touch of his hand upon her back. She turned towards him automatically, her palms coming to rest against his waistcoat. And then she forgot about dangers of any kind, including those posed by this man. Somehow her hands slid up his solid chest of their own accord, stealing around his neck and drifting through the hair that needed a trim.

It was easy in the dark. Cloaked in the blackness and silence, Glory felt free to do what she willed. She could not see herself and could barely make out the outline of Westfield's tall form. But she heard the swift intake of his breath and felt the press of his arms as they came around her, pulling her against his hard body.

Despite the darkness, his mouth unerringly found hers and with a force that made Glory gasp. She could not call it an accident, a simple brush of the lips brought on by nearness. There was no mistaking Westfield's intent as he kissed her with a passion in keeping with his strength and power.

And Glory could do nothing except respond in kind, her first, tentative responses becoming bolder until they were equals, partners in a heated exchange that left her breathless and wanting more. When at last his lips parted from hers, it was only to move to her neck, burning a path along her throat and lower, where the cap of her sleeve slipped down. And Glory reeled at the sensation. Who would have dreamed that the touch of his mouth upon her shoulder would make her whole body spark and flame?

Her head thrown back, Glory loosed a low sound of pleasure that was startling in the silence and Westfield groaned, as if in answer. He pressed against her, closer, but there was nowhere to go, and she stumbled against the crate behind her. Westfield steadied her, but then he stilled, as if catching his breath. Just as Glory was prepared to cry out in protest at the sudden loss of his lips, they were replaced by his thumb, gently rubbing her shoulder before righting her sleeve.

'Perhaps I should send a servant down here in my stead,' he said in a hoarse tone.

For a long moment, Glory was too dazed to understand him as he smoothed her hair and straightened her skirts. But when he finally stepped back, away from her, her scattered wits began to return. Raising trembling hands to her cheeks, she buried her face in them, appalled by her wanton behaviour. What had come over her?

Westfield.

Glory heard him relight the lantern, and she was grateful that its illumination was poor at best, for she was not ready for any kind of scrutiny, not even her own. Thankfully, the duke remained facing the lamp, his back towards her. So Glory turned, ready to flee from the cellar to her old room above and the life she had known before he entered it, but his voice stopped her.

'I beg your pardon.' The words were stiff, as if torn from him, and Glory paused. 'I have no excuse except that I find you irresistible.'

He turned then, his lips quirking ruefully, and Glory forgot her own embarrassment. 'And under any other circumstances, I would hope to further our association.'

Glory's pulse leapt. Was he going to offer her *carte blanche*? Although not a woman of easy virtue, she certainly had given Westfield that impression. Yet she could not become his mistress, no matter how much she loved the man. She had not only herself to consider, but her family and a business that required

an unblemished reputation. Already, she had compromised herself; to do more would assure her ruin.

'And although you are presumably unaware of
the fact, my mother has been throwing us together,'
Westfield said.

His mother? Glory loosed the breath she had been
holding. But if he was not referring to a...liaison,
what did he mean by 'association'?

'She wants me married,' he said bluntly. 'And it
seems that she has decided upon you as a suitable
prospect. That's why she had us drink the waters
together.'

Glory gaped in surprise. 'Because of the old
legend?'

Westfield nodded, his mouth twisted with disdain.
'Yes. Apparently, she thought that after one sip we
would be overcome with romantic feelings for each
other.'

Glory blinked, for she was certainly overcome, but
she did not believe that Queen's Well was responsible.
She and her whole family had been consuming the
waters since their arrival in Philtwell, without suffering the effects of any special powers.

'Although I can't countenance such nonsense, I
don't fault her choice,' Westfield said. He paused to
draw a breath before continuing. 'However, I have
obligations of which she is unaware that prevent me
from acting upon her wishes.'

Glory swallowed hard. 'Of course,' she managed.
'You are obligated to take a wife of your own choosing from your own circle.'

'It's not that,' Westfield said, with a shake of his head. 'I have…commitments.'

His demeanour was stiff, as if he were as uncomfortable as Glory. 'I hope you will forgive my plain speaking,' he said. 'But I did not want to create any confusion. You are… You deserve more than that.'

'Of course, I understand,' Glory said, though she did not. It was all she could do to comprehend that the Duke of Westfield had spoken to her of marriage.

'And I have commitments of my own, as you know. I'm devoted to Queen's Well,' she said, determined to end a conversation that had become increasingly painful. Yet when Westfield nodded, his expression once more cool and distant, it wasn't relief Glory felt, but regret.

Although they met each day at breakfast and supper, the grim group at Sutton House did little except go over what they already knew. As acting magistrate, Westfield seemed to grow more frustrated with each passing day, and Glory could not blame him, for no new suspects presented themselves, while she had buried herself among the ledgers and guest-books, looking for any clues.

At least Thad was no longer moping. Although he continued to protest the closing of the Pump Room, he had taken to poking about the house in search of clues to the Queen's Gift, a harmless enough activity.

And this morning there was good news from the outside world to enliven the gathering, the papers reporting the confinement of Napoleon on the island of Saint Helena. Only Westfield seemed oddly affected by the news, alternately pensive and impatient for more information.

'So this time it is all over, isn't it?' Thad asked. 'The war, the disruption in Europe…' He turned to Glory. 'Perhaps I shall make a grand tour after all.'

'There is always disruption in Europe,' Westfield said. 'Problems both at home and abroad are inevitable.'

'That is a rather fatalistic attitude,' Mr Pettit said, turning towards the duke with a curious expression.

When he realised the rest of the company was eying him in surprise, Westfield favoured Thad with a nod. 'But, yes, it looks like this long struggle is over, which is heartening.'

After that small concession, the duke shot Glory a curious glance, and she flushed under the unwelcome attention. Since their intimate conversation in the cellar of the cottage, she had done her best to avoid any personal contact with the man. And he, in turn, maintained his distance.

But now Glory felt his dark gaze upon her and she turned away, unwilling to let him see the feelings that she kept hidden, for fear they would spill forth at any moment. In fact, she was just about to rise from her chair when the housekeeper appeared in the doorway.

The plump female announced in disapproving tones the arrival of a lad from the village who was demanding to see either Westfield 'or his valet.'

'Send him in,' Westfield said. With a nod and a

frown, she left, returning with a young fellow hardly more than ten years of age, who clutched his cap, but did not stand upon ceremony.

'Your Grace,' he said, a bit breathlessly. 'I came right away, as soon as I saw. I left one of the other lads there, but I told him not to do anything until we heard from you.'

'What is it? Have you found a trespasser?' Westfield said.

'Worse, your Grace,' he said. 'There's a man down at the Pump Room. You'd better come take a look.'

Westfield was soon on his feet, closely followed by Thad and Glory, although she knew he would prefer she remain safely tucked away with the others. But the Pump Room was hers and she was determined to see for herself what had happened.

As she soon discovered, the downed man was someone Westfield had set to keep watch on the building during the night hours. A quick reconnoitre revealed that his daytime counterpart was standing by the front entrance, blithely unaware that his fellow was lying prone among the trees at the rear of the building.

But, apparently, Westfield's connections extended to a rabble of boys of various ages, whose duties encompassed watching the entire village for anything remotely suspicious. And it was one of these young fellows who had come across the man who was still breathing, but knocked unconscious, presumably by a large stone that lay near him.

Glory shuddered at the sight, her own encounter with falling rocks still fresh in her mind. She and Westfield could well have ended up in such a condition—or worse. Bending close, Glory was able to rouse the man with some of Phillida's hartshorn, while one of the boys ran for a physician.

With aid, the fellow was soon sitting up, seemingly unhurt beyond a nasty bump on his head. But he remembered nothing after hearing a noise in the trees during the night, which meant the Pump Room had been unattended for some time. Glory glanced towards the door at the rear of the building, and Thad, who was standing closer to the building, verified what they all suspected.

'It looks like the lock's been broken, perhaps with another rock,' he said.

Glory rose shakily to her feet. 'But why? We've closed for business,' she said. 'Isn't that what they wanted?'

Thad only shook his head, baffled, while Westfield headed towards the door. He pushed it open and carefully stepped inside, followed by Thad and Glory. Suddenly weary, Glory did not know if she even wanted to see what had been done to the interior. They had barely recovered from the previous vandalism; she was not sure that she could do it again.

But this time, Glory saw no telltale windows open, no broken glass or strewn papers, and she began to breath easier. Perhaps whoever broke into the building didn't have enough time to wreak the kind of havoc they had before. The villagers were more alert, especially the younger ones, and…

Glory's thoughts trailed off as they entered the main room, where the tables and chairs lined the walls, undisturbed. She loosed a sigh, only to follow it with a gasp as Westfield walked towards the pump itself.

'What the devil?' Thad said.

The new parquet around the pump had been pulled up and pieces tossed haphazardly aside, while the very foundation beneath had been broken, leaving nothing except a gaping hole to the earth below. Even the well itself did not appear unscathed, and Glory was only thankful they weren't standing knee-deep in the precious waters.

'You better stay back, Glory,' Thad said, walking cautiously on what was left of the floor. 'It looks like someone took a pry bar or an axe to this whole area.'

Glory simply stared, appalled, while Westfield knelt down to examine the damage. After a cursory glance, he rose to his feet. 'Well, now we know,' he said. 'It wasn't the closing of the Pump Room that they were after, although that fell neatly in with their plans.'

'What, then?' Glory asked, baffled.

'What might one look for at the site of Queen's Well?'

'The source of the waters?' Glory asked.

But Thad swung round with a cry of dismay. 'You don't think they found it, do you?'

'Found *what*?' Glory asked.

Westfield lifted a dark brow. 'The Queen's Gift.'

Chapter Twelve

Glory ordered repairs to the Pump Room, and once again Westfield set out to discover what he could about the latest attack. But he returned with nothing to report, his frustration obvious to Glory when the household convened at the supper table. It was as if the guilty party appeared and disappeared in a whiff of smoke, unseen by any of the villagers or those who watched over the properties.

Phillida did not help by speaking in low tones about the curse, as though some sort of evil spirit were responsible for the damages, and all Glory could do was shake her head in bemusement.

'No wonder you can't get a hold of him, then, dear,' the duchess said, with a wry glance towards her son.

Phillida sniffed at the duchess's teasing banter, but she offered no advice as to how to rid themselves of a ghostly foe. In fact, her sole suggestion was that they return to London and wash their hands of Queen's Well, so to speak. Considering her aunt's lack of enthusiasm for the venture, Glory was not surprised.

What was surprising was that Thad argued in favour of the spa. In a reversal of their usual roles, he wanted the Pump Room to re-open as soon as possible, while Glory remained leery. Westfield's warning about tainted waters hung heavy in her mind, especially since someone had managed to gain access to the well itself.

While Thad claimed the villain had got what he wanted and was long gone, Glory thought it unlikely that the Queen's Gift had remained hidden for centuries. Whoever was searching for it had torn up the parquet floor in vain, which meant he was still looking for a prize that probably didn't even exist. But that wouldn't stop him. What had Westfield said? *Failure breeds desperation.* Glory suppressed a shiver at the thought.

'The Queen's Gift is probably on its way to the back alleys of London to be sold for a pittance of its worth,' Thad said glumly. 'So why not resume operations?'

'Because we don't know that,' Glory said.

'He has been one step ahead of us all along, so let us not count him out just yet,' Westfield said.

'But what will he strike next?' Glory asked, anxiety seeping into her voice. 'Where else can he look?'

Even as she spoke, Glory knew the answer. As one,

the diners turned towards the mural that lined the far wall of the room. Now dim with evening, it was a shadowy presence that loomed over the assembly, taunting them with its long-held secrets.

Glory peered at the faded depiction as though Elizabeth herself would provide some answer, but the figure remained where she was, her arms outstretched, appearing to give light to the dark shape of Sutton House behind her.

'It certainly looks like she's standing in front of the place,' Thad said.

'Or the house could simply represent the owners, the Suttons,' Mr Pettit said.

'But I don't see the Pump Room or the well,' Thad argued, noticeably cheered. 'Perhaps the Queen's Gift is here.'

'I stopped looking for references to it in order to study the spa ledgers and guestbooks for mention of the Thorpes,' Glory said. 'But if you would like to pick up where I left off, perhaps you can discover a clue.'

Thad did not appear enthused at the prospect. 'I'd rather look for the gift itself than old stories about it.'

But Mr Pettit nodded. 'I have long been interested in Elizabeth,' he said. 'I would be happy to join you in the library.'

'But, Randolph, you had promised to accompany me now that the young people are bound to the house,' the duchess said, giving Mr Pettit a sharp look.

'I'm sorry, your Grace,' Mr Pettit said, smiling

serenely in the face of the duchess's plea. 'I simply cannot refuse to help the Suttons in their quest, especially if it might lead to hidden treasure.'

Only Phillida seemed dismayed by the course of the conversation. 'But if you think something is on these premises, then we cannot be any safer here than at the cottage. Why, we could be attacked at any time, right in our own beds!' she said.

'Sutton House is well guarded and is staffed with a full complement of servants,' Westfield assured her. 'No stranger can wreak havoc here.'

But what if the villain wasn't a stranger? The notion struck Glory suddenly, and she looked around the table at her companions, only to shake her head. She could not imagine Mr Pettit capable of such violence, and Westfield had already proven himself.

However, Phillida was not so easily soothed—or dismissed. 'And so we thought of the Pump Room and the cottage, yet now this...' She took a deep breath, as if preparing to swoon, and Glory saw Thad inch closer to his aunt, in case she did.

'I had never understood your interest in the spa, my dear, but I have gone along with you—until now. My nerves are such that I am nearly overcome and I must think of my health.' Phillida paused, though her expression held none of her usual drama. 'I fear I must return to London,' she said. 'Thad, will you join me?'

Stunned, Glory blinked at her aunt. Phillida had made her feelings clear all along, but her tendency towards theatrics had inured Glory to her complaints.

Indeed, if Glory had expected such a defection, it would have been some time ago, after their initial arrival in Philtwell, but not now, when Phillida had developed a friendship with the duchess.

Apparently, even a noble association was not worth the troubles of Queen's Well. And although Glory could not blame Phillida, that didn't stop the ache that came with the desertion of the woman she thought of as her mother. The three of them had been a family for so long, rarely separated, and now?

Glory looked to Thad, her heart in her throat. She was not ready to be parted from her brother, but, more importantly, she did not want him back in town without any supervision. And if Phillida had any inkling of his previous doings there, she would not encourage him to join her.

Glory held her breath as she awaited his response, but Thad shook his head, and Phillida did not attempt to persuade him. 'Very well, then, I shall be off myself, if you don't mind my taking the carriage,' Phillida said, a bit stiffly.

'Take mine, for it gets little enough use these days,' Mr Pettit said. And Phillida appeared to be cheered by the attentions of the rest of the company as they tried to change her mind.

But she was adamant in her decision. 'I have had enough of this business of yours, Glory,' she said. 'There's a reason your father never returned here, and you would do well to heed it.'

Glory said nothing, but the duchess was not as wary. 'And what is that?' she asked.

Phillida paused for effect before lowering her voice to a whisper. 'The curse.'

And even though Glory knew there was no such thing, she suppressed a shiver of apprehension for the future without her aunt.

In the wake of the departure of Miss Bamford, Letitia had lingered over breakfast until only she and Randolph remained in the dining room. When the maid had refilled their cups with coffee, Letitia stirred some milk into hers and glanced across the table at her old friend, who was proving to be more astute than she had imagined.

After their contretemps with Oberon, it was Randolph who reminded her, once he'd sobered, that she had wanted her son to feel something. And something was certainly on exhibit that night. The Oberon she'd rarely seen in the last few years wouldn't have bestirred himself over such a trifling matter as matchmaking.

While Randolph's words had dragged her from the dismals into which she had sunk, it was days of observation that had revived Letitia's flagging hopes. For even the most neutral bystander could see that the waters had worked their magic on her son and Miss Sutton. So why couldn't they see it themselves?

'I don't suppose you've found out anything about Oberon's activities in London,' Letitia said, absently stirring her coffee. Although she had written a few letters to old friends, with discreet enquiries, she had not received any enlightening replies.

'No,' Randolph said. Reaching for the newspaper Thad had abandoned, he shook it out and proceeded to put it between them, as though suddenly engrossed in reports from town. 'And I think your milk is well blended.'

Letitia glanced down to see that she was still clutching her spoon. She set it aside. 'Well, we simply cannot let things go on as they are,' she said. Miss Sutton spent her days bent over old texts, while Oberon was out and about, as though deliberately avoiding her.

Letitia frowned thoughtfully. 'The departure of the girl's chaperon, while regrettable, may work in our favour.'

The newspaper lowered slightly, and Randolph eyed her from above the edge of it. 'Tell me that was not your doing.'

'What?' Letitia asked.

'You talked that foolish creature into leaving, didn't you, by playing upon her fears? Really, Letty, you ought to be ashamed,' Randolph said. 'I'm surprised you didn't bribe the brother to go, too. I hesitate to imagine what you have planned for the girl next.' He raised the page, once more putting the news between them.

The duchess sniffed. 'I do not intend to chain her to my son's bed, if that's what you're thinking.'

'Ha! Nothing would surprise me at this point,' he said from behind the paper.

Letitia frowned. 'I assure you that I had no hand in sending that woman fleeing to town,' she said. 'It is entirely her own doing and foolish at that. Oberon is perfectly capable of ensuring her safety, and even if he weren't, why would anyone wish to do her ill? She's not even a Sutton.'

Ignoring Randolph's grunt, Letitia continued. 'And if we are tossing about accusations, what do you mean by attaching yourself to Miss Sutton, so that no one, and by no one, I mean Oberon, is able to engage her privately?'

'I am aiding her, as any gentleman would,' he said. 'And you might, as well, for the sooner these attacks are stopped, the sooner we can all get on with our lives.'

Letitia felt a sharp pang at the thought, for though she wished no ill on the Sutton family, she was not eager to return to a life that had become empty, without grandchildren, without even her son. Without love.

In the ensuing silence, Randolph lowered his paper again. 'Letty, did you ever consider that perhaps you are the one who should be taking a drink of the waters?'

'What? I have already been happily married,' Letitia sputtered, blinking at the wall of newsprint that faced her, but this time, it did not come down. Instead, she heard Randolph's voice speak safely from behind it.

'Well, perhaps it's time you were again.'

Mr Pettit had proven himself to be good company. He was quiet and agreeable, with a wry sense of humour that cropped up now and then as he joined Glory in poring over old tomes in the library. And with him present, there was little chance of Westfield cornering her alone, a situation that Glory told herself was for the best, no matter how much she wished otherwise.

But the hours still dragged and Glory became increasingly restless, eager for a change from the monotony of searching pages of scrawled signatures. Despite Mr Pettit's interest in Elizabeth, Glory was prepared to ask him to trade tasks with her, if only briefly, when she finally came across the name for which she had been hunting for so long.

Startled, Glory had to look twice, for fear she had imagined it, but Cornelius Thorpe had signed and dated the guestbook, as well as providing his place of residence with a flourish. 'Little Wattling!' she cried, startling Mr Pettit, who appeared to have been dozing over a thick volume.

'What's that?' he asked, stirring in his seat.

'Little Wattling,' Glory said. 'Have you heard of it?'

'Certainly,' he said, straightening. 'It's down in the valley, not far away.'

'Good,' Glory said, slamming shut the guestbook. 'Let's go there.'

Rousing himself further, Mr. Pettit eyed her in surprise. 'But I don't believe Westfield has returned.'

'You and I can make the trip,' Glory said. After days of inactivity, she was ready for an outing. But a glance towards her companion revealed that Mr Pettit did not share her enthusiasm, and Glory remembered that he had only recently recovered from an illness. 'But are you well enough?' she asked, trying to hide her disappointment.

'What? Oh, no, I'm quite hale and hearty,' Mr Pettit said, rising from his seat, as if to prove his words. 'But I'm not sure Westfield would approve.'

Glory bristled at the notion that she needed to seek the duke's approval for any and all of her actions. Although she appreciated his concern for her safety, she felt like a victim of his increasingly high-handed dictates.

'We'll take Thad along with us,' Glory said, getting to her feet. And before Mr Pettit could argue, she hurried off to find her brother.

If Thad had objected, Glory might have waited, but her brother was more than eager to have something to do, especially when the errand involved the possible discovery of their enemy. And soon the three of them were ensconced in the Sutton carriage, heading towards Little Wattling, with Thad talking all the while about the bruising he would give Thorpe once he got hold of him.

'But the man would have to be quite on in years, if he was an associate of our grandfather,' Glory said.

'Perhaps it is Thorpe's son or grandson who bedevils you,' Mr Pettit said.

Thad did not seem quite as confident at the thought of fighting someone who could very well be his own age and maybe twice his size. 'You don't think there's more than one, do you?' he asked.

'Perhaps we should delay our investigation until Westfield can join us,' Mr Pettit suggested, with a knowing glance at Thad.

'He is a good man to have in a fight,' Thad admitted.

Mr Pettit nodded. 'And a nobleman is harder to refuse than a mere gentleman. A duke, especially, commands respect and wields power.'

'Still, he has no more expertise in this sort of investigation than the rest of us,' Glory said.

'Doesn't he?' Mr Pettit murmured. 'I wonder.'

'He might be acquainted with some Bow Street Runners,' Thad said, referring to those in London who were charged with capturing the criminal element. 'Maybe he steps in to aid them on a lark.'

Glory shook her head at the fanciful notion. Although Westfield could defend himself more than capably, she could not picture him chasing convicts down filthy alleyways. But, obviously, she wasn't the only one who thought the duke was more than he seemed.

Glory frowned, trying to work out where his social skills and ability to handle fragile documents might figure in his 'obligations'. But her attention was soon captured by Thad, who was speculating on Westfield's involvement in the apprehension of the town's most infamous murderers.

Perhaps it was the talk of killings that bothered her, but by the time they reached Little Wattling, Glory was coming to regret her hasty decision. And she was forced to admit that pique had no little place in it. After all, she was accustomed to running her family, her life and her business. Now, it seemed that Westfield was in command of the latter two, at least, as well as a good portion of her heart.

While Glory had been kept in the library and in the dark, he was out and about all day. And once she had stumbled across him meeting clandestinely with strangers late at night, men who said 'the office' had sent them. Who could blame her for wanting to regain some control? And her trip was hardly a reckless one. All she had was a bit of faded script in an old guestbook to lead her to a family that might be long gone, their former ties to Queen's Well forgotten.

At least that's what Glory told herself as she waited for Mr Pettit, who had exited the carriage to speak with a resident of Little Wattling. Yet even as she watched, Glory could see the passer-by pointing towards the edge of town, where a few dilapidated houses were scattered before pastures and farmland.

'It appears our Mr Thorpe was a farmer and a prosperous one,' Mr Pettit said when he returned to his seat.

'He must have been to invest in Queen's Well,' Glory said.

'But he sold off all the land, as well as various houses, until only one remained,' Mr. Pettit said. Then he instructed the coachman to stop in front of the last residence that stood along the road.

'Is this it?' Glory asked as Thad helped her from the conveyance.

'No, *that* is,' Mr Pettit said, pointing to an abandoned building surrounded by gnarled oaks and growing grain, its façade faded, its roof fallen in.

'But no one lives there, do they?' Thad asked, his voice rising in some alarm. Apparently, he thought if anyone did live there, they were hardy enough to give *him* a bruising.

Mr Pettit shook his head. 'Your Mr Thorpe died more than a year ago.'

Glory breathed a sigh of relief. She had her pistol in her reticule, but was grateful that there would be no confrontations with the old man.

'What of his family?' Thad asked, glancing around as though ten strapping sons would suddenly appear out of the fields, armed with scythes and other farm implements.

'Gone,' Mr Pettit said. 'But let us ask the neighbour for more information.'

The neighbour was Mrs Marleybone, who had only a vague recollection of Mr Thorpe as a crazy old man. 'Always yelling at someone, hateful, he was,' she said.

'And his family?'

'Oh, they couldn't abide him, either, from what I gather. The wife ran off, rather than put up with him, and he had five daughters who all left as soon as they could, farmed out to relatives, married or the like.'

'None of them have remained in the area?'

Mrs Marleybone shook her head. 'When the roof

fell in, Thorpe and the last of the girls left, though I can't say where they went. She came back after he died, poking around the old house, but she didn't stay. How could she?' the woman said, inclining her head towards the remains of the family home.

'Did she have anyone with her, a lad, perhaps a son?' Glory asked, thinking of the mysterious youth who had played at least some part in the mischief at Queen's Well.

'No, I never saw a boy around, unless it was some-one courting the girls, but that would have been years ago.'

'Maybe we should take a look,' Thad said, eyeing the old structure as if the Queen's Gift might be lodged there.

Mrs Marleybone's eyes narrowed, with a local's natural suspicion of strangers poking about their property. 'I wouldn't go there if I were you,' she said. 'It's dangerous. And queer. They say the old man's ghost haunts the place.'

'Well, then, we should definitely have a look,' Mr Pettit said.

The woman shrugged, as if dismissing any interest in their fates. 'You'd better keep to the old hedge-row. Mr Dobbins won't like you traipsing through his barley.'

Nodding in agreement, they trooped off, walking through the tall grass and keeping to the uneven ground near the thicket of growth that stretched into the distance. Any path that had led to the house was no longer visible, and when they reached the broken steps that led to the front door, Mr Pettit hesitated.

'Perhaps you'd better stay back, Miss Sutton,' he said. 'I'm not sure how safe it is.'

'Nonsense,' Glory said. 'The walls look sturdy enough.'

'Looks can be deceiving,' Mr Pettit muttered.

But Thad was already opening the door, and Glory followed behind him. Although the low cottage had once been a nice home, the broken roof had let in the elements, leading to rot and decay. And despite the warmth of the day outside, it seemed dark and chilly inside, making Glory shiver.

'I don't see any signs of life,' Thad said.

'Except the four-legged kind,' Pettit said.

In fact, it was obvious the place had been empty for some time, its furniture and personal items stripped away and even some of the walls and floors damaged. The corners were cluttered with old leaves and accumulated dirt; Glory felt an unaccountable sadness at the loss.

'What should we look for?' Thad called over his shoulder as he disappeared into another room, oblivious to the melancholy that had settled over her.

'Any old papers or records, I suppose,' Glory said, though it was apparent that they would find nothing of use here. And now she rued all of the time she had spent pouring over the spa's thick ledgers.

Blindly following after Thad, Glory started climbing a broken flight of stairs, but a sound made her start. She clutched at the wall, half-expecting the building to come tumbling down around her, only to hear the flap of wings. Looking up, she saw a bird flying out of the rafters, where it had made a nest.

Still, Glory paused, aware of a gloom that clung to the upper storey. Either the sun had gone behind a cloud or it was heading towards the horizon, and this area, where part of the roof remained intact, was sunk in darkness. Glory had to squint to see Thad's figure ahead, and a glance behind her showed that their companion had not followed.

'There's nothing here,' Glory said. 'Let's find Mr Pettit and be on our way.'

'But there might be something left in the attic,' Thad said, heading towards a section that was buried under heavy slate tiles and debris. Parts of the floor up here were broken, and Glory did not care to venture any further from her place on the stairs. The wind moving through the rubble sent the old wood to creaking, and Glory heard the scurry and thud of birds or rodents. Or perhaps it was simply Mr. Pettit below them.

'No, Thad,' she called, increasingly anxious. She did not want their host, recently recovered from a long illness, to make a misstep or fall, especially since she was the one who had insisted on this journey.

'Leave that be and come along,' she said, louder. But he was already pulling at a heavy piece of wood, and Glory heard a loud crack, as though he had dislodged it.

She felt a puff of air and then the weight of something striking her shoulder. Reeling, she slammed against the wall even as her footing failed her. With a cry, she tried to find purchase, grasping finally at an exposed beam to keep from falling down the steps behind her. Shaken, she clutched her arm, breathing deeply as Thad rushed to her side.

'What happened?' he asked.

'Your wood struck me,' Glory said.

'But it can't have been my doing. Something must have fallen from above,' he said, looking up.

'I don't care where it came from,' Glory said. 'Let's get out of here before the whole place falls down around our ears.'

Thad argued even as he helped her make her descent. 'Once I get you outside, I can come back in and see what's up there.'

'No,' Glory said, in a tone that brooked no resistance. 'We should never have come in here.' She peered into the gloom, and when she could not see Mr Pettit, she called his name, perhaps a bit frantically.

A shuffling sound heralded the arrival of their companion, somewhat short of breath as he hurried from the rear of the building. 'What is it? Did you find something? I thought I heard shouting.'

'Glory got hurt,' Thad said.

'What?' Mr Pettit paled.

'I'm all right,' Glory said. She held her cloak tight to her arm, unwilling to let the others fuss over her, especially in her urgency to depart. And even when they stepped outside, away from the precarious structure, Glory could not breathe a sigh of relief.

As she hurried away, stumbling over the uneven

ground, she felt the familiar eerie sensation of watchful eyes upon her. But when she looked around, all she saw was the old house, its windows dark and forbidding now as the trees surrounding it cast long shadows. And beyond, the barley stretched into the distance, rustling in the wind.

Chapter Thirteen

As much as he might fight it, every time Oberon returned to Sutton House, he felt a surge of anticipation. Sometimes, he refused to act upon it and seek her out. In other instances, he indulged himself, peeking into the library to admire her bent head and the way the light from the window gilded her hair.

He had become completely and utterly nonsensical, he realised, but at least he restrained himself from clandestine meetings in attics and cellars—or even her book-filled lair. So why didn't he feel virtuous? Instead, he was increasingly frustrated, filled with want, a sensation wholly alien to him and yet one which he embraced.

Perhaps he was going mad.

It had happened to others. Look at old Dee himself, reduced to scrying for angels on the head of a pin or some such rubbish, useless to his family, his colleagues and his country. Maybe it would be better to consider making some changes, rather than end up becoming a liability, a prospect that increasingly occupied Oberon's thoughts.

But the notion sat uneasily upon him, and as if to assuage his disquiet, his feet unerringly found the entrance to the library. Stripping off his gloves, Oberon stood in the doorway waiting for that sense of rightness to settle over him. But it didn't.

The room was empty.

The fact that Miss Sutton wasn't where he expected her to be shouldn't have bothered him, but it did, and Oberon roamed through the house, searching for her. Yet he could find no one, and finally a servant informed him that his mother was in her room, while the others had taken the carriage out earlier.

Oberon was not easily rattled, but he felt the treacherous creep of alarm. It had been simple when he cared for nothing and had watched the world play out around him without blinking. But now he was invested in something, in *someone*. And that someone was wandering around without his knowledge—or protection. A glance out the windows showed that the shadows had lengthened into twilight, and soon it would be full dark. *Where was she?*

Was this Pettit's doing or Thad's? Or, more likely, his mother's? His expression grim, Oberon headed towards the stairs, ready to turn the duchess out of bed in an effort to find out more information. And he was already halfway up the steps when he heard the footman hurrying after him.

The carriage had returned.

With a nod, Oberon took up a place by the door, a measure of relief warring against the anxiety that continued to plague him. It was an odd sensation for a man known for maintaining his composure in the most delicate of situations. But that man seemed like a different person, one untethered to anyone or anything, unfeeling, barely alive.

Now he felt too much, Oberon realised, as he forced himself to remain where he was, instead of rushing to greet a woman who was not his relative. When he saw her emerge from the carriage unharmed, it was all he could do not to embrace her or take her face in his hands and bruise her lips with the strength of his relief. And the fact that he could not do so only increased his frustration.

It must have shown on his face, for Mr Pettit gave him a wide berth, and even Thad slipped by, without his usual enthusiastic greeting. The servants followed, and finally he was alone with Miss Sutton, although there was little privacy in the foyer where they stood. Oberon was tempted to pull her into the nearby parlour, but she seemed intent upon the stairs, and he was forced to stand in front of her simply to gain her attention.

'Where the devil were you?' he demanded.

'We went to Little Wattling in search of the Thorpe family,' she murmured.

'What?' Oberon could barely keep his voice even. 'You were not to leave this house.'

'Are you my gaoler, as well as magistrate, your Grace?' she asked, lifting her chin.

Oberon swallowed his sharp retort, for now he could see the weariness in her face, the dullness in her eyes that bespoke pain of some kind. Against all the dictates of sense or propriety, he reached out to pull her to him, but she winced.

'What is it? Are you hurt?'

Without waiting for her reply, Oberon lifted her cloak away to reveal a nasty-looking scratch below her shoulder, still oozing blood. At the sight of the wound, he swung her into his arms, ignoring her squeal of protest when her feet left the floor.

'I'm all right, your Grace,' she said. 'I am perfectly capable of walking.'

But Oberon paid her no heed as he strode to the top of the stairs. There he came across his mother, who evinced no alarm at the sight of her son carrying a genteel young woman towards the private rooms. Indeed, she walked past him without a word, which was just as well, for Oberon did not feel like explaining himself.

Instead, he threw open the door to his room and placed Miss Sutton upon his bed. Though no woman had ever graced that space, she looked…right. And Oberon suspected she would look even more so in the ducal rooms at Westfield, if only that were possible.

Calling for Pearson, Oberon ordered warm water and some kind of bandage to dress the wound even as his patient protested her presence here. Again, Oberon ignored her, leaving her side only to pour a glass of brandy. His back to her, he paused to take a quick gulp himself before turning to press the wine upon his patient.

Refusing to lie down, she sat up, her slight wince a testament to her courage and composure. Miss Sutton was pluck to the backbone, as Thad would say, but Oberon frowned at the thought of her brother and the poor protection he and Pettit had provided.

'What happened?' he asked.

'Thad was moving some wood and a stray piece struck me,' she said. 'It is a minor scrape and hardly worthy of concern.'

Oberon untied her cloak and let it fall away to get a better look. Although it was not deep, such wounds could become infected or turn gangrenous. Sometimes the worst happened, as he well remembered, and he remembered, too, just why he had stepped away from connections, from family and friends, in order to avoid the pain that came when things went awry. Yet this time, he could not turn away or run away.

Shaken, Oberon looked to her, his gaze seeking hers, but Pearson appeared at his elbow. And then he was occupied cleaning the wound, while she reported on the ill-conceived trip to Little Wattling. Oberon had to bite his tongue, steady his hand and curb his reactions until she fell quiet, her lashes drifting shut.

But he remained at her bedside, deep in thought, for the emotions she had roused could not as easily be laid to rest.

* * *

Oberon was up early again. He was accustomed to getting by on little sleep when necessary, but the last few restless nights were beginning to take their toll. Despite his best efforts, he could see no resolution to the problems here, including his own deepening dilemma. And when he looked into the mirror, the bleary-eyed fellow who stared back was a far cry from the renowned London host.

Frowning, Oberon jerked at the ties of his banyan and wondered what was taking Pearson so long in the dressing room. When a knock on the door signalled the arrival of the hot water for shaving, he called for entry, only to gape in astonishment as the door flew open to admit Miss Sutton, still clad in her nightclothes.

Although a master of all situations, Oberon found himself at a loss. And Miss Sutton seemed just as surprised as he. For a long moment, she stared at his bare calves and feet, clearly visible beneath the hem of his long garment. And somehow, her innocent scrutiny was more arousing than the most brazen stare of a courtesan. Swallowing a groan, Oberon was vaguely aware of Pearson emerging to take in the scene, then disappearing back into the dressing room, shutting the door behind him.

The slight noise seemed to bring Miss Sutton to her senses, for her gaze finally met his, and Oberon could see this was no early morning seduction, but something far more serious.

'Thad's gone missing,' she said, her voice strained.

'I went to his room to have a private word with him, but his bed hasn't been slept in.'

Normally, Oberon wouldn't worry about a fellow of Thad's age disappearing for the night. Even in this backwater, a willing woman could always be found, whether for payment or pleasure, and the boy might have taken advantage of the opportunities offered. As Thad had often opined, there was little to occupy him here, compared with London and its environs.

But nothing involving the owners of Queen's Well was as it seemed, and whoever was targeting Miss Sutton might have broadened their scope to include Thad. Suddenly, Oberon remembered the bruise the boy had sported a while ago, which he had dismissed as youthful contretemps. Now he wasn't so sure.

Miss Sutton was looking at him with such obvious distress that Oberon knew she was thinking the same thing. Unaccustomed to giving comfort—or giving of himself at all—Oberon none the less reached out to take her hand. In their current state of dishabille, it was all that he dared to do.

'We'll find him,' Oberon said. But his assurance only seemed to cause her more misery.

'We quarrelled,' she said, a catch in her voice. 'Yesterday, he put a hole in the wall of the room behind the mural, convinced that the Queen's Gift was hidden there, and I scolded him for it. After all, this is not our property.'

She sighed, her eyes downcast, her fingers holding tightly to his own. 'We've all been under the strain of the recent circumstances, and I probably said more than I should have…that he was too old to be playing at treasure hunts. He stormed off, I assumed to his room. Later, I knocked, but he wouldn't answer.'

She drew another deep breath. 'I thought he was ignoring me, as he sometimes has in recent years, and that he would come around. But after tossing and turning…well, I regretted my words and wanted to make amends this morning before breakfast.'

Her haunted gaze met Oberon's. 'That's when I discovered he was gone. And if anything has happened to him, I'll never forgive myself.'

Trusting his instincts, if not himself, Oberon pulled her close and tucked her dark head under his chin. She whispered against his chest, and the silk that separated her cheek from his overheating skin seemed at once too little and too much of a barrier.

'He means everything to me,' she said. And as she held tight to Oberon, she spoke of family loss and love that made him regret his behaviour after the death of his father. Miss Sutton had pulled her little family together, not abandoned it, and Oberon could only admire her actions.

'I've spent all these years raising him only to drive him away,' she said.

'Nonsense,' Oberon said. 'Young men of Thad's age, or any age for that matter, do not take well to scolding, especially from someone older and wiser and female. He's probably gone to the cottage.' *Or to London*, Oberon did not add.

She lifted her head, her gaze sharp, despite her distress. 'But what of the threats against the well? What if someone was out there lying in wait for him?'

'Thad has come and gone freely all along,' Oberon said. 'There's no reason to think that he's been waylaid now.' However, they both knew that the possibility existed. Miss Sutton was too intelligent to swallow his assurances whole, and Oberon would not insult her by trying to force them down her throat.

And although she had not mentioned it, or perhaps even thought it, there was another prospect that nagged at Oberon. Once he had convinced himself that Miss Sutton was not up to any mischief, he had dismissed his reservations about the family. But, in doing so, he had chosen to ignore some things that he otherwise would not have.

Now he recalled that Thad was never with his sister when these mishaps occurred, except during the most recent outing. And in that instance, Miss Sutton was struck by wood that her brother was handling. By his own admission, the boy had not wanted to live in Philtwell, and then there were the allusions to his troubles in London.

It all made Oberon wonder whether Miss Sutton's brother was up to his neck in it—right here.

After Glory was assured that Westfield would not leave without her, she hurried back to her own room to dress. She tried not to remember how he had looked with his bare feet and tousled hair, for she had more important concerns. And this time when she rushed downstairs to meet the duke, her heart was pounding with anxiety, not anticipation.

They did not pause for breakfast, but set out at once, stopping first at the Pump Room to see whether Thad was there, by any chance. But neither the guard nor the arriving workers had seen him.

While Westfield questioned them further, Glory walked towards the well to check on the progress of the repairs. They soon would be completed, making the building ready for the public, whenever the business opened again, yet Glory took no pleasure in the sight.

Weeks, perhaps even days ago, the newly laid floor and polished fixtures would have filled her with pride. She remembered her sense of accomplishment when the Pump Room was refurbished and she had taken her place in a long line of Sutton ancestors.

But now, as Glory stood looking over the pump, she knew only a great emptiness. This is what she had wanted, to pour her life into the spa that was her heritage, but suddenly, that desire seemed hollow, a desperate replacement for what really mattered.

In her yearning to fill the coming void, had she hastened its approach? Phillida was already gone, back to her life in London, and sooner or later Westfield would return to his unnamed obligations, taking the remnants of her heart with him. And Thad? Her chest constricting, Glory turned towards the duke, hoping for some good news about her brother.

'I've got quite a few people out combing the area, so, if he's here, we shall find him,' Westfield said.

The *if* made Glory uneasy, but she nodded.

'Meanwhile, I thought we should speak with some of the area's young people to see whether they might know of his plans,' Westfield said. 'Did he have any particular friends?'

Glory shook her head. 'One of Thad's complaints has been the lack of good company.' At first, especially, he dismissed the residents of Philtwell and its environs as provincial, compared to his London acquaintances.

'Still, if he's a typical young man, he might not keep his sister apprised of all that goes on in his life,' Westfield said, as he gave her his arm.

The casual comment made Glory shudder and she gripped his sleeve more tightly than necessary, for she was well aware of the trouble a boy of Thad's age could fall into. However, she didn't think there were many opportunities for such in Philtwell, least of all at the place where Westfield finally stopped.

Glory eyed the vicarage dubiously, for Reverend Longley was not one of her favourite people. A rather strict, stuffy sort, he seemed to view the spa as a possible breeding ground for licentious behaviour, which made for awkward conversation, at best.

Although Glory braced herself for an uncertain welcome, it was not the good reverend, but his son, Clarence Longley, who greeted them after they were shown into the small morning room. But while the young Mr Longley expressed dismay at Thad's disappearance, he could offer no suggestions as to where Glory's brother might be.

'So he did not confide in you?' Westfield asked.

'No,' Mr Longley said. 'I could not claim such a close acquaintance…yet.'

'But you were not at odds?'

'Certainly not,' Mr Longley said, his pale face showing surprise at the question.

'Then you never were involved in a fight with Mr Sutton?' Westfield asked, startling both Glory and Mr Longley.

'Me?' The young man laughed. 'My father would have my head if I struck anyone. And I've got nothing against the Suttons or Queen's Well, which will bring new life to Philtwell—entertainment, visitors, dances—just what we need.'

'Your father isn't as enthused,' Glory said.

Mr Longley coloured. 'Well, he has some old-fashioned ideas, but he'll come around eventually. You can't stand in the way of progress and all that.'

'What do you mean by old-fashioned ideas?' Westfield asked.

'Oh, he claims the waters are tainted somehow because they were thought to have special powers,' Mr Longley said, with a laugh. 'He can't condone anything like that because he's a churchman. And then when he heard my sister had taken a drink, he really got up in the boughs about it.'

Longley flushed again, as though he might have said too much, and Glory wondered whether the old rumours of romance were responsible for the vicar's condemnation. It seemed that more people knew about that legend than she had ever thought possible.

Glory was dragged from her thoughts by West-field's subtle questions about Mr Longley's sister, and soon she was stunned to learn that her brother appeared to have formed an attachment to the girl. In fact, Thad's interest in the Pump Room could be traced to the appearance of Miss Longley, who first arrived with some of her friends and later toasted Queen's Well with its owner.

Glory blinked, baffled by just how Westfield had discovered so much in only a few minutes of seem-ingly casual conversation. But the duke looked per-fectly at ease, as though he did as much every day.

'May we speak to her?' he asked.

'Of course,' Mr Longley said, getting to his feet as though relieved to end his own interview. He hurried from the room, leaving Glory to turn to Westfield in confusion.

'Why didn't Thad say anything to me?' she asked. Her brother had been withdrawn and silent after their arrival in Philtwell, but he'd become more like his old self lately. And yet he had never mentioned Miss Longley more than any other young resident of the village.

'And do you share all confidences?' Westfield asked.

Glory coloured, for she had said nothing to Thad of her own romantic feelings. But how could she? The object of her affections was a duke of the realm who had made his 'obligations' quite clear.

Miss Longley, on the other hand, was a sweet girl who would make a fine match for Thad, her father notwithstanding. And she proved as much when she appeared in the doorway, greeting them shyly. Pretty and soft-spoken, she was well mannered and quick to blush, which she did at the very mention of Glory's brother.

'But I don't understand,' she said, thick lashes fluttering over pale blue eyes. 'I haven't seen Mr. Sutton since the Pump Room closed, so he has not confided in me any…plans.'

'Your brother said your father might not approve of Mr Sutton,' Westfield said, with embarrassing frankness, and Glory cringed.

But instead of demurring, Miss Longley smiled. 'Oh, he has some silly notions, but he'll come around.'

'Had he forbidden you from seeing Mr Sutton?'

'No, but I do hope you will open the Pump Room again soon,' Miss Longley said, with a beseeching glance towards Glory. 'The public dances are few and far between, and my friends and I did so enjoying gathering there.'

'And were there any others, young people in your circle perhaps, who did not approve of Mr Sutton?' Westfield asked. Glory eyed him askance, for she could not imagine Thad as the victim of a jealous beau, and Miss Longley shook her head.

But Westfield persisted. 'One day Mr Sutton sported a bruise on his cheek—perhaps from some argument with a local resident?'

'I don't remember anything like that,' Miss Longley said, with a puzzled expression. 'Although there was one time when he didn't seem pleased to see someone at the Pump Room. I didn't recognise the man as anyone from the area, but Mr Sutton appeared to know him, and they left together.'

'This stranger, can you describe him?' Westfield asked.

The young woman again shook her head. 'I'm afraid that my attention was upon Mr. Sutton, so I just caught a glimpse of him from a distance.'

When Miss Longley could provide no further information, they thanked her for her help and took their leave of the vicarage. Trying to understand all that she had learned, Glory followed mutely as Westfield led her to a shaded spot some distance away. There, in relative privacy, he turned to face her, his expression intent.

'Just what sort of trouble did your brother get into in London?' he asked. 'Has it followed him here?'

Glory blanched, for she had never even considered that possibility. And yet, it did not seem likely. She shook her head, and although she had spoken to no one of that difficult time, she answered as best she could.

'Like so many other young men, he fell in with some unsavoury companions who led him into the usual mischief, mainly drinking and gambling. But I'm sure you know that such simple vices can lead to ruin when practised in excess or in certain…parts of town. It was those areas they frequented, so I cannot see them leaving London, especially for somewhere as remote as Philtwell. It is not an easy journey, with no enticements to be found at the end of it.'

Westfield looked thoughtful, but before he could comment, Glory realised that a man was hurrying towards them. Stopping in front of the duke, he doffed his cap and bowed, and Glory held her breath.

'He's been found, your Grace.'

Chapter Fourteen

From Ned Bartlett's grim expression, Oberon suspected that Thad was not in good shape. But the boy was alive, and Oberon didn't realise just how very grateful he was for that news until he saw Miss Sutton's shoulders sag with relief. If they had not been in public, he would have taken her in his arms. As it was, he had his hands full trying to keep her from running all the way back to Sutton House.

There, Oberon was glad to discover that Pearson had taken charge, so that Thad was cleaned up and tucked into bed. A whispered conference with his valet revealed the extent of the boy's injuries, but he could not keep Miss Sutton from her brother's side. And to her credit, she did not faint or wince at the sight of his bruised face and swollen eye, but greeted him with her usual briskness.

'I'm sorry, sis,' he mumbled.

'Nonsense,' she said. 'It is I who am sorry for putting you—and all of us—in danger.'

But Thad shook his head. 'Not your doing,' he muttered. Then he glanced towards Oberon. 'I gave nearly as good as I got, your Grace, but there were two of them.'

Oberon nodded. 'Are you feeling well enough to tell me about it? Because I'd like to give them a go myself,' he said, surprised at the truth of that statement.

'Not your problem,' Thad said. But, gradually, Oberon was able to coax the tale from the boy, which, as he had suspected, involved trouble from London.

It began with Thad falling in with a pair of brothers, unsavoury sorts, he admitted, who encouraged him to spend his allowance more freely than had been his wont. Soon he was frequenting low taverns and the kind of hells where a green young man with money is easily fleeced. This uncharacteristic behaviour continued until one morning he arrived home, stumbling drunk, to find his sister waiting for him.

As usual, Miss Sutton proved her worth. Instead of railing at the boy, she took measures to immediately remove him from the influence of the Fairmans, though that appeared to be a misnomer.

'If that even is their real name,' Westfield said, and Thad was still innocent enough to blink at the suggestion.

But he was not so naïve as to think he could escape his gambling debts and had dutifully paid them. No doubt he would have lost everything, like so many other young men, if not for his sister. However, at the time he was not grateful for the intervention, which likely saved them all from ruin.

Instead, upon arriving in Philtwell, he wrote to his former acquaintances, complaining about his situation. Unsurprisingly, at least to Oberon, he received no reply—until he mentioned the Queen's Gift. Then the boy received a pointed query as to the legitimacy of the story and the whereabouts of the so-called treasure. But, by this time, Thad's interest in his earlier compatriots had been usurped by something else.

'The charms of a certain vicar's daughter, perhaps?' Oberon said.

Thad looked startled at the words, but rather relieved that his secret was out, and he nodded. 'She came into the Pump Room one day and it was like my heart stopped,' he said, with a wry smile. His open admission struck Oberon with a pang of envy, for the boy had wrestled with no demons or duties.

And Miss Longley had acted upon him in a way his sister had not. Faced with gaining her approval, Thad cut off communication with his old cohorts. He'd thought himself well rid of them until, much to his dismay, the younger Fairman appeared in Philtwell. And when Thad did not greet him with open arms, a scuffle ensued.

'The two smelled a prize in the Queen's Gift and came to see for themselves,' Oberon said. 'It's just the sort of thing that would draw such scoundrels: a priceless heirloom, ready for the taking. The journey required little investment, with the potential to make much more than in years of skimming money from rigged card games and the like. And all the better, if you should find the gift for them.'

Thad nodded, his expression sheepish. 'I might have exaggerated the possibility of discovering it, too, just so they wouldn't think I was buried in some backwater without hope of escape. But when Billy came, I told him that it was just an old rumour, and even though he got the best of me, I figured he'd leave. What else could he do?'

Thad shook his head, as if only now becoming aware of his miscalculation. 'Once when I was out walking, I thought I caught a glimpse of him, but I convinced myself that it was just my imagination and that he was long gone. I didn't realise they were both here, and I never even thought of them in connection with all that happened to Queen's Well.'

For all her devotion, Miss Sutton was not blind to her brother's shortcomings and she slanted him a sharp glance. 'So you weren't trying to find the Queen's Gift for them?'

'No!' Thad recoiled in disgust. 'I was interested in finding it for us…er, myself…er, to impress someone.'

'Reverend Longley?' Oberon asked.

Thad nodded reluctantly. 'I know he doesn't think much of the spa, though Miss Longley says he'll come around, and I thought if I could make such a big discovery, that it would be…an accomplishment, what with the history and all.' He paused, a bit shamefaced, before continuing. 'And I hoped that if it really was valuable, then I could…get married.'

'But, Thad,' his sister began, and Oberon hoped she did not intend to try to talk him out of his infatuation. The boy was young and in love, and any interference would only make him more determined. But Oberon should have known that Miss Sutton would make no such mistake. Instead she reached for her brother's hand.

'You can get married at any time,' she assured him. 'Half of the family fortune is yours. I only kept control of the monies for your own sake, so that you would not fall prey to anyone like the Fairmans before reaching maturity.'

Thad had the good grace to blush at this statement, indicating that he might finally appreciate his sister's foresight.

'In fact, if you want to remain here, you can even have Queen's Well,' Miss Sutton said. 'It is as much yours as mine.'

Her offer, tendered without any hesitation, stunned Oberon. Hadn't she claimed to love the spa above all else? He turned towards her, trying to gauge her mood, but to all appearances, she was willing to give over her life's work, the object of her devotion, at one word from Thad.

'But, first, we must take care of the Fairmans,' she added, turning towards Oberon with an expectant expression. 'What do you think?'

Oberon didn't know what to think, with the latest revelations ringing in his ears and his tenure as magistrate likely coming to an end. But the Suttons were waiting for his reply, so he could only tell them what they wanted to hear.

'Perhaps we have our villains.'

Pearson insisted that Oberon change clothes in case a brawl ensued. He shook out an older coat that he deemed less fashionable and, thus, more dispensable, having already forced Oberon into a pair of breeches that had seen better days.

'I do not plan to land in the dirt,' Oberon replied.

'Nor do I, but one never knows with these low types. They do not play by the rules.' He turned, holding out the coat for Oberon, a grim smile upon his face. 'I almost feel sorry for them. They have no idea whom they are dealing with.'

'And why should they?' Oberon said. 'Like any London criminal, they think themselves far too clever for the rural population, let alone a village of this size and location.'

Pearson laughed. 'Yet, by this time, you've got more men stationed in the area than the whole of Bow Street.'

'Not quite,' Oberon said, though he had definitely gone beyond the bounds of the usual magistrate, allying himself with many of the villagers, from boys to aged grandfathers who could keep an eye out without drawing attention. And they were in addition to Pearson, himself, his grooms and the men who had arrived from London. It was all a bit heavy-handed for a couple of petty knaves like the Fairmans.

'So why don't you let some of these fellows, who are well paid for their services, deal with the riff-raff?' Pearson said. 'These two ought to be far below your notice.'

Although Oberon rarely came in contact with the criminal order, especially such characters as these, that didn't mean he couldn't handle them. And he intended to. 'I want to question them myself.'

'Personal interest leads to mistakes,' Pearson reminded him.

Although that was true enough, Oberon didn't plan on making any mistakes with two minor thieves, even if they turned out to be complete blackguards. 'I don't trust anyone else to get the truth,' Oberon said, shooting his cuffs.

Pearson's voice, behind him, was dry. 'And here I suspected you just wanted to give them a bruising.'

'That, too,' Oberon admitted, turning to face his valet. 'I only wish Thad could have a go at them himself.'

'Why did they give him such a punishing?'

'They were only going to rough him up a bit more than before,' Oberon said. 'But Thad's new boxing skills turned the scuffle into a mêlée.'

Pearson frowned. 'Do you have your pistol? Your knives?'

'Yes,' Oberon said. 'And you?'

Despite his grim nod, there was a certain anticipation in Pearson's expression. And Oberon wondered whether the man would be content strictly with brushing coats and polishing boots in the future. He shook his head.

'Jones and Thomas will be nearby, should we require any assistance,' Oberon said. 'They're at the Boar's Head right now keeping an eye on our prey and will haul them off to gaol once I've had my chat with them.'

'Right,' Pearson said. 'And your own feelings for… the Suttons won't affect that conversation at all.'

'Of course not, Pearson,' Oberon said, lifting a brow. 'You know that I am a professional and do not subscribe to unnecessary violence.'

Pearson returned his wry smile with a nod. 'Well, then, let's hope they do something to make it necessary.'

Having completed her morning calls, Letitia returned to Sutton House to find the rooms deserted. Even the library was empty except for Randolph, who was tucked in a comfortable chair by a window, bent over a book.

'Where is everyone?' Letitia asked, only to see the man start, his reading material falling to the floor with a thud. 'I can see you are hard at work,' she said, bending to retrieve the fallen volume.

'I was simply resting my eyes,' Randolph replied, with a dignified air.

Letitia read the title with some amusement. 'And yet I can see how one might doze over *A Compleate History of the Queen's Court*, in the original text, no less.'

'It is a nod,' Randolph agreed, 'but I do what I can to help the cause.'

'And whose cause is that?' Letitia asked, lifting a brow. 'It seems you have abandoned mine.'

'Never, your Grace,' he said, bowing his head formally.

'Oh, cease your toadying, for no one would believe it anyway,' Letitia said, taking a seat nearby. 'Where is everyone?'

'Ah,' he said, smiling coyly. 'Although I am not privy to all that has happened, I can tell you the whereabouts of some and surmise the whereabouts of others.'

'What happened? What have I missed?' Letitia asked, irritated by Randolph's mysterious manner and his smug expression.

Obviously in his element, he leaned back as if to present the most delicious gossip and Letitia tried not to hope that her son had compromised Miss Sutton. After all, a mother shouldn't wish for such an occurrence, though it certainly would spur things along…

'The reason we breakfasted alone is because your son and Miss Sutton had already gone out looking for Mr Sutton, who had vanished from the premises.'

'What? Why were we not informed?'

Randolph shrugged. 'Perhaps they were keeping it quiet or they were in a hurry, but Thad has been recovered and now lies in his bed, a bit bruised after an altercation with ruffians.'

Letitia gasped. 'Who in Philtwell would do such a thing?'

'A pair of nasty characters from town who learned about the Queen's Gift from Thad and thought to snatch it for themselves. Since your son and his valet are nowhere to be found, I suspect that they are off to apprehend the culprits, as we speak.'

'Oberon? Why would he chase after them? And with his *valet*?'

'He is the magistrate, is he not?' Randolph said. 'And thankfully so, for I fear after this is all over, I will resign the post.'

'But he might be hurt,' Letitia said. Although most young bucks dabbled in fencing and boxing for their own amusement, a gentleman was hardly equipped to deal with hardened criminals. 'Surely he can send others in his stead, who can better handle these thugs.'

'I'm not so sure,' Randolph said. He had taken to making such cryptic remarks lately, without any explanation, and Letitia was growing weary of it. She would have told him so, too, if she was not struck by an alarming thought.

'But if these fellows are responsible for all that has plagued Queen's Well, then Oberon has no reason to remain here any longer.' Letitia's hands tightened upon the arms of her chair, as if the force of her grip could keep everything from slipping through her fingers. 'What of our hopes for a betrothal? What of my grandchildren?'

'Future grandchildren,' Randolph said.

'Don't mock me,' Letitia said. 'I have wagered all on this and have no more hands to play. Do you think I shall ever see Oberon again once he has returned to London?'

Throughout all of her correspondence and conversations with Randolph, Letitia had maintained a light tone, persuading him to join her in a bit of matchmaking. Never had she let him see just how much it meant to her. Nor had she revealed her desperate hope that a wedding would return to her the son she had once known, who greeted her with warmth, not civility, and visited because of desire, not duty.

'Hold on, Letty,' Randolph said, reaching out to pat her arm. 'All is not yet lost.'

'How do you know?' Letitia said, cursing the quaver in her voice.

Randolph removed his hand from her sleeve and sat back with an expression of serene certainty. 'Because the timing isn't right.'

'What? What are you saying?'

'By the time Thad became interested in the Queen's Gift, the Pump Room had already been vandalised once, so these two characters, while presumably guilty of assaulting Mr Sutton, cannot be responsible for all that has happened to the well and its owners.'

Letitia felt some of the tension leave her body, though she remained sceptical. 'But why doesn't Oberon know that?'

'Perhaps his usually sharp wits are clouded by his…interest in the case,' Randolph said. 'Then again, your son plays his cards close to his chest, so perhaps he is fully aware of the timing of events. In fact, if I were a betting man—'

'Which you are,' Letitia pointed out, as hope flickered to life once more.

'Which I am,' Randolph amended, smiling coyly, 'I'd say your son knows exactly what he is doing.'

The afternoon shadows were growing long when Oberon and Pearson reached the Boar's Head, a tavern on the road to London. Leaving Pearson with a view of the front, Oberon slipped around the building into the alley at the rear, where a dark figure soon stepped from the gloom.

'Here, sir,' Jones said, by way of greeting.

'Good work,' Oberon said, with a nod. 'How many entrances?'

'Just here and at the front,' Jones said. 'And our friends are likely to be tossed out of either one soon.'

'You've been plying them with drink?'

'That, and they've been arguing. Apparently, they aren't quite sure what to do now that they've plucked their goose.'

'Yes, the boy can hardly fetch the prize for them when he's incapacitated,' Oberon said, grimly.

Jones nodded. 'The one calling himself Tommy is eager to cut their losses and head back to town, but after his initial panic, Billy wants to turn around and have another go at it.'

Or at Thad, Oberon thought, frowning. 'See if you can get them thrown out the rear.'

Jones nodded and slipped back inside the building, while Oberon whistled softly for his valet. Then they both settled in to watch, one on either side of the dark doorway. And they did not have long to wait.

Soon two drunken figures stumbled out of the tavern into the alley, loudly protesting their expulsion and threatening all manner of retaliation.

'Be quiet unless you wish to be shot,' Oberon said, quickly garnering their attention.

'What's this, a robbery?' the shorter fellow said, with a snort. 'You won't get nothing from us.'

'It's not money I want, but information,' Oberon said.

Again, he managed to get their attention, even through their haze of alcohol. 'What's in it for us?' the taller one asked in a surly tone.

'You'll find out.'

The shorter fellow looked like he was going to bolt, but Pearson stepped out of the shadows to reveal that he, too, had a pistol trained upon them. So the Fairmans changed their tune, making a show of their willingness to cooperate, while, no doubt, planning their escape.

When asked about Queen's Well, however, they maintained their innocence, and it was only after threats of coercion that they finally admitted to having a private dispute with the owner of the well, which was 'no one else's business.'

'Ah, but since I'm a patron of the well, I am most

interested in what's been happening there: vandalism, destruction of property, breaking and entering,' Oberon said. He looked to Pearson. 'Is that all?'

'You're forgetting the attempted murder upon the crags, your Grace,' his valet said.

'*Attempted murder?*' one Fairman said, sputtering.

'*Your grace?*' said the other. 'Who *are* you?'

'Let's just say that I've enough power to toss you two into an extremely unpleasant prison for a very long time.'

The Fairmans were eager to speak, then, and they confessed to having a violent argument over past conflicts with Mr Thadeus Sutton. But they claimed they were forced to defend themselves, and no amount of threats or persuasion could get them to admit to anything else. In fact, they professed ignorance of all the other attacks and denied searching for the gift themselves.

'What do we know about it?' the one said, with a bark of laughter. 'How would we go looking for the thing?'

'That was Thad's job,' the other said, muttering about the boy's inability to do it.

Although disappointing, their claims were not surprising. Oberon had suspected that the Fairmans arrived in Philtwell too late to be responsible for all that had happened. None the less, he had hoped that the mysteries of Queen's Well could be wrapped up neatly and disposed of with these two characters, but it was not to be.

'Well, then, I guess this interview is over,' Oberon said. He whistled for Jones and Thomas, but the Fairmans, having thought they would be released, made their moves. One dived at Pearson's feet, while the other launched himself at Oberon.

Truth to tell, Oberon was more than happy to oblige the fellow with a bout of fisticuffs. Not only was he eager to avenge Miss Sutton's brother, but all the frustration and pent-up feelings he had been suppressing for weeks were clamouring for an outlet. Drawing a deep breath, Oberon swung hard, landing a bellier and facer that left Fairman panting and staggering.

But the brother was fighting for his freedom and lurched forwards for more. He was desperate enough to land a few blows, including one that cracked Oberon's lip, but he was too drunk to move quickly and he finally fell, sprawling, into the dirt, floored at last.

His groan was loud in the ensuing silence, for his brother had long since been subdued. But Oberon had not let anyone else come between him and his opponent. And while his London associates stood gaping at the man they knew only as a convivial host and contact, Oberon stood over the prone Fairman and spoke with no little satisfaction.

'That was for Thad.'

Glory was pacing. Every once in a while, she slanted a cautious glance towards the bed to make sure that Thad was still asleep, but she continued moving back and forth across the thick carpet in his room. The tray that a maid had brought her stood untouched upon a nearby table; she had long since given up looking out the windows because only darkness lay beyond the panes.

Both the duchess and Mr Pettit had urged her to join them, but she had begged off because of Thad. And, truth to tell, she would not feel comfortable engaging in meaningless banter while Westfield was off somewhere, doing heaven knew what. He had not taken her into his confidence, but Glory strongly suspected that he and his manservant had set off in search of the Fairmans.

Although he was the acting magistrate, Glory had never expected him to go after the criminals himself. And considering the condition her brother was in, Glory felt her concern was justified. Her only comfort was the knowledge that Westfield was not a typical nobleman, and as she paced, she turned her thoughts to the puzzle of just who—or what—he was.

And no matter how far-fetched it was, Glory could only come to one conclusion that would explain his unusual skills, the disparity between his reputation and himself, and the obligations that he could not disclose. The duke was dangerous all right, for he was doing some sort of clandestine work, perhaps even following in Dr Dee's footsteps to serve his country. Glory bit back a snort of disbelief, and yet… Was Westfield a spy?

The sound of soft footfalls outside Thad's room made her shiver, and Glory waited, holding her breath, only to loose it in relief when she heard a low knock followed by Westfield's voice. Rushing to the door, she threw it open and let her gaze travel lovingly over his tall form, whole and solid. But then she saw his mouth.

'You're hurt.'

'What?' Stepping inside, Westfield strode towards the mirrored dressing table to peer at his reflection. He pulled out a handkerchief to wipe at a streak of blood. 'Nothing that can't be cleaned up.'

'Here, let me,' Glory said, relieved to see that the injury was minor. Taking the handkerchief, she pushed him into a chair and poured some water. 'I thought it was Pearson's job to make sure you were presentable.'

'It was dark and we were on horseback, so you can hardly fault my valet,' Westfield said.

Glory shook her head as she dipped the cloth into the bowl. 'And you simply had to thrash them,' she said, as she gingerly dabbed at his mouth. 'Why couldn't you just have shot them?'

'You are a bit bloodthirsty, aren't you?' Westfield said. 'I always knew it. From the moment you trained your pistol upon me.'

His eyes darkened as Glory's thumb brushed against his lip, and he pulled her closer until she was standing between his legs. 'I knew then,' he said, softly, taking her face in his hands. 'I knew then.'

And in that instant, something seemed to have changed between them. As his lips took hers, it felt as though all that had gone before was just a dance, a wary circling that had led up to this moment. And when Glory leaned against him, her fingers stealing into the thick strands of his hair, she felt as though everything had been settled between them.

Even though she knew it had not.

But there were no arguments, no protestations, no excuses, no second thoughts as they kissed—long, deep, indulgent kisses that spread heat throughout her body. There was no talk of obligations or conversation of any kind, their strained breaths the only sound in the silence until a voice rang out from the bed behind them.

'Did I miss something?' Thad asked.

Chapter Fifteen

Having tossed and turned much of the night, Glory rose late. Although she knew she ought to check on Thad first thing, she was not eager to speak with her brother. She could only hope that last night he had not seen much or that the laudanum the physician had given him had made him doubt what he did see.

For Glory had no desire to explain just why she had been kissing the Duke of Westfield. At the time, the duke had recovered quickly, smoothly rising to his feet and going to Thad's side to report upon his apprehension of the Fairmans. And Glory had fled to her room.

Later, when she had the long hours to consider what had happened, Glory told herself that the excitement of the moment had preyed upon her emotions. The candlelight, the quiet, private atmosphere, and Westfield's seductive kisses had worked upon her, leading to the perception that things were different.

But they could not be.

It was far more likely that the encounter had served as an end to their relationship. *That* was what had been settled, and, in effect, Glory had received a kiss goodbye. Because, with his duties done, there was no reason for Westfield to linger in Philtwell.

Blinking at the sudden pressure behind her eyes, Glory headed down the stairs to breakfast, hoping that no one else would be in the dining room at this hour. In her current state of distress, she would prefer to avoid everyone, including the duke—if he hadn't already left Sutton House behind.

That thought made her pause and Glory halted her steps, taking a moment to try to compose herself. She nearly turned to go back to her room, but a thumping noise drew her attention and she headed towards the sound, coming across a young maid who was struggling with a heavy, old-fashioned door.

'Oh, miss, would you mind helping me?' the girl asked before glancing furtively about. No doubt the servant would be roundly scolded for engaging her betters in conversation, but Glory was not high in the instep, and she quickly moved to aid the girl.

Between the two of them, they managed to swing open the oaken portal, dark with age. 'Thank you, miss,' the girl said. 'I'm to fetch a bottle of wine from the cellar for Mr Pettit, and I, well, I've never been down…there before.'

The poor maid obviously was not eager to descend into the depths below, and Glory could not blame her. Sympathy, along with a healthy dose of curiosity as to what lay under the oldest part of Sutton House, made her give the girl a nod of reassurance.

'I'll come along,' Glory said. 'I haven't been down there, either.' Of course, Thad had probably combed every inch of the residence in his quest for the Queen's Gift, but Glory had not joined him on his searches.

So when she followed the maid down wide stone steps, sunken with age, Glory glanced about curiously. Unlike the damp cellar below the cottage, with its dirt floor and musty odour, the space below Sutton House was vaulted and vast, its floor neatly tiled, its clutter nearly non-existent. It wasn't as bright as Glory would like, the only light coming from a couple of small windows, but she was not completely in the dark.

'Now, let us get down to business.'

Surprised at the change in the maid's tone, Glory turned, only to halt at the sight of a pistol trained upon her. For a moment, Glory simply stared, flummoxed by the servant glaring at her, weapon in hand. And then she realised just how foolish she had been.

She had stayed at Sutton House long enough to recognise all of the staff, and none of them would have begged assistance from a guest. Yet, Glory had fallen easily into the trap. Her only excuse was that she had been thinking, not of Queen's Well, but of something far more important to her: Westfield.

But hadn't he already apprehended the villains responsible for the spa's woes? Glory frowned. Had the Fairmans engaged a woman to work with them? The only reports of a possible accomplice had been the mysterious lad... Blinking at the woman, Glory decided that she was young enough to pass as a boy, if dressed as such. And then it dawned on her.

'Miss…Thorpe?' Glory asked, uncertainly.

'Yes. Are you quaking in your slippers, Sutton, now that I've returned to get back some of my own?'

'Your own?' Glory asked. She didn't know what Miss Thorpe had in mind, but the weapon couldn't be a good sign, and Glory was without her reticule. Her only hope was to distract the woman long enough to make an escape.

'Yes, *mine*,' Miss Thorpe said. 'You Suttons took what was rightfully ours and fled Philtwell.'

'Now, just a moment,' Glory said, outrage overcoming her caution. 'Any debt to your family was paid in full by the sale of this house, which had been our ancestral home for centuries.'

'*Blood money*,' the young woman said, practically spitting the words. 'We were entitled to Queen's Well and the Queen's Gift, not some paltry sum.'

'Paltry?' Glory said. Businesses failed all the time and the funds put into them lost. 'You were lucky to receive your investment back after the fire that closed the spa and killed my grandfather.'

Miss Thorpe took a step forward. '*Lucky?*' she repeated. 'That's not what my father said. And I listened to him for years, his bitter complaints about what was taken from him, his talk about what could have been. But the waters worked against him, saddling him with a wife who bore him too many girls and spent too freely, and you Suttons put an end to all of his chances to provide for them. *You destroyed him.*'

It sounded like Mr Thorpe was the author of his own destruction, but Glory was not about to say so when his daughter was aiming a pistol at her. She took a deep breath, determined to return the conversation to an even tone, and perhaps someone would note that she was missing and come looking for her.

'But surely you are too young to have ever even been to Queen's Well,' Glory said in a conciliatory tone.

'I'm the youngest. It fell to me to take care of him when he sank into the despair that finally killed him, despair brought on by *your* betrayal. He never had the strength to come back and take what was rightfully his,' Miss Thorpe said, her expression twisting in contempt. 'But now that he's gone I'm here to do it.'

Glory shook her head. Even if Miss Thorpe did her worst, she would never gain ownership of Queen's Well. 'You have no claim to the spa.'

'I don't care a whit for your muddy slop or the hogs that pay for the privilege of swilling it down,' the young woman said, her voice turning brittle. 'I'm here for the Queen's Gift.'

Glory felt a measure of relief that there would be no dispute over her family's heritage, legal or otherwise. But Miss Thorpe was not entitled to anything, including the Queen's Gift, should it even exist. However, Glory decided not to debate that point, for she didn't think the woman would take kindly to the news that there was no prize, as the Fairmans had discovered before her.

Glory chose her words carefully. 'You can't expect to find something that's been lost for centuries and then waltz off with it.'

'Oh, but I will,' Miss Thorpe said. 'Once it is in my possession, I can go wherever I want and do whatever I please.'

Was this wishful thinking, or did the woman really have some knowledge of the relic? Obviously, she considered it valuable enough to fund both her escape and her future. Glory frowned, considering the mural in the dining room above. 'Then you believe it is a crown?'

Miss Thorpe laughed. 'The Queen's Gift is far more valuable than a jewelled bauble, some trinket to be sold for mere money. What I'm after is power, and with the Gift, I shall have it.'

'Power?' Glory said, confused. Did the woman plan to blackmail the royal family or try to seize a title? If so, she'd likely be tossed into gaol, never to be seen again.

'Yes, power, a kind of power that very few have harnessed,' Miss Thorpe said, her eyes narrowing.

'And who is going to give you this power?'

'Not *who*, but *what*,' Miss Thorpe said, scornfully. 'The power resides in the Gift itself for someone who knows its true worth, and I have uncovered its long-forgotten secrets. Only I am the successor to the arch conjurer, the master of the uncanny arts who hid it away, lest ordinary fools seek arcane knowledge beyond their ken.'

'To he who hid it away? Do you mean Dr Dee?' Glory asked, trying to make sense of the woman's gibberish.

'What do you know of him?' Miss Thorpe asked, moving forwards, and Glory was hard pressed not to step back, away from the hatred that glittered in the woman's eyes.

'Just that he is rumoured to have visited the spa with Elizabeth, that he served as her adviser, and may have been connected with the gift she gave to the well.'

Glory's innocuous answer did little to placate Miss Thorpe, who advanced threateningly. 'As soon as I learned of you coming here, I knew you had discovered something,' she said, spitting the words. 'Why else would you suddenly appear in Philtwell to resume operations of a long-dead enterprise?'

'We returned to restore our family's heritage,' Glory said. She spoke calmly, in an effort to soothe the young woman whose sudden venom was alarming. Glory did not care to try to dodge a bullet, and she glanced around for anything she could use against her opponent.

'Have you found it? Do you have the globe?' Miss Thorpe demanded.

'Globe?' Glory asked, genuinely puzzled.

Miss Thorpe smiled, as though pleased by Glory's ignorance. 'The globe, you fool, is the most valuable of Dr Dee's possessions. His mirror was acquired by

Walpole, who did not know what he had, let alone what to do with it. But no one has ever found the crystal globe, the real source of his power.'

The woman must be referring to what Westfield dismissed as Dee's 'mystic nonsense'. And Glory had to agree with the duke, for how could an object possess any abilities? How had Miss Thorpe reached her conclusions, which seemed implausible at best? Glory peered at the volatile young woman, wondering just how credible she might be.

'But why would Dr Dee give away something like that, especially if, as you claim, no one else could use it?' Glory asked.

Miss Thorpe shook her head. 'You know nothing, do you? It has been working its magic for centuries, but soon it will work other magic, magic that *I* will direct. For too long its power has been wasted on these waters, to serve the foolish longings of your silly patrons.'

Glory blinked. 'You think something Dr Dee owned is responsible for the old legends about the water's properties?'

'I don't think it. *I know it*,' Miss Thorpe said. 'Dee bestowed his Gift upon the owners of the well, so that everyone who drank from it would experience the same romantic euphoria as had the queen herself.'

'Queen Elizabeth?' Glory asked, incredulous. In all her reading, she had never come across anything about the Virgin Queen falling in love, especially here at her family's spa.

'Of course, you fool,' Miss Thorpe said, sneering.

'But that legend goes much further back than Elizabeth's visit,' Glory said. 'The Romans were here centuries before, and the name they gave the place was Aquae Philtri, the spa of the philtre, especially of love.'

'You're lying,' Miss Thorpe said, and Glory realised that she should not have shared that particular bit of information with someone holding a weapon. Whether through madness or desperation or pure fantasy, Miss Thorpe had built her house of cards upon a faulty premise, and she would not thank Glory for knocking it down.

In fact, for one dark moment, Glory thought the woman was going to shoot, but instead, her expression settled into one of determination. 'We shall see soon enough,' she said. 'For you will find it for me.'

'What?' Glory asked, alarmed.

'I think it only appropriate that you, who stole so much from my family, should be responsible for some measure of justice.'

'But how?' Glory asked. Thad had been poking about Sutton House for some time, and he had found nothing. And, obviously, Miss Thorpe, despite all her attempts, had come up empty-handed, as well.

The young woman smiled, but the effect was disturbing. 'It's here, perhaps right where you are standing,' she said, her pale face flushing with excitement. 'I knew the moment I saw the mural that the Gift was here all along.'

'But the painting shows the queen standing outside the house, on the grounds,' Glory said.

'It's a symbol for the spa,' Miss Thorpe said, dismissively. 'And if only I had seen it earlier, we could have avoided all that unpleasantness at your precious Pump Room,' Miss Thorpe said, as she began walking around the cellar.

Glory inched away, but the woman swung towards her. 'I could have come and taken the Gift, and no one would have been the wiser. But it wasn't until I saw some writings about Buxton Hall, the site of Buxton's well, and engravings of other wells, replaced over the years, that I began to suspect the truth.'

'What truth?' Glory asked.

Miss Thorpe paused, her eyes shining. 'The original pump was here, beneath the house, which was built around it,' she said. 'This residence is where Queen Elizabeth stayed when she visited. In fact, all the guests were housed here before the inns were built, and the Assembly Rooms, and the new Pump Room.'

Glory glanced around the cellar, suddenly aware of how the space might have been used in Elizabeth's time, and she cursed herself for abandoning her older research materials in favour of the modern ledgers and guestbooks. Still, there was quite a difference between discovering the old pump and finding the Queen's Gift, a quest that was bound to disappoint Miss Thorpe. And then, what she would do? Glory did not like to consider the possibilities.

'Here,' the young woman said, suddenly. She was standing by some sort of partition that had been built in the darkest part of the cellar, and Glory shuddered, struck by a sudden coldness. Sutton House had never filled her with dread, but now she experienced the same eerie sensation that she had known so often since coming to Philtwell: a malevolent presence watching her...

Drawing in a harsh breath, Glory realised that it was this woman all along, not Dr Tibold or Westfield or the Fairmans or any nameless, faceless man. It was Miss Thorpe, and all Glory could do was turn and face the enmity in her eyes.

'Open it,' the young woman said.

Glory didn't understand what Miss Thorpe wanted until she jerked her head towards the partition. Or was it a tall crate whose top disappeared into the shadows? Stepping closer, Glory realised that there were narrow strips of blackness visible between the wooden slats, making it seem more like a cage than anything else.

The knowledge made Glory shiver, as did the thought of being locked away inside. For who would ever find her? Her heart pounding, Glory decided at that moment that she would do anything, risk everything, to avoid entering that dark chamber.

But she schooled her expression to reveal none of her intent as she turned to face her enemy. 'How?' Glory asked. 'I'll need a hammer or a crowbar.' She glanced around, eager to get her hands on something that might be used against her opponent, but Miss Thorpe shook her head.

'Just use your fingers,' she said, with a sneer. 'I thought you Suttons were clever and resourceful.'

Turning her back in order to hide her reaction,

Glory took a deep breath and began to examine the wood as well as she could in the dim light. The carpentry was poor, as though the work had been completed quickly, rather than carefully. But Glory tried not to imagine the reasons for such haste. Instead, she looked for a loose board that she could get her fingers around, in order to make some noise, if nothing else.

Finding an end that was not nailed securely, Glory pretended to work at freeing it, while banging loudly in the hope that someone, even if only a servant, would come down to investigate unusual noises emanating from below. But Sutton House was a large residence, built of stone, and Glory did not know if the cellar was even used these days. She remembered the heavy door and wondered when it had last been opened.

But Glory could do little else, so she kept at her task, while above her the household continued on, the servants about their work and the residents blithely unaware of her plight. Perhaps Westfield had already taken off for London, leaving only Thad, lying abed, and an elderly man still recovering from a long illness to come to her rescue.

They were grim prospects indeed.

Oberon frowned at his plate. He had waited in the dining room so long that the remainder of his eggs had congealed into a sickening lump upon his plate. His mother and Pettit had come and gone, and still there was no sign of Miss Sutton. Finally, he asked a passing maid to check upon her, but the girl returned with the news that Miss Sutton was not in her room.

Oberon felt a nagging unease, which he dismissed. No doubt Miss Sutton had skipped breakfast entirely in order to spend the morning with her brother. Rising to his feet, Oberon went directly to Thad's room, where he found the boy seated by the window in his dressing gown, eating from a tray. But there was no one else.

'Where's your sister?' Oberon asked.

The boy eyed him cannily.

'Perhaps I should be asking your intentions.'

Oberon frowned, unwilling to discuss his personal situation with anyone, let alone a mere boy. But how many times had he told Miss Sutton to treat her brother as the man he was becoming?

'They are honourable,' Oberon said.

Thad grinned. 'Good, because I would hate to have to give you a good bruising, though I am feeling considerably better.'

Oberon smiled at the youth's humour, but his amusement faded in the face of Miss Sutton's absence. 'Has she been here at all this morning?' he asked. 'I can't find her.'

Thad did not appear alarmed. 'You're bound to have your hands full with Glory. She's used to her independence. Mind you, she's pluck to the backbone, but you must know she doesn't take well to being ordered about. And there's no denying that you are used to doing the ordering,' Thad said, cocking his head as if to study Oberon like a sample of well water.

'Not that I'd call you arrogant, but where Glory's concerned, you're just going to have to let her have her head, loosen the leads, that sort of thing, if you mean to get on. Or meet in the middle, you might say.'

Oberon recovered himself with some difficulty. 'Do you recall what I told you last night?'

Thad looked a bit chagrined. 'Truth to tell, I was a bit under the weather, and that physician made me drink something. Why, when I saw you and Glory together, I rather thought I was dreaming the whole thing.'

Oberon shrugged off the knowledge that he should have held his tongue on the subject of his intentions towards Miss Sutton. Instead, he tried to focus on imparting some sense into her brother. 'Last night I told you that the Fairmans were not responsible for the vandalism, the destruction or the near murder on the crags. They didn't do any of it.'

Thad looked at him for one long moment, then swallowed hard as the truth dawned on him. 'Which means that Glory being missing…' he began, only to trail off, wide-eyed.

'Your sister might be in danger.'

Although Glory had hoped to lull Miss Thorpe into complacency, the young woman was too agitated to let down her guard. And she was starting to become suspicious about the noise, telling Glory to be quiet and produce results. Scanning the immediate area, Glory was tempted to duck behind the wooden structure and head for the shadows. But did she really want to play such a deadly game of tag? Any sudden movement might mean a bullet that could kill her or lay her low. And then she would well and truly be at the mercy of this woman.

And should she escape immediate injury, where would she go? Glory had never thought to wish herself back at the cottage, but there were too few places here to hide and only one way out. She glanced at the wide steps and knew she would never reach them without disarming Miss Thorpe. But the cellar of Sutton House was not cluttered with cricket bats and other potential weapons.

Her mind racing, Glory kept tugging at the loose piece of wood, which finally separated from its berth with a loud crack, nearly slicing open her palm with the rusty nail that protruded. Swallowing a gasp, Glory realised that this was her best chance, for the sharp shaft that had worked against her could work for her, especially since it was lodged within the heavy board.

Glory carefully lowered the slat in front of her, burying the telltale nail among the folds of her skirts. Although she appeared to be setting the piece aside, she simply transferred it to her left hand. And then she made a show of peering into the gaping hole she had made, her empty right hand gripping the opening.

'There's nothing in there,' Glory said, though anything could have been hiding in the black interior.

'What? Let me see,' Miss Thorpe demanded, waving Glory aside.

Glory inched out of the way, but stayed close

enough so that when Miss Thorpe stepped forwards, she was able to make her move. Swinging her make-shift weapon as best she could with her left hand, Glory could not muster the power that she wanted. Still, the board caught Miss Thorpe around the knees, and she twisted wildly, the pistol in her hand discharging its bullet.

It whizzed past Glory's ear, too close for comfort, and she was not about to let the woman load the weapon again. But that was not Miss Thorpe's intent. Her rage, her madness, or whatever drove her had reached its breaking point, and, releasing a shriek of fury, she flung the gun at Glory's hand, causing her to drop the board.

Flinching, Glory took one look at her opponent and realised that her strength was no match for that of a lunatic. Knowing her only hope lay in surprise, she did not bend to retrieve either weapon, but lunged forwards, swinging her arm with all the force she could muster. The facer that she had so diligently practised connected to Miss Thorpe's jaw with a sickening crack before the woman staggered and fell.

Above the thundering of her heart, Glory thought she heard frantic knocking, and, for one wild moment, she looked at the wooden structure beside her as if it truly held a prisoner. But then she realised that the sound was that of footsteps halting behind her. A hush fell over the cellar, then Thad's admiring voice rang out.

'Dem, Glory's floored a female.'

Chapter Sixteen

When Glory turned to see her brother and Westfield standing on the steps, she felt such waves of relief that she swayed upon her feet. The Queen's Gift, Miss Thorpe's mad actions and even her own ordeal faded at the sight of the man she had thought long gone to London—and out of her life.

He was at her side in an instant, taking her in his arms without regard to propriety or her brother's presence. And as he pulled her close, Glory felt like weeping, not because of what had happened, but for want of his embrace—and all the nameless obligations that conspired to keep her from it.

'Are you all right?' he asked, and Glory nodded against his waistcoat. *For now.*

Thad showed no surprise at the extraordinary display and strode past them to the partition. 'What's this?' he asked.

'Supposedly it's the original pump for the spa, as well as the site of the Queen's Gift,' Glory said.

'What?' Thad needed no further encouragement, but set about tearing away the shaky structure, showing no sign that he must have left his bed only recently.

Glory opened her mouth to protest the exertion, but Westfield shook his head. 'He's young and resilient,' the duke said, as though privy to her thoughts. And Glory wondered just how much of her mind—and heart—he could see.

'Look at this,' Thad called with the enthusiasm to prove it, and Glory was glad that his recent bruising had caused no lasting effects. He turned towards them eagerly. 'We need to get a lantern in here.'

Eventually, lanterns were obtained, the partition dismantled, and the pump uncovered, though Glory felt only dismay upon seeing it. More fanciful than functional, it resembled a fountain made out of heavy stone, dark with age and rather forbidding. To her mind, the new Pump Room was far preferable to trooping into a cellar, no matter how spacious, as well as being more conducive to society, if not romance.

'But where's the Queen's Gift?' Thad asked, his disappointment obvious.

Before Glory could put a damper on his enthusiasm, Westfield spoke up. 'I doubt that the Suttons would have left it in plain sight all those years, for the public would have come in here to partake of the waters. And even after they removed to the new Pump Room, family members and staff would have had access to the cellar.'

The duke walked around the original well, tapping

upon the old stone and peering into every curve and crevice. Then he put the lantern on the floor and examined the base. Finally, he knelt down to study the tiles all around it, pointing to one that looked no different from any of the others, at least to Glory's eyes.

'See that?' he asked.

'What?' Thad asked, leaning down to squint at the floor.

'The edge is damaged,' Oberon said. 'That might have happened in the creation or laying of the piece, or it could have been tampered with at some point over the years.'

That was all the incentive Thad needed; soon he was scrambling for a tool to lift the tile. 'Perhaps you should check with the owner of Sutton House before ripping up his floor,' Glory said.

'He gives his permission,' Westfield said and Glory wondered whether he and Mr Pettit had an understanding. Certainly the duke could afford to pay for any repairs to the property.

Still, she felt more comfortable with the excavation when Westfield assumed control. He was more careful than Thad, his long, lean fingers gently working at the spot in a way that made Glory flush. And when he managed to free the piece, it remained intact, so he was able to set it aside and investigate the wood flooring below, continuing with his methodical approach.

Soon, he had found a loose board beneath, as well. It covered a hidey-hole that had Thad practically capering with glee. 'Is there anything in there? What do you see?' her brother asked, crowding close and dangling the lantern even closer.

But Westfield would not be rushed, and he peered into the opening as though wary of some trap that might take any fingers he inserted. Glory could only admire his good sense when he rigged a couple of hooks and lowered them into the blackness.

His retrieval system eventually produced a heavy box, intricately carved, and obviously old, perhaps even dating to the time of Elizabeth. Now, even Glory, who had eyed the Queen's Gift with scepticism, felt a heady anticipation when the duke laid the elaborate container upon the floor.

Motioning them away with a gesture, Westfield took the same care with the opening of the case as he had recovering it, using a bent wire to lift the lid. Glory wasn't sure what he was trying to avoid, but when nothing happened, Thad moved near.

'What is it? Can you tell? Is it a crown?' her brother asked.

'Miss Thorpe claimed that the gift was a globe belonging to Dr Dee,' Glory said, trying not to laugh at Thad's reaction to that unwelcome news.

But when the lid was raised, Glory could see neither the glitter of gold nor the sheen of crystal. In fact, she thought the box empty, whatever treasure it had once held long looted and sold. However, Thad was visibly impatient to make sure, and after various attempts with wires and hooks proved unsuccessful, Westfield finally reached inside. Glory held her breath, fearful that the lid might suddenly snap shut or crush his fingers.

However, no calamity ensued, and the duke eventually removed what looked like a packet of letters, setting them carefully aside. They were followed by a sheaf of papers, tied with string that had decayed with age, proving that the materials could date back centuries.

'Maybe those are the original deeds to the well or its surrounding lands,' Glory said.

But Thad did not share her sentiment. 'If buried by Dr Dee, it's probably a treatise on mathematics,' he said, his disappointment obvious.

'*Papers?* Nothing but papers!'

The words rose into a high-pitched shriek, making Glory start, and she turned to see that Miss Thorpe had roused herself. Staggering wildly, the young woman lunged forwards and might have scattered the ancient documents, if Westfield had not bound her hands, apparently to avoid this very occurrence.

Surging to his feet, the duke managed to subdue the wailing woman and give her over to his waiting valet, who was able to lead her away. Still, she hailed curses down upon the Suttons because there was no crystal globe, no gift from Dr Dee unless he had left behind a message in the writings that he, perhaps, had penned.

Apparently curious now, Thad took a look at the pages from the box and shook his head. 'Whatever it is, it's not even in English.'

Westfield walked back to Thad and glanced over

his shoulder. 'It's not another language, but some kind of encryption.'

Glory blinked in surprise. 'You mean it's written in some kind of code, such as Dee was famous for?'

Westfield nodded absently as he studied the markings and Glory frowned. Someone, perhaps even Dee himself, had gone to a lot of trouble to bury these documents away from prying eyes and to make sure the secrets within them remained hidden. And he appeared to have succeeded.

'I guess we'll never know what was so important that it was locked away for centuries at the foot of Queen's Well,' Glory said. 'Maybe we should pack them all up again.'

'Oh, let me have a go at them first,' Westfield said, eyeing the manuscript that Thad had abandoned. While her brother poked around the box and the hole in which it had been found, as though looking for something—anything—else, Glory watched the duke with interest.

'Are you saying you know how to read such things?' she asked.

Westfield shrugged. 'It's really not that difficult.'

'A hobby of yours, I suppose,' Glory said drily. He made no comment, but she did not expect one. For she needed no further confirmation of the theory she had formed while pacing at her brother's bedside.

By itself, the ability to decipher secret messages might be unusual, but coupled with Westfield's other telltale skills, it could only mean one thing: the man was a spy.

* * *

Although Oberon rarely undertook the translation of mysterious documents, he felt fairly confident of his success. Spreading the materials out upon a table Pearson set up in his room, he first looked for any signs that code, the use of pre-arranged words or phrases, was involved. But if the writing dated back to Elizabeth, it was more likely a cipher, the kind used by Dee and others under Sir Francis Walsingham, the founder of England's first secret service.

And it was likely a substitution cipher, where different letters or numbers were substituted for the alphabet, a system that could be cracked through frequency analysis. With a knowledge of which letters and groups of letters appeared most often in English, Oberon simply substituted them for the recurring symbols on the pages before him. And while making his replacements, he watched for meaningless 'nulls' inserted to thwart decipherment, as well as the possibility of nomenclators or code words scattered throughout.

It would have been easier to simply ship off the pages to someone who specialised in such things, but they had more important work to do—even though Napoleon was locked away at last. And Oberon felt oddly protective of the materials, which probably had to do with Queen's Well and therefore would mean something to Miss Sutton.

He never expected them to mean anything to himself.

But when Oberon began to transcribe the secrets,

he found himself oddly affected. A year ago or even a month ago, he would have discovered nothing in common with a young man from another century, desperately in love with someone he could not have, or a woman whose circumstances prevented her from marrying and having a family of her own.

Now, as he closeted himself away with the writings, emerging only rarely to eat and sharing nothing of his discoveries, Oberon felt a kinship with those, long dead, who had given up so much.

And he became determined not to do the same.

Glory had settled into a routine. Although Miss Thorpe was no longer a threat to the Suttons, Mr Pettit had insisted that they remain at Sutton House indefinitely. And since Westfield was there, as well, Glory didn't have the heart to move back to the cottage. Besides, Thad was talking about making a home at the cosy residence with his intended bride, who had no interest in leaving her family and friends for London.

That left Glory unsure of her future, but she made the best of the present. Instead of re-opening the Pump Room just yet, she returned to her place in the library, where she looked for information on Queen's Well and any clues to the gift secreted beside it, simply for her own enjoyment. She wished that Westfield would join her, but he kept to himself as he pored over the documents they had found.

Life slowed to moments to be savoured: a sunny afternoon in the garden, a walk with Thad, a game of cards with the duchess and Mr Pettit, and any time spent with Westfield. Her plans for Queen's Well were put aside while she waited for the duke to report upon his findings. But her eagerness to hear them was tempered by the knowledge that he would not linger afterwards.

And so when summoned by Westfield to the dining room, Glory felt mixed emotions as she gathered with the others. But she maintained a game face as she took a seat next to Thad, who appeared impatient to get back to the life he had made for himself, his interest in the Gift having waned considerably.

Unless Westfield's document led to some buried treasure, her brother was bound to be disappointed. And yet, he was as happy as Glory had ever seen him, maturing into a man prepared to take on the responsibilities of business and marriage. And she felt a sharp surge of pride, which was eclipsed only by the arrival of the duke.

Although Glory knew she would never grow tired of looking at Westfield, she took special delight in these last opportunities to do so, her gaze lingering over his tall figure, his wide shoulders, the dark hair still in need of a trim, and the face that had grown more expressive of late.

'I've called you here because of the mural,' he said, and Glory reluctantly turned with the others towards the far wall. The room's heavy curtains had been pulled, illuminating the old painting with a beam of sunlight, but Glory could not see anything new in the fading work.

'Undoubtedly, this was commissioned by the well owners some time after Queen Elizabeth's last visit to Sutton House, to record for prosperity something of their history that might well be forgotten.' Westfield paused to draw a deep breath.

'Miss Sutton was most nearly correct in her assessment,' he said, and Glory glanced at him in surprise. 'For she noted the queen's hands were empty except for light, which might represent her patronage or approval. However, the beams stand for something far more important: royalty itself—the succession, if you will.'

'But the Virgin Queen chose no successor,' Mr Pettit said.

'No, but she had one, a son, her own flesh and blood whose birth was kept secret from all except the very few who attended her here.'

Glory blinked. In her reading, she had come across stories of the queen's favourites courtiers, possible liaisons, and even hints of such a possibility, but Elizabeth had held firm against such slander. 'You have proof?'

Westfield set the old box upon the table, the letters and papers nestled inside. 'I have the facts that were documented by Dr Dee, to assure the succession, should anything happen to the queen.'

'It seems he hid the facts too well,' Pettit said.

'Perhaps, or perhaps by the time the good queen died, her son had preceded her or was not a viable possibility,' Westfield said. 'Or perhaps those few who knew the truth would spare him such a life.'

Glory glanced at Westfield in surprise, for, as a duke, he could hardly deny the responsibilities of noble birth, yet his expression clearly showed sympathy for the child whose destiny had been denied him.

'And what of the man who won the heart of the queen?' Pettit asked.

'He was a minor courtier, who saved some of her messages, unsigned, of course,' Westfield said, gesturing to the letters. 'But by both his and Dee's account, the romance was no casual flirtation.'

'Which would explain why Elizabeth was so happy here,' Glory said.

'Perhaps that also explains how the waters got such a reputation for inciting romance,' Mr. Pettit said.

'Or rather, how its reputation became more well known,' Glory said.

'But the child put at end to all that,' Westfield said, so soberly that Glory again glanced at him in surprise. 'Before, they might have met in the middle, though clandestinely, a man of little consequence and his sovereign. But after the birth, the queen's lover feared for his life and wrote of his plans to disappear to the Continent, rather than be murdered by those who surrounded the throne.'

Glory frowned at such a bitter parting. 'And the child?'

'Your ancestor,' Westfield said.

'What?' Thad exclaimed before Glory could even form the word.

'He was given over to the owners of the well, the Suttons, to raise as their own,' Westfield said.

Mr Pettit and the duchess burst into speech, both amused and awestruck by the fact that Glory and Thad had royal blood flowing in their veins. While Thad made a great show of posturing, Glory remained silent, her gaze drawn to the mural.

'Just think of the excitement this shall cause among royal historians,' Mr. Pettit said.

'To say nothing of the boost it will give Queen's Well,' the duchess said. 'Miss Sutton, it appears that your success is assured.'

But Glory shook her head as she turned to face them. 'I don't think we should tell anyone.'

'What?' Mr Pettit appeared surprised by her words, while the duchess only smiled.

'It is their secret, not ours,' Glory said. 'I think we should put the documents back where we found them.'

Glory looked to Westfield for argument, but his nod of approval assured her that she had chosen well, if perhaps not easily, in more than one instance. And in the ensuing quiet, her gaze returned to the mural, where a childless queen held out her empty hands.

Deep in thought, Glory paid little heed when Thad and the others departed, leaving only Westfield to share the silence with her. Eventually, she heard his footsteps as he walked closer and halted beside her.

'That was quite a story,' Glory said softly.

'Yes,' Westfield answered. 'It's enough to give one pause, to consider making changes, to seize the day before the opportunity is gone for ever.'

Glory glanced up at him in confusion, and he

looked away, as though at a loss for words, before continuing. 'I realise now that closing myself off from everyone was unfair to my family, my friends and myself. For while avoiding heartbreak, I also missed out on the joys, both small and great, that make life worth living.'

Now he had Glory's full attention, for Westfield rarely spoke of personal matters—or admitted to a mistake. She stared up at him in surprise as he once more turned to face her, his expression intent.

'Miss Sutton, will you marry me?'

Glory had imagined those words so often that she suspected that she had fabricated them out of whole cloth, a wistful wish to balm her weary heart. Shaken, she rose to her feet. 'What did you say?'

Westfield stood with his hands clasped behind him, perhaps because of the seriousness of his query or to keep from reaching for her, an action that would surely affect her answer, if she'd heard him correctly.

'Will you marry me?' he repeated, his deep voice dropping to a whisper.

His seductive tone alone was enough to make Glory agree to anything and everything, so she dared not look at the man. Instead, taking a moment to gather her scattered wits, she walked to the tall windows, where the bright sunlight served as sharp contrast to the gloom that lingered in the corners. And she would have no such shadows between them.

'But what of your work for the…War Office?' Glory spoke lightly, tossing the question over her shoulder, because she did not want to see him lie to her.

'I don't work for the War Office.'

Glory turned to face him then. 'The Home Office?'

'Actually, it's the Alien Office,' Westfield said, and Glory felt some of the tension leave her body. At least, *at last*, he was being truthful with her. 'I was recruited after my father's death, and ever since then I've been doing some…'

'Spying?' Glory said.

Westfield shook his head. 'Listening, casually questioning, hosting events where certain sorts would feel comfortable and might let slip important information, bringing together those who do the real spying… But I've been thinking of retiring.'

Glory's heart leapt.

'And what of your work with Queen's Well?' he asked.

Glory smiled. 'I've been thinking of turning it over to Thad.'

Although Glory didn't remember moving, somehow she was finally in his arms again, without an impending farewell to colour her joy. And this time, when he kissed her, there was nothing standing between them. Locked in his embrace, the words that they had never spoken spilled forth in heated whispers until the prospect of someone coming upon them made them break apart.

'We can spend quite a bit of time here. It seems I own Sutton House as some sort of premature wedding gift from my mother,' Westfield said. Eyeing her with one dark brow cocked, he shook his head and warned, 'Don't ask.'

Glory swallowed a laugh before replying with all seriousness, 'And we can stay in London, as well.'

'Certainly,' he said. 'But I would most like to show you the family seat, Westfield, where perhaps we could…meet in the middle.'

Randolph watched Miss Sutton give her brother a hug and was pleased to see the boy respond in kind. Thad's brief flirtation with troubles behind him, he seemed to appreciate Philtwell, his family's heritage and perhaps even his elder sister. The boy's appreciation for her intended was obvious as he stepped back, shaking his head at the sight of the betrothed couple.

'Who would have thought it upon your first meeting?' Thad asked. Westfield's brows shot up, and the three exchanged amused glances as if privy to some shared memory.

But Westfield's mother would not be excluded. 'Once again, the well has proved its worth,' she said, wreathed in smiles. 'Despite what you might believe, the waters have worked their magic, Miss Sutton.'

'Please call me Glory,' Miss Sutton said, with endearing informality.

'Actually, it's Gloriana,' her brother pointed out, grinning like a mischievous sibling.

But the duchess seemed struck far more by his words than his manner. 'Oberon and Gloriana, just as in *The Faerie Queene*,' she said, in a tone of awe. 'Surely there can be no doubt that the waters have matched wisely.'

'Or that Miss Sutton boasts a long and distinguished heritage,' Westfield said.

The young woman blinked, apparently having not made the connection between her rather unusual name and the queen who had once borne it. But then she smiled and turned towards Sutton House, as if in mute acknowledgement of her ancestor. Indeed, the presence of Elizabeth seemed to linger over the residence, despite the changes the years had wrought.

Having become attached to the place, Randolph was glad he would be returning to hold the house for the Suttons, as he always had. But for now, he joined the duchess in a coach that would take them to Westfield and long weeks of wedding preparations. She had insisted Randolph be given his due as prime matchmaker, and he was looking forward to the festivities.

He had barely settled into his seat when she squeezed his hand. 'As a descendant of royalty, she will easily slip into her role as duchess,' she said.

'If the blood of Elizabeth runs in her veins, I think she can handle anything,' Randolph said. *Even you.*

However, just in case, he carried a little insurance with him. While Letty had been giddy with happiness over the impending nuptials, if she began meddling with her son and new daughter, he had just the thing to distract her. And he wasn't afraid to use it—on

Letty and the first suitable gentleman who came across her path.

With a sly smile, Randolph patted the pocket of his coat wherein lay the flask Thad had slipped him. After all, you never knew when you might have need of the famous waters of Queen's Well.

* * * * *

HISTORICAL

Regency

RAVISHED BY THE RAKE
by Louise Allen

Lady Perdita Brooke prides herself on her social poise...except when faced with devastatingly dashing Alistair Lyndon, who does *not* remember their passionate night together. Now Dita has the perfect opportunity to remind Alistair of their sizzling chemistry...

Regency

BRUSHED BY SCANDAL
by Gail Whitiker

Lady Annabelle Durst may be beautiful, but at four-and-twenty she's firmly—and contentedly!—on the shelf. Until her family are embroiled in a scandal, with only Sir Barrington Parker to turn to. Sensible Anna will do *anything*—even risk her reputation—to persuade this dangerous man to help...

Regency

THE RAKE OF HOLLOWHURST CASTLE
by Elizabeth Beacon

Devilish rake Sir Charles Afforde has purchased Hollowhurst Castle lock, stock and barrel. All that is left to possess is the castle's beautiful yet determined chatelaine Roxanne Courland.

On sale from 5th August 2011
Don't miss out!

Available at WHSmith, Tesco, ASDA, Eason and all good bookshops

www.millsandboon.co.uk

0711/04a

HISTORICAL

BOUGHT FOR THE HAREM
by Anne Herries

After her capture by corsairs, Lady Harriet Sefton-Jones thinks help has arrived in the form of dashing Lord Kasim. But it's out of the frying pan and into the fire... Kasim has a plan of his own: he wants Lady Harriet for himself!

SLAVE PRINCESS
by Juliet Landon

For ex-cavalry officer Quintus Tiberius Martial duty *always* comes first. His task to escort the Roman emperor's latest captive, Princess Brighid, should be easy. But one look at his fiery slave and Quintus wants to put his own desires before everything else...!

THE HORSEMAN'S BRIDE
by Elizabeth Lane

Not even a remote Colorado ranch can shelter Jace Denby while he's on the run, but one danger this fugitive doesn't see coming is impulsive Clara Seavers! Clara doesn't trust this hired horseman, but she can't deny he ignites her spirit. Even though Jace seems intent on fighting their mounting passion...

**On sale from 5th August 2011
Don't miss out!**

*Available at WHSmith, Tesco, ASDA, Eason
and all good bookshops*

www.millsandboon.co.uk

304a

0711/04b

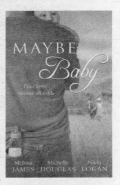

2 FREE BOOKS
AND A SURPRISE GIFT

We would like to take this opportunity to thank you for reading this Mills & Boon® book by offering you the chance to take TWO more specially selected books from the Historical series absolutely FREE! We're also making this offer to introduce you to the benefits of the Mills & Boon® Book Club™—

- **FREE home delivery**
- **FREE gifts and competitions**
- **FREE monthly Newsletter**
- **Exclusive Mills & Boon Book Club offers**
- **Books available before they're in the shops**

Accepting these FREE books and gift places you under no obligation to buy, you may cancel at any time, even after receiving your free books. Simply complete your details below and return the entire page to the address below. You don't even need a stamp!

YES Please send me 2 free Historical books and a surprise gift. I understand that unless you hear from me, I will receive 4 superb new books every month for just £3.99 each, postage and packing free. I am under no obligation to purchase any books and may cancel my subscription at any time. The free books and gift will be mine to keep in any case.

Ms/Mrs/Miss/Mr _____ Initials _____

Surname _____

Address _____

_____

_____ Postcode _____

E-mail _____

Send this whole page to: Mills & Boon Book Club, Free Book Offer, FREEPOST NAT 10298, Richmond, TW9 1BR